THE AMAZON JOB:

A CASE LEE NOVEL

Book 4

By Vince Milam

WANT TO RECEIVE MY NEWSLETTER WITH NEWS ABOUT UPCOMING RELEASES? Simply click below:
https://vincemilam.com/

Other books by Vince Milam:
The Suriname Job: A Case Lee Novel Book 1
The New Guinea Job: A Case Lee Novel Book 2
The Caribbean Job: A Case Lee Novel Book 3

Acknowledgments:

Editor—David Antrobus at BeWriteThere - bewritethere.com
Cover Design by Rick Holland at Vision Press – *myvisionpress.com.*

As always, Vicki for her love and patience. Mimi, Linda, and Bob for their unceasing support and encouragement.

Chapter 1

An intense figure stared my way, eyes dark and menacing as he spoke Farsi into his cell phone. Sitting two tables away, his presence painted this find-the-lost-scientist contract with ugly possibilities. I lowered my sunglasses and locked eyes. He paused the conversation, turned his head, and ended it with his voice considerably lowered. Game on.

We sat in a three-sided makeshift bar, dirt floor, the galvanized tin walls shared between a long row of adjoining establishments. The shop on the right sold high-end electronics. Computers, cell phones, flat-screen TVs. An old Procol Harum song echoed from a sound system for sale. The shop to the left offered vibrant-colored macaws and chattering monkeys and exotic snakes. The macaws announced loud displeasure at the nearby music selection. Somewhere a stall prepared grilled meat—type and origin unknown. The aroma and smoke wafted across the sloped bank and mixed with the inescapable funk of river, sweat, and jungle. We sat above the shore of the mighty Amazon River. In Manaus, Brazil.

High odds the guy speaking Farsi, an Iranian, was a spy. A spook. A member of MOIS, the Iranian Ministry of Information and Security. The ever-present paranoia over the million-dollar bounty on my head didn't figure into my high-alert state. Not this time. Because I'd received word regarding this performance of spook whack-a-mole prior to my Manaus arrival. Which didn't change the fact they were as welcome as an outhouse breeze.

Jules warned me two days earlier. Jules of the Clubhouse. She'd warned about a strange flocking of espionage players. Her spiderweb's tendrils picked up tingles, rumors, innuendo. But the drivers and details that had prompted spookville to pitch a tent in Manaus lacked clarity. Clarity even Jules couldn't provide.

"There is an array of interest relevant to your Amazon engagement," she'd said. "A small slice of the interest is quite keen. A slice derived from the deadlier shadows. Your walkabout scientist, rumor has it, made a remarkable discovery."

Bad news. I'd taken the job because it had presented itself as a simple search-and-rescue: find the missing scientist, a bio-prospector, and haul her back to Switzerland. This sprinkling of espionage across the engagement canvas hadn't entered my strategy.

"Let's set remarkable discoveries aside for the moment. Tell me about the deadlier shadows thing."

A request driven by *my* keen slice of interest—any information buttressing the vertical and healthy alignment for Case Lee Inc.'s lone employee. Jules adjusted her eyepatch, an affectation signaling her informational flow had been interrupted.

"Fine. I'll accept your prioritization. The gleaning of self-interest tidbits before capturing the larger picture. Not your best quality, dear. But one I have become accustomed to."

I smiled. She continued.

"Deadlier shadows. The players most prone to show are a more violent ilk. Unlike the larger clandestine cadres."

The larger cadres included the CIA, Russia's FSB, China's MSS, and MI6.

"More violent? I haven't found the Russians exactly hail-fellow-well-met."

She cracked a smile. "True enough. You *have* managed placement of quite the bee in their bonnet. To be sure." The smile faded. "But even they tend to hold a larger picture. Perhaps not awash with nuance and subtlety, but a strategic perspective nonetheless."

"Okay."

"Now back to business. If you run into players during your little jungle foray—and you may not—be aware they could belong to tribes known for extreme violence and immediate rewards."

"Thanks, Jules." I meant it. Her insights have saved my butt more than once. "Thanks, and I'll keep an eye open."

"Wholly inadequate, dear." She fired a kitchen match along her chair's arm, relit the cigar, and cast an eagle look my way. "Eyes in the back of your head, brave Ulysses. Eyes in the back of your head."

So I'd arrived in Manaus with situational awareness. Spooks of unknown origin likely present. Fellow travelers with their own focused interest in the lost Swiss bio-prospector, Dr. Ana Amsler. Strange doings on the surface, but potential blockbuster drug discoveries keyed the mike among Big Pharma listening posts. Big Pharma meant big money. And big money, in my experience, drew spooks. Bees to nectar. Fine and understood and soon-to-be white noise because I was headed into the bush. The rain forest. Where spies seldom ventured. If they did, espionage tradecraft skills were limited in value compared to former Delta Force skill sets.

I ordered a beer and bottled water, in Portuguese, from the river bar's barefoot proprietor. He wore an unbuttoned shirt as sweat sheened across his Buddha belly. When the proprietor approached, the Iranian pointed toward my small table as indicator he'd have the same. The macaws next door fired off a string of squawks. On the electronic side of things, the music changed to a French pop tune. Go figure.

It wasn't surprising that recently arrived spooks would canvas this section of Manaus. A transportation hub, it presented as run-down, derelict. It carried a movie-set air of quick scores and sudden violence. Very unlike the more modern downtown Manaus a half-mile away. Riverboats large and small nudged onto the shore, mixing with small skiffs and dugout canoes. The hue and cry of barter and sales and one-time deals carried through thick air. Floatplanes collected around nearby aviation docks. The entire scene reflected the only two viable options for this area's travel: water and air. Road passage to and from Manaus approached borderline impossible. Bridges washed out, roads collapsed.

The Iranian—clearly tasked with keeping an eye on this area—followed me into the tin-walled bar because I'd screwed up. It happens.

I'd checked the airfreight delivered to my floatplane pilot's ramshackle office. The pilot was downtown and wouldn't return for an hour, but his assistant offered storage space in a corner of the office until tomorrow's flight. I unlocked the large case and checked the contents. The morning arrival flight from the States left me naked, vulnerable. I was entering an operational area without weaponry. But my *despachante*—a professional skid-greaser—had performed his job. Underneath the tarps and hammock and mosquito netting, the Colt M4A1 semiautomatic rifle lay unmolested. As did two .40 Glock pistols.

The despachante also procured a variety of items on my behalf, now also collected at the pilot's office. After inspecting the crated Zodiac inflatable boat and the 25 hp Honda outboard, I paid the despachante. In Benjamins. He bowed and assured me 24-7 availability for any of my needs.

The small office door stood open, and the aircraft docks—where a dozen floatplanes were tied—held a fair amount of foot traffic. I didn't close the office door, didn't try and hide the loaded Glock slid into the waistband of my jeans. The office manager watched it happen. As did the Iranian standing on a nearby dock, as evidenced when I straightened up and turned. He turned as well, an attempt at hiding the fact he'd watched my activities through the small door. He wore dark sunglasses, and dollars to donuts he kept his eyes on me while shifting his body elsewhere.

Too cavalier about donning the .40 caliber comfort blanket. A mistake. So be it. The loaded Glock's cool, reassuring texture perched against the small of my back overcame any residual angst about the misstep.

I planned on waiting an hour for the pilot's return so we could discuss the next morning's flight. Have a cold beer or two then ensure the pilot was okay with the load of equipment. My cargo also included multiple five-gallon gas containers, full. But I adjusted my immediate plans with the goal of ascertaining why this spook appeared so interested in me.

The Iranian pocketed his phone, gulped beer, and poured the rest onto the dirt floor. Then hand-signaled the proprietor for a coffee. A sure sign the boss would soon appear. A boss who frowned on drinking. The guy waited, legs crossed, fingertips tapping the table, pretending I didn't exist. A rainstorm passed overhead and pounded the tin roof with dime-sized drops. The deluge cooled and cleared the air as the overhead staccato drowned the music next door. Puddles formed in seconds along the wide dirt walkway in front of the shops. And I'd arrived during the Amazon *dry* season.

I slid the sunglasses back up my nose and waited. It didn't take long. The first two strode in. Saturated from the downpour, they pulled handkerchiefs and dried their faces and beards, sidearms evident under soaked and untucked shirts. They shifted toward their companion's table, eyeballing me as they passed.

I'd rubbed elbows with spooks by the dozens and recognized low-grade operatives. Operatives better termed "experienced goon." But the appearance of Moe, Larry, and Curly playing badass rang discordant. Bio-prospectors, pharmaceutical companies, potential drug discoveries derived from nature; espionage in that realm required high-end skills, attributes not evident with this clown collection. The downpour passed as suddenly as it arrived, low clouds crossing over the river. A brief respite before the sun and steam bath and sweat returned.

The boss arrived. He'd ducked into a neighboring shop and waited out the rain. Tall and slender and fit and dry, he straightened already slicked-back dark hair, lit a smoke, and stared my way with hooded eyes. Midforties, with a mustache-goatee combination and a cruel lip-curl as permanent fixture. His assessment of me was clinical, concerted, and without artifice. He approached his seated men, leaned over, and spoke a few short sentences. The proprietor shuffled toward them, anticipating a drink order. He was waved away. The head guy didn't deign to look his way. I attempted to catch a few words. Words close enough to Arabic for a semblance of understanding. No such luck.

This could get interesting. MOIS—an outfit renowned for savage exploits. It just didn't fit under the mantle of scientific bio-exploration endeavors. And it raised the possibility these cats would go all Wild West on me. Fine. A slight shift in my seating position provided quick access if needed. I'd produce the Glock in a quarter-second and deliver four snap shots. To their heads. They were close enough to pull it off. Then drag their sorry asses downhill and into the river. Let the gators and piranhas do their thing while locals looked the other way and whistled at the sky. The head MOIS agent would make the decision. Either way worked for me.

Chapter 2

The head honcho straightened, again smoothed back his hair, and approached my small table.

"May I join you?" he asked in Persian-accented English. Not a surprise. His agent who'd made the cell phone call had sussed me as either European or American, higher odds on the latter. My physical posture, attitude, overall vibe—hard to say. And harder to hide. I raised a hand and offered the chair across the table. It kept him and his three men within the same view. He provided a snaggled brown-tooth display behind the curled-lip smile.

"American?" he asked, sitting.

"Iranian?"

I removed my sunglasses. His wolfish smile broadened, then faded. He lifted a hand and snapped his fingers, followed by a "Come here" signal directed at the proprietor. He ordered bottled water. In Portuguese. So this guy got around. An experienced operative. He used his cigarette hand's thumb and forefinger to stroke his goatee, staring as smoke curled around his face. I took a sip of beer, eyes still locked with his.

"You search for the scientist," he said.

A statement direct and definitive and unwanted.

"I'm a salesman."

He took a drag and exhaled through his nostrils.

"What do you sell?"

"Anvils. Not a lot of repeat business, but everyone needs a good anvil."

He chewed on *anvil* for a bit and said, "I do not believe you sell such things. I believe you work for a Swiss pharmaceutical company."

He grinned again. Most spooks, particularly those leading a mission, exhibited a strong element of subtlety. This guy had none, zip, zero. Bold as brass and playing against a perceived clock. Somewhere way up his food chain an Iranian minister wanted Dr. Amsler found, and found right now. Weird. Damn weird.

Well, my client *was* Swiss, but he wouldn't know that. The involvement of Global Resolutions was contracting me. They'd provided the dossier on Dr. Amsler. And paid for my services. Zurich-based, they acted as an intermediary for their clients. But this guy eyeballing me across the table figured I was a pharma company employee. Fine.

"Let me tell you what I believe. I believe it's strange running into a bundle of MOIS operatives a thousand miles up the Amazon River. That's what I believe."

My rules. When you danced with spooks, plow direct. Straight lines. Keep the conversational string away from their smoke-and-shadows world. But this guy had no issue with such an approach. He avoided conversation and fired direct statements and questions. He clearly carried beaucoup upstream pressure. Find the scientist. Or else.

"You are traveling to the Swiss base camp."

The earlier phone conversation from his guy had painted a picture. The supplies in the pilot's office. And, no doubt, the jeans-tucked Glock.

"I may go fishing. Peacock bass." I lifted the sweating beer bottle, left hand. "So why is Iran so interested in pharmaceuticals all of a sudden? I thought secret nuke-building kept you folks pretty busy."

He cocked his head and assessed me with hooded eyes. The proprietor arrived and situated a water bottle, plastic cup, and tin ashtray. A floatplane fired up below us, and I glanced as it taxied across the water, waiting. Waiting for the passage of a riverboat with sufficient size to create a large wake. Floatplanes in fetid tropical heat have an issue breaking the suction of their long pontoons. Surface chop—or a boat's wake—helped break the bond.

"Are you a Jew?" he asked.

"Nope. Rastafarian. You know—lots of weed, Bob Marley music."

His question flung the window of uncertainty wider. Were the Israelis here as well? And what the hell were these guys after?

He shook his head. The lip curl grew as he ignored my stated religious affiliation. The music next door changed to a Brazilian samba.

"The Islamic Republic of Iran is always interested in expanding its commercial interests." He ground the cigarette butt into the ashtray. "What is your name?" He pulled out and lit another cig.

"I'll keep that private. How about your name?"

We locked eyes again, silent. He stroked his goatee. I hadn't traveled under an alias for this job. Hadn't seen the need. The mission: arrive Manaus, travel to the base camp, go find Ana Amsler.

The floatplane pilot sighted a nearby riverboat with a sufficient wake and goosed it. The Amazon River was over five miles wide at this point, but—according to my pilot's office manager—planes avoided surface stretches distant from the shoreline. Out there, twenty percent of the world's fresh water flowed past. Along with massive Amazonian trees washed downstream. Out there be floatplane dragons.

Mr. Congeniality ignored my question and slid toward the issue at hand. "In the interest of business, allow me to be direct."

You haven't skimped on that facet so far, dude. I nodded as reply. Then his cell phone rang. The ring tone was the *William Tell* Overture. Why not? Everything else in this little vignette occupied weird space. I took in the table of MOIS agents. Three sets of eyeballs provided intense stares under dark bushy eyebrows. Pissant goons. My table companion pulled the phone from his pocket, checked the call, and sent it to voice mail. He refocused on me.

"This vast area," he continued, waving a hand toward the river and rain forest. "It is enormous and open for exploration. It is open to new discoveries. Discoveries that would help the world. We are a merciful people, and part of the civilized world. And yes, we have interest in development of our own drug industry. Is this a bad thing, my friend?"

His line reeked of BS but also presented an opening. A light-the-fuse opening that might display his clearer intentions. Excited folks reveal.

"No," I said, raising my empty beer bottle toward the proprietor, who smiled and nodded and pulled another cold one from the cooler. I played the pharma employee line. "No, it is not a bad thing. But these endeavors require an investment. The Swiss and Americans and others have invested millions in their bio-prospecting work."

The cig tapped against the flimsy ashtray. A thin sweat bead rolled down his cheek as he waited for me to continue.

"So I know where this is headed. You suggest taking a shortcut. Stealing."

The hooded eyes lit up, thin nostrils flared. "What do you know of stealing? Of theft? We have had our history stolen. Our glorious past corrupted. Ancient pride and power discredited. I speak about a simple business transaction. Do not portray my actions as a form of theft. You know *nothing* of such things."

Jeez Louise. Easy enough getting a rise out of this guy. Fanaticism on full display, unlike any professional clandestine player I'd run across. But instead of job-related revelations, the guy dived down an ancient-grievances rabbit hole. So I headed toward the heart of the matter.

"Why are you talking with me?"

He poured water into the cup, a purposeful movement to tamp down his emotions. His companions, silent, continued their Rasputin-like glares my way. The small scattering of other patrons ignored us. He downed the water in a few gulps, collected himself. Gave a final shot across the bow.

"Your company steals from this land. From these people. Do not speak of theft with me."

"Okay."

He waved a dismissive hand. "Enough about these things. I suggest a business transaction."

"Okay."

"We will pay you a million dollars. US. For delivery of the Swiss scientist."

"What if she's dead?"

"Deliver her body and all her possessions. Notes, computers, everything. We will pay half a million for this."

"A lot of money."

"More, much more than your company pays you. And our transaction will exist only between us. You and me. In cash."

I held back a strong urge to ask him what they thought Amsler had discovered, what magic elixir she'd found among the two million square miles of Amazonia. But he assumed I already knew or had insight or, at a minimum, understood her discovery was groundbreaking. I worked for a pharma company, after all.

"I'll consider it." Figured that would ratchet down our little chat. I was wrong.

The cigarette dangled from thin lips as he pulled a business card from his shirt pocket, hidden behind the pack of smokes. Laid it on the table while two long, thin fingers maintained pressure. The card was cream white, with an embossed phone number. No name, no organization. He tapped the smoke twice against the ashtray with his other hand and leaned forward.

"Call me if you find her, my friend. Alive or dead. Call me. Think of the money. And consider this. Either you help me, or you deny me help. Which would make you my enemy." He paused. Took a drag and exhaled across the table. "You do not wish to be my enemy."

I lifted the beer bottle as acknowledgement, tipped it his way.

"Back at you, my friend. Right back at you."

Chapter 3

My earlier Clubhouse visit had been standard operating procedure. My Zurich client, Global Resolutions, had contacted me with a job proposal. It had its appeal, but I relied on input from Jules prior to formal acceptance. Standard stuff.

I headed for the Clubhouse in Chesapeake, Virginia. Left my home, the *Ace of Spades*, docked in New Bern, North Carolina. The *Ace*. An old wooden cruiser—well used, a bit rough around the edges, and reliable as sunrise. It provided shelter and movement and protection as I cruised the Intracoastal Waterway. The Ditch. It stretched from Virginia to Florida, crossing bays and traversing rivers and canals. Long river stretches and canal sections shaded with moss-laden oaks and running past quiet hamlets. An evocative pace, quiet and isolated and removed. The *Ace*. The Ditch. Home.

The Clubhouse occupied the upstairs of a Filipino dry cleaning establishment in a run-down section of Chesapeake. I left my weapon and cell phone left on the counter—standard operating procedure—as an expressionless Filipino employee covered the items with dropped-off laundry. Entered an obscure door and ascended squeaky stairs, the metallic latch thrown after two knocks on the steel door.

I pirouetted as Jules stared down the sawed-off shotgun's twin barrels. I held cash in one hand; in the other a lone index card. Jules exchanged information using only two formats—verbal or handwritten notes on index cards. No electronic trails. She would make exceptions with me and send the occasional secure text message or dark web email. Communiqués cryptic and open for interpretation and, more than once, life-saving.

"Enter, enter, dear boy, and tell me a tale," she said, lowering the shotgun. "We have not spoken since your last little jaunt among isolated parts of the Caribbean."

"How you doing, Jules?"

I sat. She smiled and scratched under her chin.

"As well as a simple and honest broker of information might be expected. You have brought fuel to stoke the boiler."

She referenced the index card. I laid it on her desk, slid it toward her. She remained locked on me, awaiting details.

"Contact information for a Chinese spy. MSS."

"How lovely. Where might this happy occurrence have happened?"

"Panama City, Panama. The airport. A return leg from the Caribbean. He tried to recruit me."

She cackled and plucked up the card. Her fingertips evidenced the shine of applied sealant. No fingerprints.

"An unsuccessful endeavor, I take it?"

I smiled at her unserious question. "They come out of the bloody woodwork. It's like I attract them."

"Your contractual endeavors attract them, dear. Now tell me about your current fandango."

"A lost scientist in the Amazon. A simple gig. Find her. Haul her back to Switzerland."

"Yes. Of course." The Clubhouse network had already alerted her regarding the lost scientist. Did she have viable intel related to my gig? Maybe. Would she reveal everything she'd picked up? I doubted it.

"But note my dismay," she continued. "A simple contract? You have already lost sight of the one big item."

The one big item—nothing was ever as it seemed. Her personal admonition toward my simplistic worldview. Then she delivered her "deadlier shadows" assessment and the "remarkable discovery" statement and eyes-in-the-back-of-my-head counsel.

I delivered a reflexive sigh in response. As former Delta Force, cut-and-dried was my preferred realm. Good guys. Bad guys. Take out the latter. But I dealt with Jules and her peculiar tendencies because she delivered salient operational information—for a price. Information that assisted my field endeavors. And saved my scarred rear end more than once. But Jules and her associated brethren swam in cloudy water, signals unclear, motivations and actions obscured behind espionage curtains. Light years from cut-and-dried. And a pain in the ass.

"Okay," I said. "We've covered the deadlier shadows thing. Let's talk remarkable discovery. What's your best guess? Cancer cure? Fountain of youth?"

Jules shrugged. The double-barreled shotgun rested on the desktop alongside the embedded Ka-Bar knife and old wooden abacus. The knife cut the end off her cigars. The abacus constituted her accounting system.

"One can hardly separate fact from fiction with such situations," she said and puffed her cigar back to life. "The world of Big Pharma is rife with innuendo. With tradecraft often involved. Competitive advantages and such. It is a large and contentious industry, Ponce de León."

Her conversational path showed signs of fading into the pharma-world weeds, so I shifted toward tactical considerations.

"Logistics. I require a fixer. An airfreight shipment unopened by Brazilian customs officials."

"You require a despachante. I know of an excellent one."

"And a reliable floatplane pilot. A person who both knows the area and handles a tight spot when necessary."

The tight spot criteria pointed toward exit strategy development—a first consideration when entering an operational area.

"I know of just the individual. A heavy ecumenical bent, so I'm told, but first-rate piloting skills."

She slid open a wooden desk drawer and rifled through a stack of index cards. Produced two and slid them across the desktop. She waited while I memorized the contact information. Her cards never left the Clubhouse. Information digested, the cards returned.

Head tilted, she ran several black balls down her abacus's rails. I held a credit with Jules due to past provided information. A credit disappearing with great rapidity. She'd calculate the value of my Chinese spy information and factor it into my balance sheet. None of her customers had the foggiest notion about her debits and credits valuations. And no one argued.

"Now tell me more of this engagement," she said. "Share what you know, and I shall endeavor to reciprocate, albeit with details perhaps less than pertinent toward your prime concern. That of staying alive."

She chuckled, and I performed the usual informational dump. Part of my soliloquy might have represented old news for Jules. Parts, perhaps, containing new interest. I'd never know.

A missing scientist. A bio-prospector. One of a thousand high-degreed folks employed by pharmaceutical companies scouring this good earth for the next cure, the next big-bang drug compound. The bio-prospector had gone missing from a base camp deep in the Amazon rain forest. And given the base camp was run by a Swiss pharmaceutical company, it stood clear they had contacted Global Resolutions and requested someone with the appropriate field skills. Find Dr. Ana Amsler. The gnomes of Zurich had added a kicker to the contract, a first for me. Personal delivery of the good doctor back to Switzerland. Fine and no sweat. Unless she was dead. A fifty-

fifty proposition in my book. You didn't get lost in two million square miles of tropical wilderness for fun and adventure.

I leaned toward taking this gig for several reasons, and was honest with Jules about personal motivation. At its roots, the job entailed search and rescue. Search and rescue within a tough physical environment. My former Delta status ensured I had the chops to pull it off. And, while I'd visited Brazil and spoke Portuguese, the opportunity for mucking about in the vast Amazon wilderness offered a new experience. And held something of a cool factor. Hey, I'm human. And, yeah, the saving someone's life aspect had its own strong appeal.

"Not an altogether strange rationale or perspective," Jules said. "It highlights your positive attributes, dear. A can-do approach with a dash of altruism. Bully for you."

She smiled. I think.

"How did the rumor get started?" I asked. Her turn to share.

"A coffee shop."

"Okay."

"Your learned quarry, after the alleged discovery, took a brief sabbatical. In the motherland."

"Switzerland."

"Basel, to be exact." She paused, puffed her cigar. "Numerous Swiss pharmaceutical companies make their nests there."

"So she blabbed over a cup of coffee. Which was overheard and disseminated and sent through assorted clandestine grinders."

Jules wafted a dismissive hand. She owned one of the best grinders out there. Her one eye stared, unblinking. But this was the beauty of the Clubhouse. The dossier on Dr. Ana Amsler sent from Global Resolutions failed to mention operational background such as her Basel return. Valuable intel and a burr under the saddle. Global Resolutions should have included such details.

"So, bottom line, Jules. We don't know diddly-squat about what this scientist may or may not have discovered."

"Hardly the case. She has clearly discovered a method of kicking an espionage hornet's nest. No small feat."

"That's not helping me find her."

"True. And sadness reigns. Sadness and contrition." She slumped, her chair squeaked. "I have no further information. Nothing worthy of expressing. This poor creature before you is bereft of further insights. So allow a brief interlude as I admit failure and wallow in the discomfort."

I did. She cast her lone eagle eye in my direction. Cigar smoke drifted around her face. Her close-cropped DIY haircut had lost the white-spiked tips evident at our last meeting, months earlier. But she had changed her eyepatch. Deep blue replaced the usual black, the band lost amid unruly hair. Somewhere the AC unit hummed. The Cirque du Soleil poster remained taped to one of the steel walls—the lone bit of decor. She puffed. We stared. Welcome to the freakin' Clubhouse.

"A word. A whisper," she continued, straightening up. "Be aware movement is underway among less savory players. I can offer nothing more."

"There's a big bucket of unsavory players."

"Indeed there is."

She wouldn't elaborate, the informational well in that sector having run dry. We chatted awhile, and the metallic click of the Clubhouse door lock disengaging sounded. She'd pressed a hidden switch, signaling the end of our sit-down.

"One last tidbit, dear. If you engage with my world during your sojourn south, do prevent escalation."

"Always do."

"No, you do not. You cut a wide swath, Mr. Lee. And escalation will bring larger interests into the game. And the game is, indeed, afoot."

Chapter 4

I tamped down a strong hankering to confront the Iranian SOBs—all four—and clean house. But the urge, while often present, was tempered with age and experience. And provided no value for the situation. The Iranian spook had had his say and made his play. Fine. I'd hit the rain forest tomorrow, away from these clowns.

The MOIS agent removed his fingers, and I pocketed the business card. He returned to his table. I drained my fresh beer, stood, and left. Headed down the slope and back toward the floatplane collection. The sun broke through; sweat flowed.

I didn't enjoy rubbing elbows with spooks of any stripe. But this gang with their threats and attempts at intimidation raised my hackles big time. The lead guy was a bully. I couldn't abide bullies. And the outright lies about the development of Iranian pharmaceutical capabilities grated. Something didn't jibe. Plus the whole righteous indignation over the theft of his history and rightful place on the world's stage. A blindside delivery and a reflection of unstable fanaticism. A dangerous worldview, and one prone to violence. The MOIS agent was filled with a wingnut element, and his crazy zealotry owned a hair-trigger. Fine, my new friend. I owned one too.

The pilot was back in his tiny office. He filled the place. A huge man. As I approached, his voice boomed from the office's open door and window and across the floating docks. An American, he belted out the country song "Jesus, Take the Wheel." I smiled—a needed break from anger and confusion—and gave a quick thought to my reliance on Bernie taking the wheel. Bernie Anderson. My pilot.

I stuck my head through the doorway and introduced myself. He stopped singing, extended a ham hand, and threw a big smile my way.

"Bernie Anderson. You've already met my assistant, Pablo."

Pablo, now crammed against his desk as Bernie's bulk occupied all the available free space, raised a disgruntled hand in recognition.

"I have. And thanks for seeing me. I wanted to go over logistics for tomorrow."

"Fine! Are those containers yours?"

He lifted a chin toward a row of gas containers arrayed on the dock outside his office door. The man exuded enthusiasm, sweat, and humor. Bernie maintained a shaved head, and a sweat ring collected above his florid face before joining other rivulets headed south. Thick glasses eased their way down his nose, which he pushed back up with regularity. A bright Hawaiian shirt strained against his bulk.

"They are. And the outboard engine and crated Zodiac and the container of my stuff. Plus a rucksack. And me."

"Well, Case—may I call you Case?"

"Please do."

"Well, it would appear your yoke might be easy, but your burden is most definitely not light."

He laughed. You had to like this guy. He provided me background mixed with good humor. Bernie was a missionary, spreading the Word across Amazonia. Funded his mission through hauling people and equipment into the Amazon basin. Landing strips were comprised of smaller rivers and tributaries across vast wilderness tracts. Bernie, it became clear, knew the conditions and environments as well as any native, and possessed a can-do attitude. He'd lived in Manaus twenty-five years.

"Well, Bernie, I appreciate you taking my load of equipment. It's a bundle of stuff. No doubt."

"It'll take two trips, I'm afraid. You've gotta figure for APT."

"APT?"

"Added Pilot Tonnage." He laughed again and headed toward the door. I pulled away onto the dock, allowing him room. He turned sideways to exit. "Let me show you my baby."

His baby consisted of a forty-year-old Cessna 185 Skywagon floatplane. It bobbed alongside the dock, one among a dozen others. The aircraft's age didn't concern me, as long as it was well maintained. A six-seater, the two farthest back seats long-removed for cargo space.

"How long is the flight?" I asked.

"Hour and a half. I'll drop you and your essentials, then return and pick up the gas and outboard engine."

"Have you visited this base camp before?"

"Multiple times. I helped set them up. And I haul their folks in and out. But they aren't the only team prospecting the jungle, and I've helped them all. They know I'll drop everything if someone gets hurt and needs out."

"Good for you, Bernie." I meant it. The old Cessna was a lifeline.

"Give, and it will be given to you." He smiled, slapped my back—which almost sent me into the water—and added, "Let's get shade-side. It's a tad warm in the sun."

We did. The small plank office offered shade, and we stood and completed business. I paid cash and opened the door for potential insight.

"I'm here to look for a missing scientist."

"I figured."

"You know about her?"

"It's the worst-kept secret in Amazonia. I flew multiple trips on a search pattern with one of the Swiss. But we didn't have any luck. The poor lady may have met her maker."

"Did you know her?"

Insights, perceptions, small clues. Anything to help my search.

"In passing. A nice person, I suppose. One of those whiz-bang scientists, so she had a few quirks. Like they all do, I suppose. The really smart ones."

"Quirks?"

"Oh, speech patterns, single-minded focus, that sort of thing. But a good person in her heart, I'm sure. I've prayed for her often. And I'll pray you find her."

"Thanks. Could use the help. How often do these Swiss cycle out? Take a break?"

"Oh, it varies. They work three or four weeks at a stretch. I'd flown the lost one back in about a week ago."

"Anything different about that trip?"

Bernie used a sausage-sized fingertip to push his heavy glasses upward. "No. Not really. She had a pretty good-sized aluminum case with her. More scientific equipment, I suppose."

"Anyone besides the Swiss shuttling between here and there?"

He pulled a handkerchief and mopped his head.

"Had one fella just yesterday. He wore city clothes. Asked me to wait while he talked with the Swiss folks. Then I flew him back. Nice enough individual, but wasn't dressed for the occasion."

"Tall and thin? Mustache and goatee?"

Bernie laughed. "The exact opposite. Built like a bowling ball. Clean-shaven. But I'm no beauty queen myself, so I'm not one to talk."

"Did you happen to ask where he was from?"

"I tried, but he clammed up. Not in an ugly way. He was nice about it. And I respect others' privacy. Live and let live."

"Fair enough. Anything else you could share? Anything that could help my search?"

He pursed his lips and considered. Sweat dripped, voices sounded along the floatplane docks. The equatorial sun lowered, and the day's activities spread across this stretch of river began tapering down.

"It's not worth much, Case. But I'll toss it out there. She was bullheaded. I could tell from our brief conversations. Those quirks we talked about."

"Okay."

"She wasn't the type to get lost. She would know where she was going, and how to get there. I'm not saying something didn't happen with her. But I just don't see her as the type to wander around in a panic."

"That helps. Thanks."

"How long do you plan on staying in the bush?" he asked.

"A week. Ten days max. If I can't find her or a trace of her within that time frame, she's truly disappeared."

"Well, I take it you've done this type of thing before." Delivered with a slight smile. He wouldn't pry, but he left the door open for any elaboration I might want to share.

"Similar stuff." Benign enough, and as far as I'd go.

"Well, I have a few tips for you, which we'll go over during the flight. Piranhas, gators—that sort of thing. It might help. I want you to find her. Or her remains. Her family must be distraught beyond belief."

We made plans for an early a.m. meet-up. We'd fly at dawn. A handshake and I strolled away, aware that eyes on the riverbank watched. Bernie hummed an old gospel tune behind me. Dusk approached.

A mile or so back to the hotel, and I walked busy streets. Safety in crowds. Not safe from being followed, but no one would try whacking me while dozens of locals pressed around. An opportunity to stretch my legs and reflect on the mission.

Find a disappeared scientist within a vast area of Amazonia. Challenge aplenty. And now the Iranian BS. Clearly tons of pressure on the head guy. It's why he pushed, offered big bucks, threatened. I wished I knew more details about the rumor Dr. Amsler slipped into whirling winds at a Swiss coffee shop. If her discovery held global-interest water, why weren't the big boys here? CIA, MI6, Russians, Chinese? I couldn't be sure they weren't, but given my past with the Company they would have shown by now. Would have appeared and attempted to leverage my efforts for their own purposes. Nope, just Iranian agents. Unpleasant assholes.

I could turn the tables and follow those guys, suss how they operated in Manaus. Who else they contacted. Meet the players. Or skedaddle early a.m. Keep low, sidestep their presence, and do my job. Head up the Amazon River. Find the good doctor. With an added new wrinkle if I found her—I wouldn't be able to return to Manaus. The MOIS muscle would be after her. And me. I'd talk options with Bernie in the morning.

Citizens of Manaus strolled, laughed, called to friends across small streets. I lowered the high alert dial a bit, certain the MOIS agents—who may have followed me—would wait for my jungle return. With Ana Amsler.

I ruminated on the nature of this gig. After several tough and gnarly bloodletting contracts, I'd asked Global Resolutions for lower-key jobs. They'd responded with a contract that, on the surface, appeared pure gumshoe. In the Caribbean. It had turned into a chaotic space with contract killers, terrorists, and a rogue CIA agent. So much for sedate sleuthing engagements.

This contract had the earmarks of a challenging environment—the Amazon rain forest—but one with a great big plus: isolation. Me, the bush, a missing scientist. Well, that whole premise was now shot to hell. Still, gone tomorrow morning. Unfettered, focused, a specific mission with few incidental entanglements. All good. So I began shedding the MOIS encounter as ugly noise from the sidelines and looked forward to a shower and a good night's sleep. Decision made. Leave Manaus in my wake, focus forward. Focus on the mission. Keep it simple, Case. Don't get wrapped around the axle over a run-in with spooks a thousand miles up the Amazon.

I passed through small sidewalk tables set up outside my hotel and nodded toward the front desk staff with a smile. The room offered AC, and I took full advantage. Soon enough I'd be bivouacked in the jungle. But at least equatorial jungles cooled off once the sun set. Concrete jungles less so. I stripped and stood under a cold shower while the day's stench—both real and perceived—washed away.

I dried in the now-cool air when the room phone rang. An unwanted intrusion. I picked up and waited for whoever was on the other side to speak first. The AC hummed. My wet footprints tracked across the exotic hardwood floor.

"Mr. Lee? Uri Hirsch. I'll be waiting at a table outside the hotel entrance."

He hung up. Great. Uri Hirsch. Whoever the hell he was. I stared at the Glock I'd brought from the bathroom and tossed on the bed. My lone trusted companion, who would join me and address this phone call from out of the blue. Jules was right. I'd forgotten the one big item.

Chapter 5

I eyeballed the immediate area outside the hotel's entrance, right hand under my loose, untucked shirt, and scratched my side. I didn't itch. But the ruse kept five fingers poised alongside the waistband-hidden Glock. A half-dozen tables and chairs in either direction. A waiter worked the few patrons. Evening's start, and Manaus slid into its after-work relaxation rhythms as the day's heat and hustle abated.

He sat at the far end of tables on the left, smiled, and raised a hand toward me. Bernie had nailed the description—a human bowling ball. Had to be the same guy. Thick, round, and bald except for a dark friar's fringe of hair. He sat with his back against the building's outer wall, lighting provided by a few electric sconces along the hotel's facade.

As I approached, right hand resting on the pistol's grip, he popped a tiny hard-boiled quail egg—shell and all—into his mouth. He chewed with mouth open and motioned toward a seat opposite him at the small table. Which would expose my back street-side. And hide his movement below the table. Movement that might involve weaponry. Not going to happen.

"Scoot over," I said, standing near him.

"First, I don't know you well enough for such intimate seating," he said, chuckling. "Second, there is not sufficient room for us both along this side of the table."

"The hell there isn't. Move your ass over."

Raised bushy eyebrows, a shoulder shrug, and more open-mouthed smacks. He scooted his chair farther down, remained against the wall. I moved a chair nearby, back now protected. He grabbed his glass and gulped white wine. Then burped, covering it with the back of his ham hand. Round head, round body. But not soft. Bowling-ball hard. The dude had forearms the size of Popeye.

"Have an egg," he said and signaled the waiter. "Or try the bread. Or both. The eggs are better." He emphasized his assessment with a quick wrist flick. Another tiny egg entered his maw. "I'm Uri. Uri Hirsch."

His English had an accent—European, perhaps, or the Levant.

"So you said on the phone."

"And you should introduce yourself. It would be the polite thing to do."

"You already know my name. Want to tell me about that?"

The waiter appeared, and he ordered another wine and a cafezinho, Brazil's ubiquitous tiny cups filled with nitro-grade sweet coffee. I ordered a Grey Goose on the rocks. No immediate danger vibe, no mental alarms, emanated from this guy. He lacked menace, unlike the Iranian. He also lacked table manners.

"I'm Mossad." He popped another quail egg, the shell crunching as he chewed, and talked. "You've heard of us."

He placed a business card on the table. Uri Hirsch. Mossad. And contact information. This cat didn't try and hide anything. An Israeli spook. Great. Just freakin' great. Which card-carrying member of spookville might drop in next? The Russians? The Brits? The heat and insects and crawling critters in the deep jungle had never held such appeal as at this moment.

"Yeah. I've heard of Mossad. Once or twice." I pocketed his card. I was collecting the things like at a real estate convention.

Uri chuckled again. "You are an interesting fellow, Case Lee. I've met people who are much more interesting, but you do have an active background."

"Good to know. Maybe I should get a Facebook page going."

"Maybe you should tell me why you are in Manaus."

"Maybe you should shove it where the sun don't shine."

He delivered a belly laugh, choked a bit, and swigged water from the table's shared bottle. Pedestrians—individuals, friends, lovers—meandered past. Traffic was light as Manaus adopted a slow-paced nighttime mantle, and locals grabbed the opportunity to socialize.

This guy had tracked me though flight manifests. Mossad had the ability—as did many others—to backdoor airline information. The name Case Lee blinked a few lights. Followed with a search of likely hotels. Money exchanged, guest registrations checked.

My mental processes tugged me in two directions. Leave, exit, and focus on tomorrow's kick-off. The mission. And tell this guy adios. Can't say it's been fun, but best of luck with whatever spy dance you're engaged with. Or play espionage poker with the Israeli on the off chance he could provide something that would help my search. With reluctance I chose the latter.

He drained the water bottle, cleared his throat, and smiled again. "Good, good. I always enjoy interactions with your kind. Emotions on your sleeve: red, white, and blue. Good. You are here to find Dr. Ana Amsler."

"Why are you here?"

"Ah. An answer more complex, I'm afraid. Are you hungry? I am."

"No, thanks."

"I believe I will try their fish. Something fresh from this magnificent river flowing past. Do you have any idea how impressive such a sight is for an Israeli? We are a dry country, in case you aren't familiar with our geography."

"Do tell."

"I *do* tell. And I will tell you we also have interest in Dr. Amsler. Perhaps."

"Perhaps?"

This guy wasn't playing his cards close to his chest. Blunt and forward. Same as the Iranian.

"We both know of the rumor. Such as it is. But we would not expend limited resources on chasing such a rumor except our sworn enemy *is* chasing the rumor."

"Okay."

"You may run into them. MOIS. Iranians."

"I'm not part of your geopolitical battles. It's between you and them. Leave me the hell out of it."

The waiter arrived with the drinks, and Uri placed his food order. My neck became stiff from looking in his direction, so I shifted for a more face-to-face position. And moved a bit farther from his reach, back still covered.

"I would love to do so. Unfortunately, they are here. A fact. And I am here because of them. And you are here to find whether the rumor is real."

"I'm here to find Amsler. Period."

Man, what did these guys hear in the rumor mill? Global Resolutions had provided no insights, no clues in Amsler's dossier. And Jules had provided zero specific insight as well—a rare and inopportune Clubhouse failure. Or she knew more details regarding the rumor and opted not to share for whatever convoluted Clubhouse reason. Hard to say. Our drinks arrived. I took a hefty swallow.

"So what I'm seeing is spook-on-spook movement around a rumor," I continued. "Do you really think I give a damn?"

"You will soon. Quite soon. But first, understand the context. And do call me Uri."

"Okay. Context."

"The Iranian government desires expansion of their terrorism support. This is well known. And desires to wipe Israel off the face of the earth. Also well known."

He'd lost all pretense of bonhomie and now delivered a hard stare. He took a sip of coffee, followed with a slug of water—while remaining eye-locked with me.

"Yeah. I get that. And it's awash with politics and fanaticism. I don't swim there."

"Don't confuse worldviews. They wish to wipe us out. We wish to survive. They spread their religious dogma. We don't. For instance, I'm an atheist."

I chewed on that, took another swallow of Grey Goose, and asked, "So let's play this out, Uri, old buddy. I find Amsler. Then what?"

"Then I convince you to hand her over to me."

"Fat chance."

"It's your best move. MOIS will forget about you once I have her."

"Not interested in MOIS."

"Maybe not, my friend." He paused and drained the cafezinho. The tiny porcelain cup appeared dollhouse scale in his paw. "But they will be *very* interested in you."

How would he know that? I hadn't revealed the riverbank sit-down with their head guy. So I opened the lid on the can-of-worms.

"I've met them."

His hand halted, a tiny egg positioned between thumb and forefinger.

"When? And with whom?"

I described the vignette, figured nothing to lose. Plus, this guy—while not an ally—was, in the immediate picture, less of a threat.

"What did their leader look like?" Uri asked, both forearms now on the table.

"Thin, fit, goatee, smoked a lot."

"And you didn't kill him?"

"Can't say I did. Sat in a public place, daylight, while three of his spooks watched. No, Uri, I didn't whack him."

I failed to mention the possibility, and the urge, as I sat at the table during our visit. Uri and I shared unblinking stares. He lifted a thumb toward himself.

"I would have."

I finished my drink with a brief reflection on the violent world Mossad and MOIS inhabited. Little or no nuance there. His food arrived and he attacked, using a fork and knife combination to shovel the dish home. He continued with a food-filled mouth as he talked.

"Farid Kirmani. Remember the name. Kirmani. You chatted with one of MOIS's head killers. We've crossed paths before. In different parts of the world."

"I'm not interested. Well outside my realm of concern. So tell me what you have on Amsler. Every bit of intel helps. Because I'm headed deep into the bush. A helluva lot more than a brief base camp visit attired in business clothes."

"So you've met Bernie. Another interesting man. A bit heavy on the Jesus metaphors, but a good pilot."

"Amsler?"

"Nothing you don't know already."

Man, did he have that wrong.

"I had hoped the Swiss collection at the base camp would have revealed more," he continued. "But they are most protective. Protective of their work and of Amsler. My charm and good looks failed to open any cracks in their protective shell." He chuckled. "And as for your not interested dismissal, you no longer have such an option."

"How's that?"

"When Kirmani delivered the friend-or-enemy ultimatum, he was not kidding. It is unfortunate, Case Lee, but you are now an official enemy of his. Which makes me your friend."

He cast a casual smile my way.

"How do you figure?"

"Because a MOIS agent followed me here. And out there," he said, pausing to wave an oak-limb arm toward our immediate environment of city street and traffic and pedestrians. "Yes, out there they have seen us break bread. Have a drink. Why, we're close personal friends. Kirmani will not like that. Or you."

He'd set me up. Knew how this would play out. A forced enlistment on the Mossad side. Dragged me into spookville's muck and mire. And put a target on my back. My blood rose and anger bubbled.

"Thanks, you son of a bitch. But know this. I'm gone in the morning. So screw you and your grand plans."

He shoveled more food into his wide mouth, a contented expression across his face. Content with the food, the setup, my response. A Mossad spook. One who reinforced pretty much all I knew about them. They also played for keeps.

"Don't you want to position on the side of God's chosen people?" he asked, pausing to wipe his mouth with a linen napkin before gulping more wine.

"Thought you were an atheist, asshole."

"Any port in a storm." He smiled large. "So let's talk about what happens if you find her."

I shifted position again and scanned the surroundings. MOIS agents observed us, somewhere. This guy might have been full of BS about their current watchfulness, but I didn't think so. So how would they now react? Try and whack me? Wait for my return from the jungle? I considered my options and paid little heed to the Mossad agent.

"They will not kill you now," he continued, glomming onto my adjusted physical demeanor. "They will wait. Wait until your return to Manaus. Then they will kill you."

I continued a focused scan, sought a glimpse, an indicator. Even within this setting's minimal light I'd pick out one of the MOIS agents from the riverbank bar.

"Although, and this is important, Case Lee, Kirmani may want another chat with you prior to tomorrow's departure," he added. "What with us breaking bread together."

"You said you knew about me." My eyes remained on the surrounding area. People wandered along both sides of the street; several vehicles rolled past. "Then maybe you understand stabbing me in the back isn't a wise course of action."

I shot him a quick glance, locked eyes again.

"You are upset. I understand," he said. "Now get over it. And let's talk about what happens if you find Dr. Amsler. As I have mentioned, the smart move is handing her over. At such point, you are no longer involved. And in no danger."

I wasn't paying any more attention to this asshat alongside me. A search and rescue and deliver gig. Now warped and shredded with deadly espionage maneuvers. At least in Manaus. Once in the bush, I stood on home turf. My turf. And my rules. Screw Uri. Screw MOIS. And screw the fresh-painted target on my back.

Did this guy really think I'd hand over Dr. Amsler? Moron. But my immediate concern focused on the next ten hours. The time between right now and when I crawled into Bernie's plane. I could retreat to the room, shove a chair under the door handle, wait till dawn. An option, but one seldom pulled from my playbook.

"I'll take a stroll. Don't try and follow me. My sincerest hope is I never see you again."

I stood, adjusted the Glock for easy reach while walking.

"Do you believe that wise? You would be safer in your room. I say this as your new friend, a fact you will come to understand."

And there stood the vast chasm between spooks and Delta. Faced with my situation, they would lie low, focus on their next clandestine steps. Survive until daylight. Delta training pushed for the specific acknowledgement and recognition of the enemy. And an opportunity to hunt them down.

"Leave me the hell alone, Hirsch." I locked eyes one last time. "And I'll do the same."

I walked away, headed for an opportunistic arena. A place, a stage, for the opening night of the killing floor.

Chapter 6

The distinct likelihood this would become violent perched over my movements like a vulture. I had no desire for engagement. None. This was geopolitical kabuki theater between two lower-level sworn enemies. Iran versus Israel. Lethal jousts across the tournament field of a nebulous rumor. The big players weren't involved. I would have smelled them by now. The Company, for sure. They would have contacted me given our recent and semi-acrimonious relationship. The Russian FSB—still mightily pissed at me—hadn't triggered any personal alarms. The Chinese MSS, always a behind-the-scenes player, were a no-show. The Brits, MI6, were exceptional pros and would sniff around if wafted aromas of legitimacy floated past. But nothing. Nada. Another wild rumor on their radar, lost among sea clutter.

Just an appearance by the Iranians. Which prompted—as per the Mossad agent—an Israeli presence. And nothing either MOIS or Mossad would say fell into the truth-be-told slot. They hated each other, plain and simple. Which left Case Lee—or anyone else—a pawn or tool or handy leverage for operational advantage.

I strolled the Manaus streets, window-shopped, and observed reflections. If I was being trailed, it didn't show. In a city of half a million, evening foot traffic afforded plenty of nighttime cover for any tails. So I employed a well-honed tactic that would nail anyone ghosting me. It held risk, upped the odds of confrontation. But I didn't have time for this mess, and my involvement irritated me big time. It both diverted from the mission and layered a patina of two-bit intrigue that held no coin in my personal realm. I knew the perfect place to find some simple answers. *Teatro Amazonas.* The Manaus Opera House.

In the late 1800s, the rubber barons of Manaus considered a grand expenditure for their newfound wealth. They decided what the backwater jungle town needed was an opera house. A sky's-the-limit decision in favor of conspicuous consumption. So they imported artists, designers, and materials from across Europe. Roof tiles from the Alsace region, fixtures from Paris, marble from Italy. Sure. Smack dab in the middle of the Amazon wilderness. Why not?

Twenty years later it shut down. The invention of synthetic rubber doomed the natural rubber market. The building, ornate as a wedding cake, sat idle for a century. In the early 2000s, Manaus—now a large city—fixed it up, cleaned it up, and reopened the place. It would be closed this time of night, but an on-duty guard or two would open a discreet door for an earnest tourist with a few Benjamins in hand. If I was being followed, my trackers would join me on the inside, an enclosed space where their intent and mission and threat level could be discerned.

One thing was now clear. This wasn't a miracle cure Amsler might have discovered. No sir. To suck MOIS operatives into the middle of Amazonia—and have them pursue a rumor with such intensity—required the discovery of something nasty, deadly. Something—a plant or a bug—that delivered toxic death. Even the head moron at Case Lee Inc. could figure that out. And I'd researched enough about bio-prospectors to know remarkable compounds and drugs had been derived from nature's toxic grab bag. With a bit of tweaking, potent toxins could be altered. Save lives. A new anticoagulant from the saw-scaled viper's venom in Africa. And promising research into treatments derived from other examples of nature's nasties. Good stuff.

But conversion from toxic to life-saving took time and investment and concerted lab effort. Iran wasn't headed down that path. The world's leading backer of terrorist activities smelled an opportunity. Smelled an opportunity to develop a new tool for terror. A new tool against the West.

And Mossad may or may not have arrived because of the Iranians. Never trust a spook. Uri Hirsch could have been sent to snatch the discovery for Israel, which had an uber-fortress mentality and would leverage any advantage.

Either way, I donned no caped crusader attitude and kept my focus on the prime mission, aware that wild rumors were just that. So find Ana Amsler. Get her to Switzerland. And haul ass away from the entire mess. Let others figure it out. You gotta keep it real, or the weirdness affects you. And not in a good way. First, ascertain hindrances, threats to the mission. The here and now. Did MOIS actors threaten the key component of the mission—me?

The opera house was washed with minimal light. Sufficient for viewing the ornate pinkish exterior. Double grand steps led upward toward the building, the tiled dome displaying the Brazilian flag's colors. I stopped at the plaza in front of the building and surveyed my backtrack. There was no production, no opera or show or event this night. A somewhat thinned crowd for this part of town, but sufficient foot traffic and darkness could hide a decent tracker. Fine. Let's get up close and personal.

"Boa noite." Good evening. Addressed toward the cluster of three unarmed security folks relaxing at the main entrance. I continued in Portuguese. "I just arrived in Manaus, and I'm flying out early in the morning. But I can't miss the opportunity to see the famous opera house."

"It is quite grand, is it not?" one replied.

"Magnificent." It was too elaborate, too fussy for my taste. But I wasn't here to critique architecture. "Truly magnificent. I would like to see the inside if I may."

"It is closed."

"Yes. Closed. I understand. But I could not forgive myself if I missed this opportunity for a view of such a wonder."

"It is closed," said another. His chest swelled with official finality.

"But I have tickets for this evening."

They looked at each other, and back to me.

"There is no performance tonight," said another.

"This is true. Yet I have tickets. Allow me to show you."

I pulled three Benjamins and handed over one each.

"For a short time. A view, an appreciation of such an amazing creation. Nothing more."

They each produced a flashlight and inspected the banknotes. Each bill then disappeared into pockets, and one of the guards head-signaled a "follow me."

We strolled alongside the building, passing several entrances. At the back, a tucked-in door—perhaps a performers' entrance—stood shadowed and quiet. A key ring jangled, the door unlocked, and I passed inside.

The guard delivered a closing remark. "Vinte minutos." Twenty minutes. Which meant up to an hour. Fair enough.

Musty, thick, dark—an enclosed fetid staleness. The century-long hiatus hadn't done this structure any favors. A performers' entrance, backstage. Through doorway curtains on the right, dim lights cast long hazy shadows. I entered into the theater seating. The low illumination highlighted elaborate frescoes and detailed fixtures with an aura of another time, long past. Four layer-cake tiers with private boxes overlooked a stage. For all its grand exterior, the actual theater wasn't large. It would seat maybe six, seven hundred patrons.

The grand chandeliers overhead remained off, but several tiered patron box seats were subtly backlit. Stage illumination was provided through a semicircle of low-intensity floor lights. A grand and glorious anachronistic setting with a tawdry touch. Rug runners along the seating aisles covered exotic flooring—mahogany, rosewood, and a rare timber I'd never identify.

Stairs to my right led upward. I took them two at a time. If MOIS heavies followed me, they'd enter through the same now-unlocked door. They'd avoid interaction with the guards out front who now, without doubt, were huddled and discussing how best to invest their hundred dollar bills.

Third tier, and I circled. Wall murals, ornate wainscoting, an overabundance of decoration. I had the weird sense of moving through a baroque dollhouse. Passed through a curtained divide and settled in a private box overlooking the stage. Drew the Glock and waited as my eyes adjusted to the dim and shadowed environment. It didn't take long.

Sounds of the actor's entrance door pulled open. The curtain divider rustled. Leading with a drawn pistol, the first MOIS operative eased through the heavy material. His two cohorts followed. The same three who'd watched our little chat at the river bar. They huddled and shared low mumbles. These goons represented muscle more than finesse. Their tradecraft relied on intimidation and force and killing. And, given their current state of indecision, not the brightest bulbs in the basket. One of them pulled a cell phone and made a call. Not a challenge figuring the call's recipient. Their boss. Farid Kirmani, according to Uri Hirsch.

Call made, they waited, wavering on the correct course of action. Better wait for the boss's directives than make a move that could run counter to Kirmani's desires. Five minutes, then ten. I remained still, watched and listened. The stage's curtain backdrop displayed a scene from ancient Egypt, faded and blurred. The three continued their low mumbling, aware I had entered. Entered and now shared this strange quiet space with them. The silhouette of a decent-sized lizard moseyed along my personal opera box's top rail, unalarmed. High overhead, several bats flicked about, hunting. The back door sounded again, and doorway curtains parted. Kirmani strode in as if he owned the place, surveyed the situation, and lit a smoke. The flick of his lighter was audible three levels up.

"Anvil salesman. I have researched this word. You are a funny man," he said, his voice echoing across the enclosed and layered space. "And now, funny man, you and I will talk."

With a low voice he conveyed instructions to his three henchmen. My ears strained in the vain hope of understanding a word or two. No such luck.

His men, pistols drawn, spread out. One crossed through the floor seating, headed for a stairway. Headed for me. Another slid along an outside wall, hunted toward the back of the theater. The third returned through the heavy curtains across the near-stage doorway we'd all entered through. He'd check behind the stage's backdrop and search backstage nooks and crannies.

"You should have told me you were a partner with the Israelis. This is important information."

He flicked ash on the carpet, took another drag, and stroked his goatee—all the while scanning the theater's upper levels. Well, that laid out his interpretation of my sit-down with the Mossad agent. Partners with the Israelis. Thanks again, Hirsch.

"So we will talk," he continued, climbing the five side steps onto the stage. "And you will provide answers. Then we are all happy. Do you understand?"

He shifted from near center stage and strode toward the stage-right exit. Leaned against a pillar, feet crossed, smoked. Not a care in the world, figuring he had me on high ground, surrounded. Advantage MOIS. Wrong, asshole.

"You Americans have an expression I most enjoy," he said, wandering back toward center stage. He spoke toward the tiers of private box seating. "We can do this the hard way, or we can do this the easy way." He shrugged, took a drag, and tilted his head back to exhale smoke upward, smiling. "Either way, funny man, we will talk."

My threat meter pegged. All signs pointed toward something other than a tense discussion. I'd seen the aftermath of MOIS's work in Lebanon during Delta Force days. Ugly stuff. Beyond ugly. These clowns intended capture—either through intimidation or a crippling gunshot. Then Kirmani would guide his men. Produce knives and begin removing body parts while he asked questions. I had no doubts about their intention, driven by gory Lebanon flashbacks.

Well, now I understood who and what I was dealing with. But they damn sure didn't. So welcome to the terminal world of Delta, you SOBs. Welcome to *my* world.

Chapter 7

A puffed-cheek slow exhale and momentary slide into the Big Lost—resigned to the inevitable, acceptance of a stand-alone position. But no questions, no remorse or hesitancy. A brief mental collection spot for well-honed skills and appropriate attitude. Into the breach. Not my call, not my preference. But yet again, my reality.

A hard blink, lips tight, a slow deep inhale. A quick head roll and loosened neck muscles. Full and absolute commitment, the kill switch thrown. All right. Let's rock and roll. Four armed MOIS agents against one former Delta operator. Man, were they screwed.

"You should know my men are quite prepared to kill you." He ground his smoke against the polished wooden stage floor and lit another. Cleared his throat and continued. "But know also I do not wish this. I wish to talk. Nothing more."

My thoughts went briefly to outside interference, outside actors. Gunshots—booming pistol shots—would blare cacophonous inside the opera house. But the sound would be muted, obscure, anywhere on the wide plaza surrounding the building. And the only plaza occupants were three unarmed Brazilian guards. Extra players in this situation added unwanted complexity. But it was my firm belief that the guards would acknowledge the muted booms among themselves and wander farther away. Edge toward the nearby street and sidewalks. Acknowledge but ignore. An hour or so from now, relock the back door. Say nothing. Allow the next day's tour guides to make the discovery and claim total ignorance of nefarious activities. Clean hands.

Kirmani barked a command for his men and continued to address me. "Show yourself, my friend. Show yourself, and allow my men to bring you here. Then we talk. Simple, no?"

He'd keep one man on the ground floor, watching for movement toward any of the multiple exits. The other two he sent up into the box seats. After me. The best hunting tactic was bait the vignette. Bait with the sound of my location. I picked the preferred spot for subsequent action. The opening act.

I scooted along the third tier hallway at the back of the seating boxes toward the hallway's end, stage right. Cracked the last box's curtain and kept an eye on the hallway.

"Well, here's the deal, my friend." The place had great acoustics, my voice carrying across the cavernous space. "I have nothing to discuss with you."

Not a Bard-worthy delivery, but it would draw the killers he'd sent upstairs.

"And there, my friend, you are most mistaken. I am certain you have much to tell me."

Kirmani paced center stage, barked more orders toward his men. I considered and rejected a long pistol shot. Always sound policy—take out the leader. But I calculated a hundred-fifty-foot distance, the target in motion, the light poor at best. Oh, I'd hit him alright, but a kill shot wasn't assured. And a wounded boss would trigger his three men into a full-on assault. I planned on one at a time. Better odds.

"I'm just not feeling the love, buddy. Sorry. So why don't you go piss up a rope?"

Enough. At least two, and perhaps three men would arrive at my spot soon enough. A quick move away from the box seat, a silent sprint, after which I assumed a one-knee position in a dark corner at the end of the hallway. Used the wall as a stabilizer, alongside a heavy split curtain that hid descending stairs toward the second level. I cracked a fold of the material pressed against the opening's side and glanced downward. Another curtain draped the stairway entrance below. A dark, dark tunnel.

On the right, the long curved hallway was in deep shadow. Anyone from that direction would creep along the inside wall, searching. By the time we saw each other, the split-second response boiled down to who was the better shot. I was more than okay with that.

"How long have you worked with Mossad, Jew-lover?" His voice indicated a move toward a protected position. Perhaps tight against stage right's exit. "How many of my people have you killed?"

None to date, bud. A number subject to immediate change. Then movement, slight, dimly perceptible. The center split of the downstairs curtain. A small opening, performed either with a finger or a pistol's barrel. This guy wasn't half-bad. He stood back from the minute opening. Viewed up the stairs while hidden in near-blackness. I couldn't make his position. A half-dozen lead-induced holes in the curtain was an option, but a poor one. Amateurish. I'd wait. I continued a focus downward from my protected kneeling position, as well as cast quick glances toward the right, in anticipation of a wall-crawler any second. Breath steady, adrenaline controlled, confidence sky-high.

A full minute, and another, as the cautious downstairs MOIS agent and I stared at each other, unseeing. Soon enough he'd opt to slide through the curtain and ascend the stairs. And take his last steps on this good earth.

No movement on the right, the hallway quiet. No wooden under-floor creaks, no moving shadows. But another worked his way toward the last sound of my voice. No doubt. Down the stairs, the curtain slit widened, slow and sure. The pistol's two-hand grip eased through the opening. His head and body followed. Another quick hallway glance. All quiet.

Explosive booms, double tap, death. Two successive shots, tenths of a second apart. Both struck the MOIS agent center-chest. Gone before he hit the floor. An immediate rightward swing of the Glock, along the hallway. I adjusted position. Sat flat, back against the wall, knees propped as arm rests. Still buried in black, aim rock-solid.

My shots triggered assailant number two's fire and verve. Big mistake. He started a dash my way, footfalls well received even on carpet. Headed toward the customer box where I'd last spoken. I was thirty feet farther down the hallway, pressed into darkness. A motionless real-life gargoyle. He wouldn't look my way, but rather focus on my last known location.

He appeared, teeth bared, and ran with gun held chest-high. Fifty feet, forty, thirty. A slammed stop at my previous location's curtained entrance. Bait swallowed. He gathered himself for a burst-through but didn't get the chance. I took methodical aim, squeezed the trigger, and delivered a roared headshot. As he crumpled, a bloody haloed mist—shadowlike—hung in the thick air. Then it fell, dissipated.

My ears rang. I shot a glance down the stairs in case one of them chose this attack point again. Silence, frozen silence. I liked my position, my Alamo, but movement gave me more advantage at this point. One MOIS goon left, plus Kirmani. Time to hunt.

Unexpected massive booms blared from the theater's interior. Somewhere on the ground floor. Two shots in rapid succession, followed by a third. Three seconds later, a fourth. All from the same weapon. The last shot a coup de grâce. What the hell? I popped upright, sought targets.

Then a clang—a metallic exit door handle bar pressed. Followed by a more muted click as the door closed. Someone split, left the opera house through a primary exit. I eased along the hallway, adrenaline meter pegged, rapid glances toward my back trail. And with a poor grasp of the situational arena.

Footfalls. Someone tromped up the steps toward the stage. A shuffle of clothing, rustling, and a critical grunt. Followed with the crinkle of paper or plastic. I stopped outside a central box seat's curtain, straining to hear. What bloody weirdness was this?

"Was Farid Kirmani one of the two you killed?"

Uri Hirsch. My Glock eased open the curtain split, providing a view of the theater. He stood center stage, unwrapping a candy bar. As he worked the wrapper, his pistol's barrel pointed in assorted directions.

"Or are *you* dead, Case Lee?" he continued. "I sincerely hope not."

He took a bite of the candy bar. I shook my head while he chewed.

"You're one strange dude, Hirsch."

I passed through the curtain and stood in the private box.

"You are wrong. And this is not decent candy," he said, inspecting the halfway exposed treat. "Brazil grows a great deal of cacao. You might think they could do much better than this."

The acoustics were so good neither of us raised our voice.

"Sorry you're disappointed with your snack. And Kirmani wasn't one of the two."

Freakin' surreal. I stood on the third tier of an empty opera house in the middle of Amazonia conversing with a Mossad spy who stood center stage, munching chocolate. While three dead MOIS agents lay strewn about. Man, I needed a career change.

"A pity. He must have been the one who ran."

"Yeah."

"And so, my friend." He deigned to look toward me. "We have a new situation."

"Manaus is loaded with new friends. Who would have thought?"

He chuckled and took another bite. And spoke with a mouthful of candy bar.

"He will hide. In a city of half a million, this is not so difficult. I will search for him, of course. And kill him, if possible. But that doesn't relate to your new situation."

"You talking about standing here with three dead Iranian spies in an opera house a thousand miles up the Amazon River? I think you nailed it, Hirsch. Definitely a new situation."

He delivered a sharp laugh, a bark. "No, no, Case. The upcoming situation. Kirmani will contact Tehran. And request many more MOIS agents. Perhaps a dozen or more. And they will kill you on sight."

"Not too long from now *I'll* be out of sight. Upriver. Middle of the jungle."

He finished the candy, crumpled the wrapper, and shoved it into a jacket pocket. The pistol hung from his trigger finger as he belched.

"Yes. Fine. You go. I wish you well. Godspeed and such. But at some point you must return."

"Working on alternatives." I wouldn't reveal any more.

"Yes. There are alternatives. But be most assured, MOIS will place their people in anticipation of your altered plans. I speak from experience."

"Yeah, well, so do I. So count me less than frantic over the future plans of MOIS."

"You do not fully understand. Perception as differentiated from reality."

"Let's stick with reality."

"No, let's consider perception. MOIS now perceives the US and Israel as a team. The Great Satan and the Little Satan working together. A team focused on preventing Iran from achieving their goal."

"And what goal is that?"

"Why, the acquisition of Dr. Amsler's discovery. Which they hope will crush Israel. And bring the US to its knees. It is not complicated, my friend."

Spooks. With their constant end-of-the-world scenarios. Enough. Adios time, hunker down for the night. Get out of Manaus early a.m. Kirmani wouldn't expend effort coming after me. If smart, he'd hide from the crazy Mossad agent. And I didn't believe he was stupid. Time for an exit. This bloodletting chapter of the Amazon job was over. Finito, Benito.

"See you, Hirsch. Actually, I hope I never see you again. But good luck and all that."

I turned and started through the drapes toward the hallway, headed for the down stairs. Hesitated, turned back, and rolled the dice. Why not, in this bizarre situation?

"How nasty do you think this stuff is—plant or animal—the good doctor discovered?"

He stuck a finger into his mouth and extricated a chewy bit of candy from a back tooth.

"I do not know. It may be nothing. It may be everything."

"Great answer, professor."

"It is." He inspected his now-removed fingertip. "When our sworn enemy is in pursuit of a maybe, my people take it very seriously."

"I've noticed."

I slid through the curtains and sought the nearest exit. His voice carried after me.

"You have my card. My phone number. Call me at any time. You will need help at some point, Case Lee. Help from a friend."

Chapter 8

Dawn. Bernie fired the Cessna while I untied the dockside pontoon. The old plane listed left—Bernie's Added Pilot Tonnage. The Amazon River rolled past as the day's first rays highlighted the indescribable and inexorable current, ocean-bound. Our protected floatplane area contained backwash and small whirlpools. The opposite shore, five miles distant, was discernable as a haze-covered green horizon. The Amazon jungle. I slipped into the copilot seat and donned a communication headset.

Bernie let the engine warm, idled into the river, and waited for a riverboat-induced wake of sufficient size. He slapped my thigh and spoke through the headset.

"A glorious day. Glorious. A few rainstorms between us and the base camp. But not a worry, and good morning!"

"Morning to you, Bernie. I'm glad to be underway."

And more than glad to have Manaus in the rearview mirror.

"Alright, alright. We're loaded up, revved up, and here we go."

He goosed the throttle. A two-tiered riverboat passed across our takeoff path, the lower deck filled with supplies, the upper with people. Headed upriver for a village, a town, new starts on life. Bernie was one of those pilots who rested a hand on the full-bore throttle as if more power could be eked out if needed. We lumbered along, accelerating. Hit the first half of the boat's wake, lifted, splashed down. The wake's other side did the trick and we were airborne. Bernie kept it straight until we climbed several hundred feet and hung a right. We were underway.

The massive Rio Negro—its tannic waters refusing an initial mingling with the Amazon's—appeared west of Manaus. We kept left and followed the Amazon River. Bernie kept us in a steady climb.

"So you've taken malaria pills?" he asked, cutting the throttle back as we reached cruising speed.

"Yep. All set."

"Good. Now, I don't want to treat you like a nimrod, Case. But can I share some experience with you? Amazonia experience."

"Knock yourself out." I patted his leg. "Every little bit helps."

"Some folks get offended."

"Not me."

Only a fool would bypass the opportunity to garner inside info before a weeklong push into the Amazon jungle. I took pride in my outdoor skills, but awareness and local perspective and survival tips were gold-standard commodities before such an excursion.

"Well, let's start with water."

"No shortage there." I smiled as the world's largest river flowed below us.

"Actually, there is. This is the middle of the dry season. Rivers and tributaries and creeks are dropping. It's a big deal."

"Okay."

"You've gotta think scale. Take the entire US west of the Mississippi River. Now dump twenty or thirty feet of standing water on it. That's the peak flood season here."

I'd read up on my destination. Knew of the annual floods. Still, flying over this vast jungle-covered area brought it home unlike any form of research.

"Help me understand the wet and dry seasons from an operational perspective."

"Well, it's not flat down there. A good thing."

He laughed and winked my way. Then used a sausage-sized forefinger and pointed toward each of the Cessna's instrument panel gauges. Pilot habit—checks and confirmation.

"Some areas—the size of small US states—remain above the floodwaters," he continued. "Plus thousands of small hills and hummocks become islands. Just figure about half what you see down there is submerged six months of the year. Trees and all."

"So you work through half-submerged trees to access those dry land islands?"

"You got it. But with the waters receding, rivers and creeks are returning to their normal channels. Which will make navigation and movement easier for you."

"Good to know." Better than good to know. Much better. I began hatching a search plan.

Bernie shifted his bulk, sought a more comfortable position. The plane shifted with him.

"But low water brings a few other potential issues." He turned his head and smiled my way. Bright teeth flashed across a florid face. "Now, I'm not trying to freak you out. Just tossing a few things on the table."

"Toss away."

"Piranhas."

"Okay."

"The big silver ones in the deeper big water. The little bluegill-sized red bellies up the smaller tributaries and creeks."

"So stay out of the water."

"Nah. Not really. You can swim and bathe with them. Until the water gets too low. Then they concentrate. You don't splash around when they're stacked up at low-water season in another month or so. But they're a consideration. If you have a wound or cut that might bleed, you'll want to avoid a swim."

"I have a feeling this isn't mentioned in the visit-the-Amazon tourist brochures."

We both laughed while he checked the instrument panel again and sang a bit of a gospel tune, his voice a sweet tenor.

"Oh," he added, "They're also quite tasty. For fresh fish, they're easy to catch and good to eat. But that reminds me of something else."

"Okay."

"Don't pee while you bathe or swim."

"Don't plan on a lot of swimming, Bernie."

"I enjoy it. It's refreshing when you're sweat-covered." He pointed an index finger downward. "Just don't pee when you're in the water. Candiru. A tiny, tiny little fish. The locals claim it follows the urine stream, enters the penis, and locks tight."

"Ouch."

"Yowza. One mighty big ouch. It may not be true, but better safe than sorry."

"Sorry on a scale seldom reached."

"For a fact. One wonders what the good Lord had in mind. Now, let's talk gators and snakes."

"They truly have left a great deal out of those tourist brochures."

He chuckled and pulled two cool guarana drinks from between the seats. We both popped tops and drank.

"Now, alligators. Technically they're caimans, but who's arguing? Not too much of a worry during the day. But do *not* visit the water's edge at night."

"Got it."

"And you'll run into snakes. Most are harmless. But the anaconda is another reason to avoid visiting streamside at night. That's one big snake."

"So I hear."

"I'm talking thirty feet long. Big around as your waist. And keep an eye peeled for the fer-de-lance and bushmasters. They will kill you."

"So what I'm hearing is stay away from snakes."

He laughed. I joined, but with less enthusiasm. A lot less.

"Oh, and bullet ants. Take a wasp sting's pain and multiply it thirty or forty times. Another yowza."

"Makes me want to run naked through the bush. Take in all that nature offers."

"You'll be fine. Be aware. It's not a benign environment."

The downside presented by Amazon critters wasn't a dissuader, nor did it implant fear. Stings, critter bites—part of the deal and accepted. A matter of simple precautions, and never let your guard down. This wasn't an English meadow that flashed past below us. And *flash* the appropriate word—flocks of bright red and yellow and blue parrots flew formation over treetops, visible as neon colors against a green horizon-to-horizon backdrop. We rode in silence, the propeller droned, and smaller tributaries glistened as we passed overhead. Bernie plowed through a couple of rainstorms. The plane's cabin cooled prior to breaking into bright sunlight and warming again.

"What about the locals? Natives?" I asked. I wasn't counting on encounters with rain forest folks, but preparedness was the name of the game.

"Ah. A favorite topic of mine. Congregants. More or less. Perhaps less than I would like." Said with a wide smile. "The Rio Urucu area you'll be in has several tribes. I haven't had much contact with them."

"Friendly?"

"Depends on the day of the week. And the hour of the day. And maybe the moon's phase. Would you fish one of those sandwiches out for me? Help yourself as well. Part of the in-flight service."

The paper sack behind us contained a bag of Brazil nuts and several sandwiches. I handed one over, and Bernie dug in.

"So, any tips in case we do bump into them?"

"Smile. Extend an open palm. Leave. Go explore another spot."

I caught myself performing an unconscious scratch of the scar left by a New Guinea tribal arrow. Bernie's advice held real-world water.

"Okay. Anything else about the flora and fauna? Land sharks? Jungle krakens?"

He chuckled. "I've laid out a few things to be aware of. But it's a place like no other. An amazing spot on this grand ball we call earth. The Amazon rain forest is filled with wonder and beauty." He sang a gospel line. "Let your worries go, and trust the Lord has a plan."

Bernie Anderson extended an acorn-squash-sized fist. I bumped it with mine and grinned, so relieved at having Manaus behind me. Filled with positive mission-oriented anticipation. Headed into my kind of turf. My kind of operational area.

A couple of items remained unresolved. We'd been airborne for a while, and the mission's exit required addressing. Along with a warning.

"I won't return to Manaus. With or without Dr. Amsler. What are other options for an Amazonia exit?"

"Can I ask why?"

"Better if you didn't. Call it personal reasons."

A lousy response given recent events. Valid under other circumstances; sufficient and final. But reality shone bright—Bernie was exposed. Seen with me. So I delivered a tangential warning.

"There's something associated with my personal reasons you should know about," I added. "There are bad characters in Manaus keenly interested in Ana Amsler."

"Was the fellow in business clothes one of them? The round one I flew here the other day?"

"No. I mean, he's associated with the whole mess. But I don't believe he's a threat. There are others. Be careful for a while."

He chuckled. "You make it sound very mysterious. But I'm not worried."

"I'm talking bad, bad dudes. Among the worst. I'd appreciate it if you'd heed my words."

"The Lord is my strength and my shield."

"Yeah, I get that. But on a more secular and tactical level, watch your back. I'm serious."

"So you seek options other than Manaus." He chomped the last bit of sandwich before answering. He'd moved on from concerns about his safety. "Coari."

A finger directed my attention toward a spot on the horizon. Toward evidence of a town, a small city, along the main Amazon River's bank.

"When you're ready and—Lord willing—successful, I'll pick you up at the base camp and drop you at Coari. In a pinch, you could travel by boat. It's about sixty miles from the base camp. Down the Urucu and Amazon rivers."

I considered a danger zone revisit for emphasis. Opted for a mission-oriented tack and kept things light. Plant the danger seed now, fertilize later. I'd bring up Manaus issues with him before final departure.

"I assume they have a runway? Nothing against slow floatplanes, bud, but Amsler and I might like something that could land us in Rio de Janeiro or São Paulo. Like, sometime this month."

Bernie patted the top of his baby's instrument panel. "Pay him no mind. The race is not to the swift and the battle not to the warriors."

"Hope you're right. I'm in the 'avoid battles' mode. Now, about that runway?"

"One commercial flight a day. To Rio de Janeiro."

"Good. A solid alternative."

"Plus plenty of plane traffic between Coari and Manaus. Floatplane traffic. Remember those? They look a lot like your current conveyance. The one making a door-to-door delivery. At a remote base camp in the middle of the Amazon jungle."

Delivered with a wry smile. Man, I liked this guy. And wished he'd heed the danger warning with more intent.

"Got it. And nothing against your baby. Speaking of imminent delivery, who's the base camp boss now?"

"Dr. Rochat."

The dossier on Ana Amsler included a few tactical considerations. The Swiss base camp held five or six scientists at a time. The lead scientist—the base camp boss—rotated out every three or four weeks with the rest of the team as the new team arrived. I'd deal with Dr. Kim Rochat, PhD in biochemistry and molecular life sciences. She hailed from Switzerland's French-speaking area.

"What's she like?"

"Solid. A nice person."

"Anything else?"

"A good leader. And great to work with. I like her."

Knowing Bernie, I'd now plumbed the depths of his opinion regarding another person. One final stab at information gathering. Bernie helped search for Amsler. He might have insights into her discovery. A long shot.

"So who flew with you on your air search?"

"The Doc. Dr. Rochat. Since she's team leader and all."

"Did she happen to mention anything about a discovery Ana Amsler made? Some remarkable discovery?"

Bernie adjusted the plane's throttle. A flock of electric-red parrots skirted treetops, their plumage highlighted against the shades of green.

"Yes. And it was kinda weird."

"How so?"

He glanced my way and struggled with delivery, context.

"Well, the Doc didn't detail what Ana found. Remarkable discovery, I think she said. But her tone was strange. Fearful."

"Fearful?"

"Yes. That's the weird part. I mean, her body tightened and face tensed. Not the reaction you'd expect when discussing a potential miracle cure."

We started our descent in earnest.

"It made my gut knot," he continued. "And since you tossed in the possible involvement of men with ill intent, the knot—a tight one—has reappeared."

"Good. Maybe it'll keep you on your toes."

He shot a quick glance and shook his head.

"I'm not much of a ballerina. But it reinforces my initial impression when I talked with the Doc. I think Ana Amsler found something bad. Real bad. Something I don't believe people should mess with."

Chapter 9

The Urucu River narrowed and meandered. Smaller rivers fed it from all directions. Bernie turned west and aimed at one of the larger tributaries, hemmed with dense overhanging rain forest. A rapid descent, and we dropped below treetop level. The walls of massive trees and green growth flashed past less than twenty feet off each wingtip. A poor time for pilot error. Splashdown brought relief and new appreciation for a guy who'd handled these landings for decades.

We cruised up the unnamed river toward a bend, the water with a slight off-color but otherwise clear and inviting. Until my mind wandered toward piranhas. And the urine-flow-seeking tiny critter.

Camp smoke clung to the treetop canopy ahead. As we rounded the bend an organized tent camp appeared on a steep-sloped bank, well above the high-water mark. A half-dozen aluminum skiffs were arrayed in a neat line along the shoreline. Bernie edged the Cessna onto the bank for offloading.

A small, fit woman descended wood-reinforced steps cut from the riverbank. She strode toward us as the engine died, wearing khaki shorts and a two-pocket khaki work shirt. A navy Houston Astros ball cap above Ray-Ban aviator sunglasses. And bright purple bootlaces with her hiking boots. Dr. Kim Rochat. Had to be. She removed the sunglasses. Instead of sliding them into her shirt's neckline or one of the shirt pockets, American style, she popped open a Ray-Ban belt case and secured them. Because, being Swiss, it's where they went. Bernie squeezed from the pilot's seat, stood on a pontoon, and made introductions.

"Dr. Rochat, this is Case Lee."

I stepped onto shore and extended a hand. We shook.

"Mr. Lee. I was told someone would arrive soon."

Up close, her eyes jarred. Ice-blue. Siberian husky blue.

"Glad I'm here. And ready to get started. Let me unload. I've got work assembling the inflatable boat while Bernie makes another trip. Fuel and the boat engine still sit in Manaus."

"We will depart this afternoon?"

I blinked. She didn't. Her eyebrows were white-blond. Her voice carried a French lilt.

"We?"

"But of course. I will accompany you."

She emphasized her statement with two fingers extended and pointed my way. Like a kid shooting an imaginary pistol. Three other Swiss scientists made their way from large, neat tents and descended the bank to join us. Introductions and handshakes all around.

"Well, the thing is, I work alone," I said, addressing Kim Rochat.

"I will provide assistance. I am prepared for departure at any time today. My preference is to leave as soon as you are ready." She assessed me stem to stern with pursed lips. "You are American, Mr. Lee."

A series of statements, not a single question hidden among the bunch. And accompanied with several finger-pistol gestures.

"That a problem?"

"I do not know yet."

Delivered with a half-smile. I held up a forefinger.

"Excuse me and hold that thought. Bernie could use a hand."

Delivered with my own half-smile. Bernie and I wrestled the crated Zodiac from the cargo area and carried it ashore. Next came my large case of equipment and special tools. The unloading tasks allowed weigh time. Weigh the pros and cons of Kim Rochat as a search partner.

My initial reaction—kneejerk. Based on habit and experience. Now tempered with the acknowledgement that we weren't entering a hot-fire zone or human-induced danger. Rochat might provide field insights. A plus. A second set of eyeballs, another plus. And, yeah, she was cute as could be. Although the finger shots would take getting used to. And the statement about my country of origin—a dig? Maybe. Maybe not. But then again, I'd made a cultural broad-brush mental assertion with the Ray-Ban storage. Within ten minutes we had the floatplane emptied. And I'd emptied most of my pushback against Dr. Kim Rochat as a search party member.

"If you'll give a shove once I've fired her up," Bernie said, pouring sweat. He pushed the eyeglasses back up his nose. "A strong shove. Put me in the center of this river. I'll return in three or four hours."

As he lifted his bulk into the plane, he shot a question toward the camp. "You need anything, Doc? While I'm in Manaus?"

"No, thank you, Mr. Anderson."

The floatplane fired, I shoved, and in short order Bernie had navigated the river's tight turn. Couldn't see it, but I heard the takeoff as baby received full throttle. As the noise faded, she sidled alongside me.

"And so. We shall depart this afternoon, Mr. Lee."

"Yeah, well, there are a few items we should discuss first."

"Items?"

"Items. First, do you mind if I tour the camp?"

Lay of the land, enquiries, habits and peculiarities of Ana Amsler—grist for the search mill. The other scientists headed up the riverbank. I stood face-to-face with Kim Rochat and wore a small sincere smile. An emphasis we were on the same team. With the same focus. Find Amsler.

In lieu of answering my camp tour question, she removed one hand from a hip and with a half-hearted flourish waved an arm toward the carved-out steps. Accompanied with either a half-smile or half-smirk. Hard to say.

"Like your bootlaces," I said and turned toward the steps. I did appreciate them—a splash of color revealed that the base camp boss had a lighter side.

Several small generators hummed nearby. Paths between tents covered with small tree limbs, split, flat side up. A series of jungle timber sidewalks. Sturdy living-quarters tents organized around two larger tents. Kim pointed at one as the kitchen and mess hall. The other, their field lab. The tent floors consisted of thick plywood laid across more timber, dry and above the mud. Three Brazilian camp workers occupied the kitchen and prepared the noon meal.

Kim explained that the initial setup—boats, tents, plywood, generators—were shipped upriver via riverboat. Bernie flew in personnel and ongoing necessities. The Swiss had done this right. Not the Taj Mahal, by any stretch, but comfortable and functional and professional.

"Could I look around Ana's tent?"

"Dr. Amsler?"

"Yeah. Ana. And this brings into play one of those items."

She raised an eyebrow.

"I understand it's a breach of Swiss protocol, but let's drop the formal names. Okay? I'm Case. She's Ana. You're Kim."

She blinked, frowned, and digested the item. For a good five seconds.

"If you insist."

"Great. Thanks. Now, Ana's tent?"

"Why would you wish to enter her tent?"

"Not sure."

A poor answer. She responded with a head tilt and furrowed brow. I was facing a high-end scientist. "Not sure" failed the scientific method test.

53

"There might be clues, indicators, evidence of habits," I added.

She nodded and said, "Yes. Then it will be fine."

Amsler's tent contained no away-from-home items. No photos, no sketches, no personal decor. A bunk draped in a mosquito net, a simple desk and chair, and a bookcase half-used for clothing and toiletries. Spartan. Alongside the desk, a small tin bucket half-filled with dirt. And long cigarette butts. I pulled out several—each smoked for a puff or two and ground out.

"Davidoff," Kim said, standing nearby with arms crossed. "Swiss cigarettes."

"She's a one- or two-puff smoker?"

Kim shrugged.

"I don't see any photos or remembrances. Does she have family?"

"She never spoke of such things. Dr. Amsler is a private person."

I considered probing the private person line but opted for a neutral-ground noninvasive path.

"How about a cup of coffee? Could we do that and discuss a few more items?"

"But of course."

I loved the Swiss-French accent. She led the way into the mess hall. Two cafezinhos soon appeared.

"Okay. About you joining me on the search. First, we may be out there ten days. That's a long time given the environment."

"I am most prepared for such an endeavor."

She pulled off the Houston ball cap and scratched her head. Her hair—like her eyebrows a white-blond—was clipped a uniform two-inch length. A jungle cut. I couldn't tell if the head-scratching represented an affectation or, well, a head scratch.

"Are you an Astros fan?"

"No. My brother works at the Texas Medical Center in Houston. This," she said before sliding the cap back on, "is a gift from him. You have brought your own boat."

"Yep. Bernie will return with fuel and the engine."

"We should use one of our boats."

The row of aluminum skiffs bankside. A solid point and solid offer. A fifteen-foot skiff offered more room and more comfort for a two-person search party. If two became a reality.

"That would be great. Thanks. *If* you come with me."

"I will join you on this search, Mr. Lee." She delivered another finger shot.

"Case."

"I will join you on this search, Case." No finger shot.

I pulled the contract card—potent and perhaps unfair given I dealt with a Swiss-scientist mindset.

"My contract does not require me to take anyone along."

A potential showstopper for Kim Rochat, so she countered with a mighty solid statement.

"I could show you where Dr. Amsler did *not* go. Areas where the rest of my team explored. And I could show you where, I believe, she *did* explore."

A helluva hole card, for sure. Fruitless search days avoided. I pulled a detailed area map from a cargo pocket along with a red pen.

"Let's start there. If you don't mind, I'll ask questions while you point out those areas."

She sipped her coffee and stared at the map. Lifted her head and locked eyes.

"No."

"No?"

"You must commit, Mr. Lee. Commit and take me with you."

Not a bad poker move. A bit out of place coming from a Swiss scientist. But solid, and a hand well-played. We stared, unblinking, while I chewed on an answer. One of the Brazilians thwacked a cutting board with a knife, slicing food for the pot. Dregs from the nitro-grade coffee remained on my tongue. Kim fired another salvo.

"Be most assured of my commitment regarding Dr. Amsler. She is alive. This I know. Now we—you and I, Mr. Lee—must find her."

Yeah, well, I wasn't committed to shoving off with Kim Rochat in tow until the sixty-four-dollar question was addressed.

"Tell me about her discovery."

Silence from the other side of the table, along with pursed lips and averted eyes. Ten seconds ticked off. Two other scientists chatted outside the mess hall. Food prep continued behind us. She understood this bridge would get crossed. Had to. And crossed before any commitment to her joining. She glanced my way, eyes filled with concern, awe, and a touch of fear.

"A plant."

"Okay. A plant."

"One which—and this aspect is most incredible—emits an airborne toxin. A neurotoxin, Dr. Amsler believed. A toxin beyond any ever discovered. Beyond belief."

"How potent are we talking about?"

She shifted her gaze toward the tabletop.

"You must understand we are able to synthesize and alter such compounds. My profession is capable of delivering remarkable results with such alterations."

"Understood."

She lifted her chin with a touch of defiance. "Wonderful, life-saving results."

"Yeah. I understand. And no one is blaming anyone for anything. No finger-pointing."

A quick nod of appreciation or acceptance or perhaps relief at my statement.

"Now, how toxic *is* this plant?" I asked.

Nostrils flared, jaw muscles clenched, she leaned across the table.

"It could save lives. Yes. In the appropriate hands."

"In the wrong hands?"

"It could kill millions."

Chapter 10

Oh, man. I'd suspected, wondered, considered. Kim's statement validated my suspicions and altered the mission's scope. And not in a good way. For starters, Case Lee Inc. wasn't in the high-caliber toxin-handling business. In any way, shape, or form. And I wouldn't allow MOIS or Mossad or pick-your-outfit to get their hands on this stuff. If it was real.

And Kim's statement provided back trail clarity. The Manaus violence. Not definitive—a thin-ice assumption anytime you dealt with spooks—but now it made more sense. Dark, death-dealing sense. My anger toward Ana Amsler rose. What the hell was she thinking? I visualized the Basel coffee shop. In a city home to over thirty pharma companies, many of them cutting-edge research outfits. They'd budget funds for industrial espionage. No doubt. A line item on their corporate financial spreadsheet. Masked as "Competitive Analysis" or some other BS. There wouldn't be a bar, restaurant, or coffee house there without a couple of folks performing "competitive analysis." The money was too big, the opportunities too lucrative. And Ana Amsler barfed up her discovery while on home turf as she drank coffee with an associate. *Pass the cream and oh by the way there's this airborne toxin I've discovered in the Amazon rain forest. World's deadliest. Isn't that exciting?*

How the overheard conversation filtered into the global clandestine world would remain a mystery. So be it. What mattered was it tied with the Iranian's interest. And Mossad's. And helped explain the frantic and violent Manaus kick-off.

"Do you think it's real?" I asked. A question prompted by incredulity or fear or straw-grasping.

"Ana is not the type of person to exaggerate about such things."

"Do you think this plant killed her?"

"No. She would take appropriate precautions."

Still, the world's deadliest toxin. The standard precautions rule book wouldn't apply. And she'd dealt with this stuff in the middle of a jungle. Fair odds Ana Amsler lay stretched out somewhere in the bush, well past her expiration date.

"How would she have approached this whole thing?"

"Whole thing?"

"Recovery of this plant. Collection of a sample."

"A meticulous approach, I would say. Quite methodical."

Yeah, fine. So maybe she had success collecting a sample. Then she disappeared. Which threw open a barn-door-sized possibility. Was Ana Amsler a card-carrying member of wingnut central? A weird, jaundiced view on my part—fair enough. But a consideration. Or maybe I'd hung with Jules too long.

"What else did she tell you about the discovery? Implications? Possibilities?"

Kim stood and wandered toward the kitchen staff, tiny porcelain cup in hand. One of the Brazilians smiled, nodded, and poured her another cafezinho. She returned, sipped, and finger-tapped the tabletop—a moment for Dr. Kim Rochat to gather her thoughts, to choose her words with care.

"She described the find. The discovery. She did not discuss possibilities. She *did* inform me there would be special equipment required from our company."

"Did you order it? The equipment?"

"No. It was custom-made. She returned to Switzerland and supervised the construction of the apparatus. I approved the expenditure."

Kim had faith in Amsler. Faith at least in her scientific approach. Which raised the question—did she have faith in Amsler as a person?

"Do you consider Ana a friend?"

Another long tabletop stare. "Not a friend as much as a professional comrade."

"And you're confident she'd conduct herself as a professional regarding this discovery?"

A raised eyebrow and raised hackles as response. "Of course. How else would she behave?"

"Well, she did run her mouth at a Basel coffee shop."

A deep dive stare into the cup of sweet black coffee. "So I have been told."

No point pounding on Amsler's misstep. It would put Kim into a defensive posture. And hinder further intel gathering. Kim had shot straight with me, and the questions I tossed her way had a clean purpose—to paint a legit picture of Ana Amsler. Maybe get into Amsler's head. But the object of my mission remained enigmatic, so I moved forward and nailed down chronology.

"How long ago did she make the discovery?"

"Six weeks past. An approximation."

"She returned here a week ago?"

"Oui. This is correct."

"Did you see the equipment she brought with her? The custom-made equipment?"

"No. She was quite secretive about it. Which is not unusual. Not unusual for Ana."

The paint-by-numbers picture of Dr. Ana Amsler remained unclear. A loner, focused, and—as Bernie had said—bullheaded. Fine and dandy. But my portrait of her had a shadowed off-kilter element lurking in the background. Couldn't paint over it.

"When she returned, did she head into the jungle right away?"

"Only after two days' preparation."

"So she's been missing five days?"

"This too is correct."

Her information jibed with the Global Resolutions dossier.

"Does your entire team venture out each morning?"

"On most days we explore in pairs. Our standard regimen unless the day is spent within our small laboratory. Ana, however, would leave alone. The only one of us to do so. I addressed this with her several times, and yet..."

Kim shrugged and lifted a hand toward the heavens. Clearly her team-leader role, at times, fell on deaf ears. She explained they'd begun searching for Amsler the day after she'd ventured out. After two days, she called Bernie and an air search was conducted. All of it in vain. Ana Amsler was either dead or was enjoying an extended and secluded camping trip at the discovery site. Or she'd headed farther upstream on a weird *Heart of Darkness* voyage. And maybe she'd bypassed the base camp at night and headed for parts unknown, with some unknown rationale at the wheel. I broached the last two possibilities with Kim.

"Such activities and choices would have no scientific or rational basis," she said, her hackles raised "No. We shall not consider these things and focus instead on her being lost or injured."

Yeah, well, Kim. You never know. Folks peg the peculiar meter with greater regularity than we want to believe. But no point digging the wingnut hole any deeper.

"She has a satellite phone?"

"Of course. With a small solar charger."

"And you've tried calling her?"

One raised eyebrow as response. Along with a dealing-with-the-village-idiot look. But I had to ask. Folks *do* miss the obvious.

"Okay," I continued. "Now, there's something you and your teammates must know. Please take this very seriously. None of you can return to Manaus."

"I do not understand."

"There are dangerous people seeking Ana. They're in Manaus. I ran into them."

"Dangerous people?" A slow blink; a quizzical look.

"They want this toxic discovery of hers. For bad things. Evil purposes. And they'll kill to get their hands on it."

"This would hardly appear possible."

"It's more than possible. It's a reality. They will kill for it. In the literal sense."

She pulled her ball cap off and scratched her head. Weighed my declaration.

"Bernie presented a viable option," I continued. "There's one flight a day from Coari to Rio de Janeiro. He'll do a Coari shuttle for you and your people. Don't go to Manaus."

Ball cap returned, she squared her shoulders and said, "My team's safety is the first priority. I do not understand why Ana's disappearance could cause such an activity. You have experienced this danger?"

Yeah. And stamped expired on two of their birth certificates.

"Yes. These are bad, bad people."

"Then we shall utilize Coari. I will alert my home office and the rest of the team."

"Good. Thanks. It could change after we find Ana. Maybe. But for now, do not under any circumstances visit Manaus again."

"Yes. I understand. There is no point repeating such statements."

Fair enough, but if Uri Hirsch was right, MOIS would send another contingent of killers. And I wasn't leaving any gray areas regarding this dangerous reality.

She scratched a bug bite. I slid the area map between us. I'd flown sufficient warning flags about Manaus. Time for a move onto the search area.

"Okay. Please show me where your team has searched. I'll mark those areas in red."

She complied. I supposed she took my return to map activity as a definitive sign. An acquiescence that I'd let her join me. The more I thought about it, the more I vacillated, unsure and concerned. The gig was now awash with a darker, more toxic palette, and exposing Kim to whatever I'd find didn't sit right.

The Swiss bio-prospector team worked farther upstream from the base camp. Their tributary meandered for miles, and they had concentrated along the east side. She explained Ana worked even farther upriver, focused as well on the tributary's eastern regions.

"You and the other team of scientists would rotate out, right?"

"This is correct."

"And both teams worked through the rainy season?"

"Again, correct."

The Brazilian staff wouldn't permit us to sit and talk without sustenance. They brought over thin-sliced bread, cheese, fruit, and several bottles of cold water. Hungry, I dug in.

"You have satellite images overlaid on topo maps. These would highlight the areas above flood water," I said. Neither the cheese nor the bread had much flavor. The jungle fruit—rich beyond compare. I leaned over a napkin as the juices dripped.

"Yes. We conduct methodical searches. It is the appropriate manner for such research."

"The daily rain didn't alter your field schedule?" Asked with a mouthful of mango. I must have resembled Uri Hirsch.

"Yes, it did. We would spend many days in our laboratory." She pointed out a screen window toward the base camp's other large tent. "The rain is most challenging. But yes, we would venture out."

"With everything flooded, how'd you get to dry land?"

"We have, of course, GPS."

"Understood. How'd you physically get there?" She raised both eyebrows. Another dealing-with-the-village-idiot look. The fruit was so good I didn't care. "Mercy, this is good." I held up a chunk of unidentified buttery fruit, smooth as pudding with a lemon hint. "You tried this?"

"Every day, Mr. Lee. As to arrival at the nonflooded areas, one team member stands forward with a long knife. A machete. The other team member drives the boat."

"So you cut a treetop tunnel?"

"If one wished to view it as such. Oui."

"How did Ana do it? She explored alone."

"As I understand, she would cut a path and use a paddle."

Ana Amsler was a determined person. I imagined she would whack a limb with the machete, forgo the paddle, and pull herself forward with the tree limb stub. Repeat until she made her destination.

"We chose high ground along the main river channels. We did not cut through more than a few hundred meters."

"Okay. Good to know. When Ana left here the last time, how much higher was the water?"

She pursed her lips and hesitated, scientific gears turning.

"Between four and five meters."

Twelve to fifteen feet. Quite a drop over the last six or seven weeks. And a key to the search. Two of the other scientists wandered in and sat with us. Kim relayed the decision about Coari as the new exit town for the team. Then she wandered off, stating she'd inform the home office of the decision. Satellite communications with broadband for cell phones and computers kept even the most remote locations connected.

I chatted with the other team members, asked about Ana, probed for other hints and clues. Not much there. The overall impression—Ana Amsler wasn't popular or much admired. But I was dealing with Swiss folks. Folks seldom prone to opening personal kimonos.

I wandered toward the riverbank. Inspected the aluminum skiff lineup and selected the one least-used. Removed the smaller outboard motor and fuel tank. Kept the paddles and a small anchor. Shifted my gear into the boat and waited for Bernie's return.

The job's contours had been altered, no doubt. But I remained focused on the primary mission. Find her. Take her, or her remains, back to Switzerland. The Iranians and Israelis and whoever else avoided, sidestepped. If Amsler possessed a toxic care package, I'd deal with it at the appropriate moment. I sure wasn't toting it around with me. And odds existed—reduced odds after I'd met with Kim Rochat—the toxic plant was less potent than Amsler had declared. Either way, I wasn't fooling with it. The contract was stark: bring Amsler home. It didn't say a thing about her special little treat.

Bernie's baby hummed in the distance, headed our way. Somewhere around the river's bend he splashed down and cruised into sight. Ran the pontoons onto the shore, killed the engine, and threw open the door.

"Good to go, good to go," he said, delivered with a wide, sweaty grin. "Would you mind lending a hand?"

We unloaded the plane. The new outboard motor and a dozen gas containers. Kim and two other scientists joined us.

"I've gotta run," he said. "One last trip this afternoon. A short one. You have my number, right?"

"I do."

"Call me anytime, day or night."

"I appreciate it. Now, there's a change in this team's travel plans."

I looked toward Kim. She nodded and explained to Bernie the new base-camp-to-Coari logistics.

"Suit yourself," he said. "And good luck on the search. I'll pray for success."

"Help me wrestle this crated inflatable boat back into your baby. I'll take one of the camp's skiffs. It's a donation, Bernie. Me to you. Sell it back to the despachante."

He grinned widely, thanked me, and we squeezed it back into his plane. I was less interested in the inflatable boat and more focused on a chat with him away from the others.

"And you have *my* number, right? Call if you have any questions. Or concerns. Or want my perspective on events in Manaus."

He squeezed my shoulder and shook it. "You make it sound like a James Bond movie. We're talking about Manaus. Where we're pretty far removed from much excitement along those lines."

"Do you believe in evil? True, walking evil?"

His expression became rock-hard. "Of course. I know it to be real."

"It's real in Manaus. Right now."

He returned a grim nod.

"Watch your back, Bernie. For the next couple of weeks, watch your back. Do it for me. Please."

We shook hands, I shoved his baby into the river, and he roared away. I mounted the new outboard motor on the skiff and arrayed the gas tanks at the stern and amidships. The Swiss disappeared, back to their lab and computers and field notes. Kim joined them.

Between the floatplane unload and skiff prep, I'd sweat-soaked every square inch of clothing. The river called, invited. A hundred yards downstream, toward the river bend, the base camp became obscured by jungle. I created a small tepee from shoreline sticks and stripped. Socks, underwear, shorts, and shirt—all quick-dry material. I rinsed everything, squeezed out what water I could, and draped my attire around the tepee. Then stood at the water's edge. Gotta trust somebody, and Bernie claimed no worries until the water dropped to its low point. Still. Piranhas were there. Right there. Guaranteed. Get a grip, Case. You're former Delta. Get your butt wet.

I did. And it felt great. Can't say it was relaxing. Cool water, a thorough rinse, but minimal splashes. Just in case. Bernie's yowza factor. Ten refreshing minutes later I pulled skivvies and socks from the driftwood and air-twirled them for a final dry. Donned everything but the shirt and flung it around my head on spin-dry. And noticed Kim standing fifty feet away, arms crossed, a half-smile and full head-cock.

"You understand not to urinate while you bathe?" she asked.

"Yeah. So I've been told."

"You carry multiple marks. Battle scars, I would assess."

Bullets, shrapnel, blades. A recent arrowhead. All totems—life markers on the Case Lee path.

"Yeah. Something like that."

She cast a glance up the shore, toward the base camp.

"My things are in the boat."

Kim Rochat represented solidity, leadership, smarts, and commitment. No downside with her joining me other than some moronic Lone Ranger ache or tough-stuff strut or a mental buildup for flying solo. I didn't know for sure. But I knew it was time to jettison that crap.

We locked eyes, a decision made. I'd cross the Rubicon into uncharted toxic turf. With a Swiss scientist and the clock ticking.

"Alright, Kim. Alright. Let's go find her."

Chapter 11

Underway and filled with purpose. The weather fine as the four-stroke outboard kicked us upriver, making watery tracks. The mission more muddled but real and here and now. Man, it felt good—movement, a plan, a goal.

And a mission. One officially kicked off at last and more low-key and appropriate for a guy who now emitted the occasional involuntary groan when bone-tired and rising from a comfortable chair. It wasn't the years as much as the mileage. And while not a classic sleuthing job, this engagement held its own powerful appeal. The jungle, my skill set, a dash of intrigue. With no indicators the body would take a hammering during the search. Kim glanced my way from the front of the skiff and shook her head. Must have been the mile-wide grin the chief bottle-washer of Case Lee Inc. carried.

"It is quite nice, isn't it?" she asked, an arm waved toward the passing green.

Another attribute of a four-stroke outboard motor—quiet running. No shouted voices required across the short distance between us.

"All good," I replied, keeping us centered in the tributary. A river among other parts of the world, over a hundred feet wide with dense green-hued jungle walls. A small tributary in Amazonia. "First things first. We both have satellite phones. Let's exchange phone numbers. Just in case."

We did.

"Now, turn them off. Both of us."

"Why would I do such a thing?"

"Because we could be tracked. GPS. Lots of Hoovers float around up there."

I pointed toward the sky. Spy agency satellites—the US's NSA as a prime example—might track our movement. A long shot and a dash or three of paranoia, sure. But possible.

"I shall turn off the navigation function."

She lowered the Ray-Bans, looked over their upper rim, and began disengaging her GPS.

"Not sufficient. If they want in, they get in. Trust me, Kim. They have the capability."

"And how shall we find the search areas? I have the coordinates programmed into this device."

She lifted the phone and displayed it with a slow side-to-side rotation. As if the boat's official moron couldn't grasp the coordinate concept.

"You know the general area. Activate the phone, acquire a relative position, and turn it back off. Navigate from there." I smiled. "Repeat as needed." Pointed toward the sky again. "Don't want them tracking us."

Lifted eyebrows and lifted Ray-Bans and crooked neck as she looked at the sky. I took the opportunity to lay claim to nonmoron status and reviewed the search plan with her. She accepted it without argument or alteration. Accepted, maybe, that I knew what I was doing. The initial goal—observe where she and her teammates had explored in both the high-water conditions as well as during recent weeks. A view of their treetop tunnels benchmarked my search. Provided examples corresponding with Ana Amsler's explorations. The first area was thirty minutes upriver and allowed time for more intel gathering.

"So what does a bio-prospector look for?" I asked.

A troop of howler monkeys vocalized from nearby trees as we sped past. Their raucous calls faded, replaced with the steady hum of the outboard engine and the light rush of humid air.

"Unknown macro- and microorganisms."

"Okay. So you stomp around in the jungle and look for unknown plants and animals."

"Hardly. It is quite a systematic approach." Kim aimed her finger pistol my way. "For example—plants, fungi, and animals." Three hand-pistol shots.

"For commercial use. Things that might benefit people."

She smiled. "But of course. The commercial aspect is one incentive. For many of us, the motivation is much more than money."

"Okay."

"Our research focuses on biochemicals. Biochemicals, Mr. Lee, which might be synthesized and, if needed, altered. New drugs and new compounds."

"Case."

"As you wish. Case. We approach a search area."

I cut the engine back and maneuvered close along the left bank. The Swiss team explored the right side, westward, and the farther back from the wall of dense foliage the better for the capture of machete-work pathways fifteen feet above us.

"We are close," she said and pulled her phone.

"Don't tell me. Leave the phone off."

"Why should I not tell you?"

Her word order or word usage or the French lilt made for a great conversational tone. It struck me as a flavorful add-on within an already exotic environment.

"It's best if I find it. Recognize it. Without knowing the exact spot."

I kept the engine past idle and made slow headway against the mild current, hugging the left bank and eyeballing the right bank's upper tree line. Found it. Nothing leapt out, no obvious indicators. Then a change, an inconsistency among the tree foliage. Several branch stubs, a subtle opening high in the air.

"That's it."

She returned a nod with a slight eyebrow lift behind her shades. Was she surprised? Maybe. A legit perspective given she knew nothing about me other than I was sent under contract. A proof-of-the-pudding moment.

"Don't let me know when we approach the next one. I'll find it on my own."

The afternoon sun blazed, the heat oppressive. Kim, her back toward me, would dip a handkerchief in the water at regular intervals. She removed the ball cap, draped the dripping cloth over her head, and pressed the cap back on. A cool reprieve from the heat, repeated often. She adjusted, worked with the environment. Understood what worked and what didn't. Good for her.

I ran us at a moderate speed. Too slow and we'd never make headway. Too fast, and we'd whip past entry points. Eyes peeled, a well-honed skill set utilized. Several miles upriver I found the second tunneled entrance. Same indicators, subtle but discernible. This little training exercise would pay off, big time. The pathways of my quarry would hold similar signs. I swung the boat across river and beached it beneath the overhead alleyway.

"Why do we stop?"

"Checking one of these high-water islands you folks concentrated on."

"Why?"

"To capture a feel for the environment."

"This strikes me as peculiar. We have a great deal of river travel before we enter Dr. Amsler's search area."

"Yeah. I know."

A small headshake as she removed the wet handkerchief and scratched her scalp. The vertical midline of her shirt, dark with sweat, clung to her back. I killed the engine as the boat's bow scooted onto the few feet of beach, its prow nudging the wall of green. Birds called and insects buzzed. Rain forest noises, unchanged for millennia. The scrape of our aluminum hull against riverbank an alien call, invasive.

Kim unsheathed her short machete and stepped onto the bank. She turned and captured the sight of me prepping a personal webbed tool belt. It contained my own machete, a Ka-Bar knife, and soft-sided water canteen. A built-in fanny pack held a first aid kit and energy bars. The belt also held a holstered Glock.

She stowed the sunglasses—a deep-shaded world awaited. "Is this necessary?" A finger shot toward my weapon.

"Hope not."

Which she met with a hard stare and furrowed brow.

"There's an old expression," I added. "Better to have it and not need it than need it and not have it."

"An American expression?"

"I suppose."

"But of course." She turned toward the jungle wall. "Shall I lead?"

"Knock yourself out."

Her machete strokes would be more indicative of a Swiss scientist trail than my more experienced jungle traverse technique. A technique with less machete work, more sidesteps, faster pace. This was a Swiss scientist pathways lesson within a vast wilderness.

"Does this mean yes?"

"It does. Yes. Please lead."

Deep shade and instant cooler temperatures. Eyes adjusted to our intrusion into this muted light and life-filled world. We worked our way uphill, a gentle slope, the high-water mark discernible as we crested the small hummock. A uniform line of jungle debris adhered to tree trunks and bush tops.

"If we find something interesting," I said as Kim whacked brush and overhanging tree limbs, "something we could toss in a blender and create a concoction to cure the common cold, let me know. I'll split the patent with you."

"You are making a joke?"

"Sorta."

Squawks erupted overhead, but their source remained hidden by thick-tiered branches. I heard quick, short scampering sounds through the jungle floor detritus around us. I scanned the surrounding area with constant glances toward the immediate travel path.

"Watch for snakes."

"I am aware of snakes, Mr. Lee." She whacked another limb.

"Case."

"Yes." She directed a backhanded machete swipe at an obstructing frond plant. "So you say. Often."

She halted and slapped her exposed thigh. An insect. The slap was accompanied by a Swiss word I didn't understand. High odds it wasn't a word used among polite society.

"Alright. Seen enough. Let's get back underway."

Shade and lower temps didn't offset the exertion of wielding a machete. Sweat poured down her face. She strode past me, leading again, and shot me a "waste of time" look. It wasn't. She'd cut a trail, and I now understood what to look for. Each scientist would have their own approach, sure, but the frequency of blade swipes and the linear nature of advance would remain somewhat constant.

At the boat she grabbed a mess hall pitcher. Dipped it in the river, bent at the waist, and poured semicool water over her head. Full sun radiated off the aluminum boat, the metal hot to the touch. She offered the pitcher, and I repeated her performance. Whether an act of simple companionship or an effort at keeping the hired hand upright was unclear.

I goosed the engine and headed farther upriver, farther into the wilderness. The treetop tunnels lowered as we progressed, reflecting the drop in water level over the last months. The last hacked path appeared at shoreline level, and Kim announced we were approaching the farthest upstream exploration area for the rest of her team. We had entered Ana Amsler's area. The search zone. I slowed the boat to half-throttle.

I well understood Amsler's technique. Amsler the loner. The hardheaded scientist. She'd suss the dry areas, the large islands of potential, each night at the base camp. Study the satellite images overlaid on topographic maps. Choose the next day's exploration area. Areas farthest away from the others. Ascertain the GPS coordinates. A daylight start, her boat loaded with fuel, a GPS enabled phone, and minimal supplies. A solid approach from Amsler, and a valid assumption on my part. Not rocket science. With such a light load, the little skiff would scoot at full throttle. And she'd keep it at full throttle for several hours, covering multiple miles upriver. We didn't have the luxury of speed as we searched and hunted for signs, so I'd figured three or five days to cover the most probable areas. Scour her trail for indicators, clues. But we did have one ace in the hole.

"Okay. What we're looking for is very specific," I said and waited for Kim to turn around and face me. She did. "A treetop tunnel. About fifteen feet above us."

She lowered her Ray-Bans and nodded. Ice-blue eyes, unblinking.

"And one of two things corresponding with the overhead path. One—another entry point at ground level near the overhead. Where she went back in with her custom-made equipment."

"I understand."

Her attention meter pegged. Right up Kim's alley—specific and methodical.

"Or two—a nearby smaller river or creek that could have accommodated her boat. Used for closer access to her objective. Her discovery. A small creek wouldn't have been discernible during high water. She may have used one several days ago."

"We should focus on the smaller river premise."

"Why?"

"There was no sign of her boat during our airplane search. If she had entered near her earlier location—the treetop tunnel, as you call it—and an accident or injury occurred, the boat would have remained. We would have seen it. A smaller waterway nearby would hide her boat due to overhanging jungle. Is this not so?"

Yeah, it was so if you held with surety a view of Amsler as still around. Hurt, perhaps. Lost. I wasn't so sure; I maintained the possibility that Amsler had skedaddled with her toxic bundle downriver toward heaven-knows-where. But no point cracking open the weirdness door. Not now.

"What's important is we dismiss nothing and absorb everything. Any sign of her and her travels."

She nodded, those ice-blue eyes focused over the top of the sunglasses.

"We're working a puzzle," I continued. "We require all the pieces. All the data."

The last bit seemed to salve Kim's thoughts toward our search methodology.

"I understand." The Ray-Bans went back up her nose. "We shall do as you recommend."

She turned back around, sat straight, and officially began her personal search for her Swiss colleague. I smiled, amused at the scientific mantle she wrapped around her demeanor. Not my cup of tea, but it had a strange appeal coming from Kim Rochat. Maybe it was the French inflection or the tightly wound demeanor of the small and fit scientist. Hard to say.

I kept us in the waterway's center. I wasn't buying that the entire Swiss team had searched the west side of the river. Not with Amsler. I spotted the first overhead indicators an hour later. Westward, sure enough. I slowed to a crawl and eyeballed the shore and adjacent foliage for signs. Nada. And no smaller creeks as inlets nearby. We moved on. I found the second air tunnel occupying the east side. When I pointed it out, Kim frowned and shook her head. A violation of team protocol. An unauthorized departure from agreed-upon methodology. But again, no further signs or indicators of a follow-up entry point.

The river forked. I slowed and idled against the current, considered my quarry. Kim expressed, in no uncertain terms, that the right fork constituted the correct route. And it could have been. Maybe. I kept right, and we found one more Amsler high-water access with no accompanying clues. Then nothing. A full hour pushing upstream and no signs, no access points. Late afternoon, and time to make camp. A river bend held a sandbar and offered a small open area adjacent to the jungle.

"That's it for the day," I said as the boat's bow pushed onto the sand. "Let's settle for the night and hit it again at daybreak."

No argument from Kim. Together, we fixed a large rain tarp ten feet overhead inside the jungle wall. I strung my hammock and mosquito netting and helped with hers. Shared a trick or two regarding hammock sleeping preparations. Worked with her to secure a small jungle stick perpendicular to the hammock rope at both ends. Each one acted as a rafter, jutting out in both directions. When the mosquito netting was situated, the sticks held it away from the hammock. Otherwise, critters could bite Kim through the netting where it draped against her body. I also emphasized tight netting knots farther up the rope. It would keep creepy-crawlies from working their

71

way along the rope and joining her during the night. She nodded approvingly during the setup.

A large tree, victim of high water, lay across our camp and provided a working surface, a rain forest table. We collected fallen limbs and started a fire—it would cool off once the sun set, and the damp woodsmoke kept the insects at bay. You could go old school to start a fire with damp wood. It took time and effort. Or use a small road flare and let a couple thousand degrees of heat kick things off. Between futzing around or striking a flare, I preferred the latter. Kim pulled dried food and aluminum pots from her camp collection.

"How about fresh fish?" I asked, assembling a travel fly rod. "Bernie says they make fine fare."

"What does?"

"Piranhas."

"I believe such tales of their density are much exaggerated."

"Yeah, maybe. Let's see."

I'd brought several twelve-inch lengths of flexible wire leader to prevent sharp teeth from cutting my monofilament line. At the end of the leader a decent-sized feather streamer. I didn't sweat color or shape too much—these were piranhas, after all. I cast midstream and stripped line. I was beginning to credit Kim's skepticism when, close to shore, a hook-up. It was the size of a healthy bluegill perch. But with razor teeth on prominent display. Mercy. I changed flies—it had destroyed the feathered presentation—and cast along the shore. Two line strips and bingo, another. And another streamer destroyed. Kim sidled up as I cast again. And caught another piranha.

"It would appear they are quite numerous," she said.

"After I catch supper, feel free to take a dip."

"Dip?"

"Swim."

"Most amusing. No, thank you."

I caught two more and called it good. Cleaned the fish and tossed the heads and guts into the water six feet from shore. Flashes beneath the surface appeared—a few silver darts grew to dozens. No more heads, no more guts. Yowza.

After supper I fed the fire more logs and branches as night approached. Before it was too dark, I ran two perimeter lines of thick monofilament around the camp—one at two feet off the ground, the other at ten inches, the lower one for any gators or anacondas taking a midnight ramble. At each tree I bent the line around, I attached a small LED light—much like the one on a cell phone—six feet high. A monofilament trigger line then attached to the perimeter line. Each LED was powered with a small battery. I had packed several dozen of the small devices and plenty of thick monofilament.

"And this is for what?" Kim asked.

"Critters. Both four- and two-legged."

I explained the trip line would engage the LEDs and light up the camp's perimeter, as well as frighten away whatever caused them to trigger. The lights also emitted a small electronic whine when activated.

"You have plans to sleep with your weapon?" she asked as I unholstered the Glock and tossed it into the hammock.

"My version of a comfort blanket."

She went about her business, prepared for sleep, and muttered a few things in Swiss French. I may have heard the word "Rambo." We settled, and I ensured she tied a tight knot in the mosquito net where it draped below her hammock.

"Keeps the ground dwelling insects out. Usually."

"Yes. Fine. How often do you plan on shifting position during the night?"

Peculiar question. And I said so.

"You have assembled our hammocks so we share a common tree," she replied. "A quite small common tree."

True enough. We shared a small diameter tree as one tie-off. The other ends of our hammocks were attached to separate trees.

"Each time you shift or turn, this small tree reacts. And I bounce."

"I'll try and keep it to a minimum. Good night, Kim."

A resigned exhale from the nearby hammock.

"Good night, Case."

It wasn't.

Chapter 12

My eyes popped open and the adrenaline meter pegged. High-pitched electronic whines as LED lights flashed on. Situated smack dab in the middle of Amazon wilderness the high-pitched noise and bright light made for a hell of an alarm clock. Pistol in hand and a quick exit from the hammock. I ripped through mosquito netting and plopped on the ground. Jaguar, gator, or one of those giant anaconda snakes. Didn't matter—I wasn't a menu item for any of them.

The jungle-side of our camp now illuminated, I stood with a two-handed grip on the Glock. Searched, strained for movement. And found it. Multiple figures in deep shadow, retreating into the dense rain forest. I dropped to my knees. Not good.

"What is the issue?"

The electronic whines, lights, and my hitting the dirt woke Kim. She sat up.

"Hit the ground!"

"What?"

No time. I scrambled the few feet toward her and flipped the hammock. She wasn't heavy enough to break through the netting and hung suspended, cocooned, a foot off the ground.

"What are you doing? Stop this!"

I whipped out the Ka-Bar knife—another comfort blanket—and slashed through the netting. She tumbled onto the ground. A few choice Swiss expletives joined her attempt to stand.

"Down!"

No time for discussions. I grabbed her shirt and jerked her toward dirt and safety. She gripped my wrist with both hands, furious. We performed a mad scramble with accompanying khaki shirt tug-of-war toward the protection of the fallen tree across our campsite.

"Stay down!"

"What is it? What are we doing?"

A distinctive thwack against the other side of the fallen tree trunk was her immediate and unwelcome answer. Followed with two more in rapid succession. Arrows. Not good at all.

"What was that?" she asked, now with semiacceptance of our hunkered-down position. "This noise. What does this mean?"

I responded with the Glock lifted over the log and pointed high toward their general direction. I had no intention of hitting any of them, but I was damn sure intent on delivering a message. We're armed. And we'll fight. Three massive booms from the pistol echoed through the dense environment. And three white-bright muzzle blasts even in the LED-lit environment. A quick glance toward the other half of our search party revealed a small Swiss scientist, eyes wide as headlights, short hair disheveled and mouth open.

"Those thunks were arrows. Stay down, Kim. Give them a chance to scoot away."

"Why are they attacking us?"

"Because we're on their turf."

She digested this information and asked, "What do we do?"

"Get the hell *off* their turf."

The rustle of bodies against branches and fronds and ground cover, retreating. Whether this activity would continue or they'd gather and come at us again would remain an unknown. We'd depart, as in right freakin' now.

"Give them another thirty seconds. Then we grab our stuff and toss it in the boat."

"It will take time for arrangement of our equipment."

I shot her a no-nonsense eye lock. There were another few minutes on the activated LEDs before they'd flick off. I'd activate the ones at our back side, toward the river, to give us an additional few minutes. We wouldn't require it. Speed, rapidity of movement was now paramount.

"No arranging. Throw everything in. You got that?"

She scowled and returned my stare. Helter-skelter packing wasn't in her wiring. I lifted the Glock and ripped off two more shots. Cacophonous nighttime explosions, two more special delivery messages.

"When I say go, you grab what's not tied down. I'll get the tarp and hammocks and our rucksacks. Make a pile. Right here. Understand?"

"But of course I understand!" She pinballed between battle fear and spitting rage and acquiescence to necessity. "Have you considered the possibility of communication with these people? With something other than your gun?"

"No. Ten more seconds. Then we go." I got in her face. "Do. You. Understand?"

A quick eye-roll accompanied a terse "Oui."

"Go!"

I leapt up and scoped the surroundings. No threats visible. Which meant diddly-squat. I slid the Glock into my pocket. I hated these moments: the split seconds when the intent and actions of your enemy remained unknown. I'd caught an arrow in the recent past, and the thought of another ripping through the air toward me had my hair standing on end. But gotta move; gotta shake, rattle, and roll.

Kim, to her credit, bolted up and began collecting camp equipment. Ka-Bar in hand, I sliced through rope supporting the tarp and the hammocks. I grabbed our rucksacks and created a pile. Kim added to it. I dashed toward the boat and tripped those monofilament lines. Tight whines, bright light. A quick one-eighty and back toward the pile. Gotta move. Those cats could be notching arrows right freakin' now. We donned rucksacks and captured two armfuls of possessions. I produced and flicked on a small, high-intensity flashlight.

"Stay behind me. The river's edge is not our friend."

She nodded back. We halted five paces from the boat. Sanctuary within spitting distance while my back provided a perfect target for a decent archer. Heart racing, I shined the light along the left bank. Clear. On the right bank and adjacent to the boat, a set of bright eyeballs at the water's edge reflected back. A gator lay in wait.

No time, gotta move. If I were leading the tribesmen's greeting party, I'd circle. Come at us from the river side. Which they could be doing, right now. Screw this noise. I dropped my armful, pulled the Glock, and—holding the flashlight alongside the weapon's short barrel—took careful aim. I didn't miss. Violent thrashes, water spraying, then quiet.

"One dead gator. Let's load."

"Caiman."

"Whatever. Get this stuff in the boat. I'll go fetch the rest."

She did. As I collected the final articles of equipment, I heard rustling nearby. Movement on the left. Not good. Not good at all. A mad dash with arms full toward the boat.

"Get in!"

Kim didn't understand life-saving frantic activity and paused, considered her boarding process. I tossed my armload into the boat's center then lifted and tossed Kim on top of it. In return, she again did her level best to teach me a few Swiss expletives. Everything loaded, I shoved us off the bank and into the river. Leapt in, scrambled past Kim, and fired the engine. Roared away, full bore, into the night and upriver.

A quarter-mile later the boat and my adrenaline surge slowed. They wouldn't follow us through the night, tracking our river route as they moved through jungle. Well, they probably wouldn't. And *probably* got you killed. So I formulated a different overnight sleeping arrangement. An unexpected alteration driven by high-risk realities. Aggressive natives, flying arrows. But I held no animus toward our attackers. It wasn't only a matter of invading their turf; we'd entered their culture and beliefs and Amazon tribal perspectives. Accepted and dealt with as best we could. The prime strategy—haul ass. Fair enough.

We cruised silent for fifteen minutes. Sufficient moonlight allowed a decent view of our surroundings. Kim sat in the bow and swung around, facing me.

"I have processed our rather rapid exit."

"And?"

She cracked a smile. "I must say, the entire event was most exhilarating."

"Here's hoping a first and last time for you."

"To be sure, your initial performance was most uncomfortable."

"Sorry."

"No. I do not believe an apology is proper. You have experiences, life events, which I do not possess. Your actions reflected those experiences."

"Okay."

"And I shall heed your directives if we encounter such a situation again. Be most assured."

Good to know. I had no plans for further high-torque encounters during our time together, but her acknowledgment of certain skill sets showed both self-awareness and character. I appreciated it.

"So it is I who should apologize," she continued. Arms lifted, extended either side as an airplane, she experienced the cool night air passing as we worked upriver. She threw her head back and spoke toward the stars. "And again it must be said, such a level of excitement has affected me. A strange sense of enjoyment. A most peculiar reaction."

"It's called an adrenaline rush." I smiled back. "You may want to experience it next time under more controlled environments."

"No, I would disagree." She lowered her head, eyes crinkled, one side of her mouth lifted. "I might suggest the lack of control was a prime variable. Do you perform such activities on a consistent basis?"

"Try not to. There were times and places when such things happened often enough. I avoid them now."

She shifted and rummaged around for the bowline. Found the tied-off section and repositioned herself on the cross-seat between us. Stood, leaned back, and used the taut nylon rope for support and balance, the boat-driven wind at her face. And, yeah, she looked pretty fine standing there, silhouetted in the moonlight.

Several minutes later she twisted her torso and asked, "Have you killed many men?"

Used to think it came from out of the blue. But the same question posed often enough through the years convinced me that macabre interest was hardwired in people. And, as usual, the question was triggered by a recent violent event. Plus, Kim the scientist collected informational markers. Delivering an honest answer would enter her Case Lee data bank. And perspectives formulated based on body count. But unless you'd been there, done that, the picture she'd paint would bear little likeness to the real me.

"I won't answer that."

"Three or four? Three hundred or four hundred? A range is sufficient."

"Nope."

She faced forward again. I had to smile given the high odds she was formulating a different approach to the same question. Seconds later she performed a panicked duck while her free hand waved frantically. A dark-winged creature flicked away.

"What was this?" she yelped.

"A bat."

She dropped the bowline and sat, facing me. Head cocked, another of her clinical assessments underway.

"Bad people." It would be a while before I tired of her Swiss French accent. "The very bad people you referenced. I feel it appropriate you elaborate on these people. We have been through an ordeal. It is time you tell me."

I did. Not the gory details, but I ID'd their source and, more important, their operational approach.

"It is quite unbelievable the Iranian secret service would become engaged with our situation," she said, sitting up straight. "Quite unbelievable."

"The world's largest state sponsor of terrorism. They'd love to get their hands on nukes. Amsler's discovery, if it's real, might offer a near-term alternative. A massive death-dealing terrorism opportunity."

"It is a fantastique possibility. Beyond belief."

"I met them in Manaus. They're real."

"And did this meeting lead to bullets and explosions? On the streets of Manaus?"

"It led to awareness. They are violent men. Killers. And they seek Amsler's discovery. Sabe?"

"You ask if I understand?"

"I do."

"I understand you are Américain. Which, of course, presents a good versus bad worldview. This I understand. Oui."

I considered a snarky response. Yeah, I had a good versus bad worldview. No apologies. But I wasn't here to leap cultural chasms.

"You've gotta trust me on this one. I have no reason to lie."

She gave a Gallic shrug and raised her chin. "I shall take your assertions under advisement."

"You do that."

On our left, an opening. A wide and still lagoon. Perfect. I cut the engine back and idled into the open space. A thick bed of lily pads covered the lion's share of the lagoon's surface, and I edged against them. Killed the engine, crawled past Kim, and dropped the small anchor.

"We'll spend the rest of the night here. I don't think they intended chasing us through the jungle. And if they did, they won't cross the river at night."

"You suggest we sleep in the boat?"

"More than a suggestion. I'll move the fuel containers to the stern. You move the hard-surface equipment into the bow area. The middle, between the two bench seats, is home for the night."

She stood, hands on hips, and performed another assessment, this time of the overnight proposal. I waited. After a few *hmm*s and a brief sigh or three, she began shifting our material. We placed rucksacks as pillows and layered the hammocks and light blankets as a bed. Situated ourselves and pulled the tarp over us. Under the current conditions, snug as bugs.

"Case?"

"Yes."

"Should we have concern over the bats?"

"Nope."

"Other creatures? Caimans?"

"Nope. We're good, Kim."

A small hand rubbed my chest. I didn't see that coming.

"You should understand these battle scars you carry do not bother me. They are most appropriate. And provide a strange comfort. Comprenez vous? Do you understand?"

Maybe. The scars indicated I'd lived through scrapes and had experience handling dangerous environments. I supposed she might find comfort there. Or the chest rub signaled something else. And while I had more than a passing interest in exploring that path, if my interpretation proved wrong—well, it would get mighty awkward in our little floating bungalow. I chose the safe route, with yearning hesitation.

"Yeah. Understood. Let's get some sleep."

She did, curled against me. Sleep danced at my perimeter and refused engagement. For starters, I could smell her. Don't know what or how it happens or why it's true, but women smell good. They just do. Might have been the Delta Force years, shoulder-to-shoulder with other men under less than hygienic conditions. Helluva contrast. Or life alone aboard the *Ace of Spades* where the aroma of old damp wood and diesel exhaust mingled with, well, me. Never could figure it out, how women pulled it off, but it's true.

I slid back the edge of the tarp and stared at the swath of overhead stars—poured across the sky by the bushelful. Thoughts of another woman came easy. Rae. Rae Ellen Bonham, my murdered wife. A bounty hunter killed her. A killer who sought collection of the bounty on my head. Rae, dead and not gone. Images and remembrances and small vignettes washed in. I'd learned to accept them and relish them and refuse them the chance to drown me with sorrow and remorse. It wasn't easy.

I didn't mind a quick wallow among the pleasant and loving times past. As long as it didn't dictate my attitude every waking hour. But pinballing around with those special thoughts were images of Ana Amsler. And a discordant hunch. Yeah, we'd continue upriver for a while. The right thing to do. But Amsler was a weird duck. A contrary duck. And a small grating voice said she'd taken the left fork into the river arm now far behind us. She would head toward an area not part of the team's game plan. A rock-solid part of a do-her-own-thing Ana Amsler plan. My quarry. I was getting into her head. And it wasn't a good place.

Chapter 13

Howler monkeys woke us at earliest dawn. Perched among the trees lining the lagoon, their loud ruckus greeted the day as they laid claim to treetop territory. No rain during the night, the morning cool. Our surroundings bathed in the low-light clarity movie directors called the magic hour. Each detail of the lily pads, rain forest, and morning sky stood in subtle definition prior to reflective squinting under a blazing sun. Kim and I sat up, yawned, and scratched our heads—actions reminiscent of the tree-dwellers watching us.

"Quite the morning alarm clock, is it not?" She produced the ball cap and resituated it.

"Wouldn't want to make a habit of it. Those things won't win any awards for tonal harmony."

When the raucous critters took a break—dead quiet. Until soft blowhole exhales no more than five feet away. Kim latched on to my forearm. The strange sound startled me as well. It was two botos. Rare Amazon River dolphins. Pinkish-white, curious, and content to check on their lagoon's new addition. They hung out with calm, minimal movement no more than six feet away. Time was irrelevant as we shared both space and a primal connection. Then they slipped away, a departure filled to the brim with yearning and loss. We sat in a dreamlike state, amazed. A true magic moment, one etched forever.

"I do not know what to say," Kim whispered. "Such beauty."

"Gotta say *that's* about as good as it gets." The howlers kicked off another round as shards of bright sun struck the treetops. "But the band has gotten back together, so let's move toward a friendly shore and take care of morning business."

We did. Morning ministrations, energy bar breakfast, coffee made over a tiny propane burner. As we waited for the water to boil, Kim took over the rearrangement of our boat.

"Let me lend a hand."

"No. Thank you, but no. Allow me."

Her scientist mind had a specific layout for our stuff, so instead I assumed master and commander position over the coffee preparation.

"What is the plan for today?"

A light grunt as she spoke, moving fuel containers.

"We'll search for access points at low speed another hour-and-a-half upstream. At that point we'll have reached the limits of Amsler's exploration."

"And you know this how?"

She stopped her work and focused on me squatting alongside the small pot, burner, and French press prepped with ground coffee.

"If she left at the crack of dawn and raced full-speed upriver, there's a point where an overnight stay becomes mandatory. And you said she returned every evening. Except for this last time."

"And if we do not find her access point upriver? What are our next steps?"

"We go back to the split in the river. Take the left fork."

"Dr. Amsler would not have…" Her voice tapered off, followed by a shrug and a nod and a return to boat rearrangement.

We cruised, eyes peeled on both sides. Nothing. Nada. Ninety minutes later I idled the engine. The slow current began pushing us downstream. Full sun exposure, the morning coolness long gone. And without our movement-generated breeze, broiling.

"I would ask another thirty minutes. We must be certain."

She'd turned and lowered the Ray-Bans for the request, no trace of demand or superiority. She wanted surety. Go the extra mile. Fair enough. Thirty minutes later she turned again, shifted position, and faced me.

"Enough."

Short, sweet, to the point. I turned the boat and goosed it. With the current we made good time. Slowed and scoped the section we'd flown past last night after the hasty exit from Flying Arrow Resort. As we approached the less-than-hospitable camp spot, I asked her to hunker in the bottom of the boat. I did the same. Didn't relish a view of outsider-seeking arrows whipping our way. We passed unmolested, the tribesmen having slid back into their world, unseen and unknown.

At the fork I edged onto the riverbank and we both stretched our legs. Made sandwiches and ate more glorious fruit from the base camp kitchen.

"I must say, this is most discouraging," she said between sandwich bites.

"Nature of the beast. Searches take time. We're doing it right. So don't get discouraged."

Back after it, headed up the left fork. I cut back to low speed again and worked upriver. No discouragement from my perspective. We were on her trail. I felt it, sensed it. Amsler was a hardheaded solo player. She'd come this way. But as the afternoon progressed, nothing. No signs.

A tinge of doubt, despair. Just a bit. After the right-hand fork proved fruitless, I considered another possible facet of Amsler's discovery. She hadn't been searching for her toxic find. Nope. She'd come rip-roaring upriver toward a specific spot. Toward a satellite image anomaly. A high-ground inconsistency. Something overlooked by others. While the rest of the team played cards or watched movies at night, she'd pored over the topographic satellite images. Yeah, she'd made a beeline for a certain place. No exploration. She sought with specificity. A gut feeling, but of a type I'd long relied upon. It seldom failed me.

It was during a late afternoon shore break when I heard it. A plane. Another search effort, maybe. It was possible my client had hired another searcher. Or Kim's company had hired their own team. But it didn't sit easy. I'd turned on my satellite phone every couple of hours, checked messages. Bernie knew my phone number. He would have called and left a message if he'd planned a flight in my direction. Call it paranoia. Fine. But it didn't sit right.

A slow upriver traverse left us exposed. And sure enough, the plane passed well overhead, turned, and made a lower pass. It wasn't Bernie's aircraft. One more pass and it turned northeast, toward the Swiss base camp.

"Turn your phone on and call your team, please," I said.

Kim stood in the middle of a backward-leaning stretch. She'd waved at the plane.

"Why would I do this? We talked this morning. Who do you believe occupied the airplane?"

New searchers, new contractors hired to join the effort. Or vicious killers. Sufficient time had passed for the arrival in Manaus of Kirmani's reinforcements. A bit of a stretch, sure, but this gig had a dark side and there was no point avoiding acknowledgement of that.

"I don't know. More people searching, maybe. Would you call your team, please?"

She did. And reported that all remained normal. Although they had no awareness of an additional search party. My mind flashed to their possible assault tactics if the plane held MOIS agents. They'd chase us via boat. A floatplane could land them close. But the plane couldn't maneuver through winding narrow rivers with any speed. Their quarry—us—would scoot away.

And the closest boats for them to access were at the Swiss base camp. Oh, man. But I dialed the paranoia down, focused on the mission.

So back at it. A rainstorm passed overhead, and we both donned rain gear. Kim hunched under the oversized jacket and appeared small and fragile. Marble-sized drops pounded, each delivered with either tiny explosive splash points on the river or with resounding whacks against the aluminum hull. We continued the search.

"Another hour or so and we'll make camp. Fix a meal, walk about. Before dark we'll anchor again. Sleep on the boat."

Kim nodded, still facing forward, and continued eyeballing both sides of the river's green walls. She gave no other response. The rain passed and she shook out her raincoat, neatly folding it within easy reach. Resumed her focus. Random slight headshakes accompanied her usual body movements. She was clearly struggling with the situation. The Swiss team leader couldn't fathom her fellow scientist, her compatriot, acting in such a manner. Or maybe Kim sensed failure. Failure at finding Amsler, a failure of leadership. The blues are a prickly business.

"She was here," I said.

"There is no supporting evidence to indicate so." She spoke toward the bow point. A shift in her position brought us face-to-face. "None. Your statement is pure speculation."

"I smell her. Maybe not literally. But I smell her. She was here."

She dropped a hand over the side and skimmed the water's surface. A sixty-second silence.

"You have greater experience with such things. Perhaps you are right. Perhaps."

She delivered the statement with the slightest of smiles. An improvement. A touch of optimism, hope. All good. It wouldn't last long.

Chapter 14

An uneventful night, a cloudy morning, the trail unknown but near. Had to be. And the nagging questions over yesterday's floatplane. A quick shore breakfast, filled with a sense of Amsler's proximity. I asked Kim to call her camp once again. She did. No one responded.

"There could be many reasons for such a lack of communication." She prepped her boat seating area for the day ahead. "We do not carry phones with us at all times. I will try again later."

I didn't like it. Not one little bit. But we headed upstream, slow, seeking. Kim and I both alternated between sitting and standing, the air thick and sticky. The wall of trees became closer, joined overhead. A vivid green tunnel constricted as the river narrowed, hemmed us in. We continued focusing on elevated access points. I spotted a hyacinth macaw eyeballing us with intense scrutiny as we passed underneath, its spectacular blue plumage combined with a bright yellow chin and eye patch. Other parrots and toucans and monkeys called and rustled overhead. Out of direct sunlight the sheen of sweat remained, but the accompanying thin rivulets stopped.

There it was. Clear as day and twelve feet in the air. The hacked stubs of tree limbs, headed inland. Everything changed. My quarry's trail, spotted. Everything in me was elevated: my focus, my sense of joy, and, yeah, personal affirmation. Not a done deal, but a hot trail. I was closing in. Kim spotted it as well and whipped around, a bright smile and eyes sparkling. She remained silent, but her body language spoke volumes. I killed the motor, and the slow current backtracked our progress.

"She returned and entered here again. Somewhere along this bank," I said, eyes peeled.

Three hundred yards downriver and nothing. I fired the engine, and at Amsler's tree tunnel we pulled ashore. Webbed belt, fanny pack with first aid supplies, water, extra ammo. Glock holstered, machete in hand. Good to go.

"Let's walk upriver. Look for signs."

Kim scoped me with an unknowable eye crinkle. But she gave no argument and nodded agreement, glacier-blue eyes still lit with excitement. Several hundred yards later a small creek stopped our progress. We stood shoulder to shoulder and searched the area. It was quieter here, fewer signs of life, less overhead action from birdlife. Few insects buzzed. Not a major change in our environment, but discernible. The small creek gurgled over a fallen branch prior to joining the river. A nick in the branch said it all.

"No," Kim said. "No, this is not the place. We must continue our search."

"This is it."

"She did not return here."

"Yeah, she did. This creek held another eight or so inches of water when she came back. Her boat's light load drew six inches of water. And she risked a broken boat propeller. Damn the torpedoes, full speed ahead."

I led. Kim, her daypack adjusted, followed without comment. Amsler had toted a heavy equipment container. She'd have sought the closest access point and avoided a long haul inland. Two hundred yards up the creek, it shone as if lit with spotlights. Markings of a boat pulled ashore. Remnants of soft-sand footprints, even after heavy rainfall. And the drag marks of a heavy container. I had her.

After a violent wander through spookville and fruitless search days, I had her. Amsler's discovery and, maybe, Amsler's demise. No victory stake pounded, no need for high-fives. But a welling of satisfaction, of alright. A touch of *You can run but you can't hide, Amsler*. And a brief pause for fulfilling accomplishment. Yessir. I had her.

Kim stared and absorbed the signs. She got it. Whipped around and squeezed me in a wild-abandonment bear hug. Even kissed my cheek.

"It would appear you do possess certain skills, Case Lee." She banged my chest with both her palms. "An explorateur extraordinaire, to be sure! My heart pounds!"

Another smack on the cheek, and she pushed away. Her celebration faded, although her smile remained.

"We must now proceed with the utmost caution," she said, adding several finger shots as emphasis. "An amazing discovery lies ahead, but one also most dangerous."

"Agreed. Let's move slow. Eyes, ears, noses. Crank up the senses, Kim. I need your help for this little exercise."

She nodded back, still smiling. I was too. But with tight lips. The drag marks and occasional machete swipes discernible near the creek faded into deep jungle. A not quite hair-on-end sensation filled me. A sixth sense kicked in. There was something bad wrong with this place. Nothing you'd put your finger on, but a dark-alley vibe. A time, place, texture thing. Not right and filled to the brim with potential danger.

Six paces and the land began to rise. The drag marks continued, the machete cuts fewer. Amsler had hurried, plowed through vegetation. But a root scrape here, a furrow in the detritus there. Headed inland. And this place was quiet. Weird quiet.

As we progressed, the rain forest became sick. There was no other way to explain it. What should have been flexible branches snapped when pushed aside. The rich green foliage was now muted, ill. Leaves yellowed, stems drooped. The normal vibrancy of a rain forest gone, drained. Amsler's way forward became an easy follow as the vegetation's usual resilience to intrusion was now lost. Twigs underfoot snapped instead of the usual yield and spring back. There was something wrong, unhealthy.

Signs of a staging area appeared. We stopped in an area of prep, deployment. Feet had scuffled, the heavy case opened. And a different track added. Two tread lines appeared, faded, appeared again. Miniature tank tracks. A machine running on treads. And a smell I knew too well. It permeated the area, sat as a morbid wet blanket across the landscape. Unreal and otherworldly and horrific. Kim gripped my upper arm.

"This is most dangerous," she said. "Can you feel it? We are near. And my skin is covered with bumps."

"I can feel it. It's like another world. Surrounded with potential life, but quiet. Devoid of movement and activity. Too still."

"What is this smell?" she asked.

"Death."

We locked eyes. The sweat faucet stopped. A near-chill washed across me. I'd experienced dead zones before. Areas where human-driven battle and explosions and carnage held center stage. But not here, not now. There was an environmental terminal illness dominating our setting. Strange. So damn strange.

"Amsler deployed a small tracked vehicle here. Radio-controlled. She walked alongside, driving it."

She released my arm. I trailed Amsler and her machine. Foliage cracked when we brushed it aside. I maintained an intense focus on Amsler's trail. Cautious, we'd stop dead after two or three steps. I sought surrounding visual clues, anomalies. Kim neither spoke nor prompted me to move forward during the stand-stills. We both conducted overhead searches as well, seeking birds. Seeking life. None. Nothing.

Thirty slow-motion paces later, the trail changed. Amsler had stopped and shifted her feet. Her remote controlled driver's spot, where she'd sent the treaded vehicle ahead.

"We don't go any farther after the vehicle," I said. "Amsler stopped here. So do we."

"Are you most certain she went no farther with her equipment?"

"Yeah. I'm certain."

High odds the small vehicle was equipped with a live camera feed. Amsler could steer it without personal visual directions.

"She is not dead," Kim said, a personal buttressing of hope. "We must assume this."

"Poor assumption. All we know is she's not dead right here."

"And our next action? If she did not progress from this point, it would appear this is the edge of a safe zone."

"Nothing safe about this. Any of this. And she moved on from here while she sent the vehicle toward her objective." I lifted my chin toward Amsler's still-evident trail markers ahead. A few foot scuffs, a hacked branch every few paces. Kim squinted, then nodded.

"I do not understand. If she guided the equipment from here, why did she move forward again?"

"Don't know."

I squatted and sought a view through the underbrush where the small vehicle had passed. Nothing. A slight stinging across my eyes—whether real or imagined, unclear. I stood and performed a slow pirouette, senses cranked, the shift of my jungle boots on dirt and fallen leaves the lone noise.

A slow-moving insect flew toward us from our back trail. Dragonfly-like, although unrelated to any dragonfly I'd seen. It wasn't surprising—millions of undiscovered insects resided in remote jungles around the world. Large—a good ten inches long—with two sets of wings as a standard dragonfly, but with a leisurely wing beat. A floating motion, passing close. A jet-black body with translucent gossamer wings. A distinct electric blue dot at each wingtip. It hovered near us and continued on its way through the jungle. The same direction as Amsler's tracked vehicle.

At intermittent intervals I'd lose sight of it before it reappeared, wings stroking slower than the second hand on a watch. Thirty yards away it faltered, missed a stroke, fluttered on its side in midair, continued. Five or so paces farther, one set of wings ceased operating. It spun, helicoptered, as it dropped and disappeared from sight. Dead.

Chapter 15

"Did you observe this?" Kim asked. While I stood on tiptoe attempting to maintain sight of the insect, she dipped low and found a view spot beneath much of the foliage. "Most amazing."

"Yeah. Amazing."

A nearby tree, two feet in diameter, was wrapped with a climbing vine as thick as my wrist. A perfect stairway upward. I sheathed the machete and began climbing. Kim watched, silent. Every third foot placement caused the circling vine to break apart, and I slid past lost ground. I'd performed such a climb numerous times in the past and vines never broke. They were tough and resilient and clung to the host tree's trunk. This one was brittle and unhealthy.

Ten feet up, then twenty. A leg-lock around the trunk. And a view so bizarre, so insane it could and should have been a warped artist's rendition. Three massive trees were centered in a circle of death. Their canopy huge, thick, and draping. For fifty yards in every direction stunted, dead, and dying vegetation. The circular area was marked with a yellow-brown coloration. The three trees—healthy. From the air or from satellite photos their massive canopy would hide most of the underlying dead zone. An area with carcasses littered about. I was surprised there weren't more. Several dozen monkeys in strange suspended decay. Hundreds of birds. But the lack of even more carcasses said the rain forest animals had learned. Learned to avoid this area. Stay away or die.

"What is it you see?"

"A hellscape."

The trio of trees weren't the killer. Surrounding their base in an irregular pattern, a beacon of purple. It leapt out—the lone living color below the trees' green umbrella. The strange mottled purple of strap-leaved plants. Long leaves, waist-high, pointed upward. They stood sentinel around the trunks of the host trees. And nestled against this patch of purple, Ana Amsler's small-tracked vehicle.

In brushed aluminum, the size of a large microwave oven, and covered with functional apparatuses, it had the appearance of a Mars rover. I fished a set of small binoculars from my fanny pack and scoped the scene. The plants—still and upright and perhaps the deadliest thing on earth. I didn't have the foggiest notion what to look for, so I focused on the machine. High-

93

end construction. Of course—Swiss. A miniature car battery provided power and contributed the lion's share of the vehicle's weight. Several devices jutted, one of them the camera for navigation.

"Well?" Kim asked below me.

"Well, I'd like you to climb up here after I get down."

"But of course."

The binoculars provided the required magnification. The small vehicle also displayed an articulated robot arm and a strange lineup of small polished aluminum canisters mounted in a bandolier with space for five. Four remained. Mounted along one side of the rover was an aluminum tube the size and shape of a gift-wrapping tube. At its base, a tank—a compressed air tank, with actuator. The rover's cannon. Had to be. The toxic sample delivery system.

The entire machine was impressive. A miniature mobile sample collection device. The air cannon angled at forty-five degrees, pointed toward an area ahead of us. Toward another part of the safe zone. Or semisafe zone. Hell, for all I knew, I'd drop out of the tree like the dragonfly any second.

I returned the binoculars and paused for a final look. A grove of three massive trees, strange purple strap-leaved plants at their base. A kill zone extending fifty yards in every direction. All shaded by the massive canopy of the apparently immune trees. Yeah, Amsler had picked up on something from the satellite images. No doubt. An overlooked clue. And made a beeline to this area. As I climbed down, I gave a final glance, a final capture of nature's most lethal circle. Oh, man.

"Stick these in your pocket," I said, handing her the binoculars. "And don't linger up there long."

The circling vine didn't break under her weight as it did under mine, and she shinnied up the tree. At first, she didn't speak. Kim stared with mouth open and gave a slow headshake.

"Mon Dieu!"

"Amen."

I had a powerful urge to get out of there. I don't scare easy. But fear of this, the drop-dead unknown, grabbed me hard.

"Incredible. Fantastique!"

"Yeah. Incredible. It's those purple plants."

"Oui. So it would seem."

This wasn't a plain vanilla world-class toxin. No, ma'am. It was airborne. There was no conjecture about mortality when blown by the wind. No confusion about death administered. A minuscule skin touch or inhalation—done deal. Oh, man. It didn't get any worse than this. A little gift from nature's gumbo any terrorist organization would drool over. And kill to get their hands on.

"So, let's be clear. Wind will carry this stuff."

She remained focused on the dead zone.

"Incredible."

"Kim."

"Incredible. Oui, oui. A wind, a breeze."

"Okay. So I've become very interested in current wind conditions. Would you help me keep an eye on the treetops? Movement up there means air movement down here."

And air movement at ground level would trigger two folks hauling it like greased lightning. Oh, man.

"One can hardly describe such a scene."

"Yeah. Got that part. Breeze, Kim. We don't want to be downwind of this little patch of wonder."

"Clearly a symbiotic relationship with those large trees."

"And it's unclear whether hanging this close won't kill us with residual effects."

"Plants do not simply spew toxins into the environment."

"Yeah, well, those purple ones didn't get the memo."

There was no point becoming too emphatic, too forceful with Kim regarding personal danger. A high-end scientist was situated over my head, enraptured. An element of scientific fascination would play out. But long discussions weren't on the agenda.

"Plants only release toxins when touched or ingested."

"Okay. Let's talk botany later. Check the rover. The robot vehicle. We have to talk about it."

"Spores? Fungi related to the purple plants? Or a release from the plants themselves? Incredible."

"I mean, we could be breathing the stuff right now. So use the binoculars, please. Focus on the rover."

"Yet there are microbes that appear unaffected! Note the decomposition of the animals. The monkeys and birds decompose at a remarkably slow rate. Yet they *are* decomposing, so there are life forms resistant to the toxin."

"Kinda doubt we fall in that category. Use the binoculars, please. Check out the rover."

"Rover?"

"The robot vehicle."

She did.

"How large a sample is needed?" I asked.

"One could not imagine such a thing. Such a discovery," she said while scoping Amsler's custom-built contraption.

"Kim?"

"One could not dream of such a thing."

"Kim? Sample size?"

She glanced down, irritated at my constant questions.

"Quite small. Once analyzed, the synthesis process can begin. Variants created in the laboratory."

High odds the Iranians wouldn't have the expertise for such work. Which opened the door for other possibilities, other players. I reserved head time for later conjecture, but not now.

"You see those little canisters? The small tubelike containers? Are those collection devices?"

"It is most possible."

"And the articulated arm. Could it collect a sample and place it in one of those canisters? And seal the canister?"

"This is again most possible. What a discovery! Mon Dieu! The implications are enormous."

In ways you'd never imagine, Kim Rochat. There was no doubt her mind reeled with the scientific and medical possibilities. A bio-prospector perspective. A toxin altered, life-saving compounds created. A valid viewpoint and, in another place at another time, appreciated. But mine was a radically different perspective. One based on an ugly slice of human propensities. Evil intent.

"We gotta go. Amsler circled this area and found an open spot. And aimed the air cannon toward it."

"Cannon?"

"We gotta go, Kim. Come down, please. Now."

I checked the treetop foliage. It was calm, still. For the moment. I don't mind admitting a part of me said screw it and let's scoot. But the mission—a concept hammered into my psyche—said seek answers. *Then* screw it and scoot.

"I must take a photo."

She wrapped her binocular arm around the tree and began digging for her phone with the other hand.

"No. No photos. Or GPS coordinates."

"Do not be absurd."

"Photos are an open invitation to put a target on your back."

She hesitated, hand inside a cargo pocket. "I do not understand."

"Evil people would kill you for a photo."

Raised eyebrows from above. But she stopped retrieving the phone.

"Come down, please."

She did, wearing a confused frown.

"Let's go find where Dr. Amsler shot those canisters."

The trail continued circling the dead zone. Amsler had stopped, guided the rover, collected the sample. She had been focused, intent on the objective. My mind's eye could see it. Once the robot arm dropped the canister down the air cannon tube, she circled. Sought a tree and limb-free trajectory. Then she used the remote control and aimed the device. Pushed the handheld fire button. A blast of compressed air sent it soaring. Rough guess—a lightweight projectile could carry a hundred yards. Maybe a few more. But it was aimed ahead. Toward an intersection with the trail before us. There was no telling what we'd find at the sample landing area. I half expected a stretched-out and decomposing Swiss scientist.

The target area was marked with sunlight. An opening below the sick overhead trees, limbs, vines. I halted. Kim edged against me, seeking. We crept forward. The trail dead-ended, a small operational turnaround spot evident. The spot was marked with a pair of heavy rubber gloves dropped on the jungle floor, turned inside-out.

"Those look familiar?" I asked.

"Yes. For protection. We have many such gloves in camp."

"So let's say she fired the air cannon this direction while standing here. Or standing nearby. The canister lands. Its outside surface is toxic, right?"

"Oui. One must assume so."

"So she dons the gloves, picks it up, and then what?"

A puffed-cheek exhale from Kim.

"Protocol would dictate its placement inside a pressure-sealed container. Again, we have numerous such containers at camp. Prior to shipment, this would be placed inside another container."

"Okay. How big? The pressure-sealed container?"

She described a lunch-box-sized receptacle.

"What color?"

"Red."

So Dr. Ana Amsler, PhD in more stuff than you could shake a stick at, walked out of here with a red bundle of potential hell unleashed. She kept her handheld control device and collected the rover's case she'd dragged. Left rubber gloves behind. And took off on a personal mission I'd yet to understand.

I couldn't shake off an absent element of the situation, a facet of this entire scenario outlined in bright neon, highlighting a missing piece. Amsler could have collected another sample of a decomposing monkey or bird and discovered which microbes were immune to the toxin. A possible antidote. But nope. She collected a world-class airborne-capable toxin and boogied. Headed downriver. She took off and went incognito. And now walked around somewhere on this good earth with the world's deadliest toxin tucked under an arm. Or under the bed. Maybe she kept it on the kitchen counter. A card-carrying member of wingnut central. She had to be. The question—where was she? Well, question number one, anyway. The follow-up had far greater implications—what did she intend to do with it?

"She is alive," Kim said, consternation displayed across her face. She'd grasped the implications—big time. She removed her ball cap, scratched her head. "Oui. She is alive, but where?"

"Yeah. Where." I shifted inside Kim's personal space, leaned down, and locked eyes with her. She paused mid scratch. "I gotta know something. Tell me the truth. Just how batshit crazy is Amsler?"

Her crestfallen expression and lack of protest and quick sidelong glance told me pretty damn crazy. Silence. Then cap back on, a finger shot delivered.

"We shall discuss this later. First, we should leave this place. On such an action we can both agree."

Yeah, agreed. With one major hitch. MOIS showed up. And added to the killing floor.

Chapter 16

In my world, reliance on good fortune led to dead-and-maybe-buried. But I'd take a bit of luck when it came. Amsler's toxic canister pickup spot positioned us near the river. The high-torque whine of a two-stroke outboard engine funneled upriver, loud enough to alert us. The Swiss used two-stroke outboards at their base camp. High odds that this boat lacked Swiss folks. And high odds the occupants of yesterday's floatplane flyover filled this boat. A boat loaded with trouble. Lethal trouble.

The engine cut off downstream, followed by the soft scrape of aluminum hull against riverbank sand. A half-assed attempt at stealth. Overconfident SOBs. It was strange, given they knew about me through Farid Kirmani, who would have painted a violent portrait. But they arrived brazen, assured, cocky. They'd soon enough lose that attitude.

I sheathed the machete—no more bushwhacking—and signaled Kim to do the same. I gripped her upper arms in a firm but gentle hold. Things would become gnarly, starting now, and any mistakes would have fatal consequences. Communication became vital, no misinterpretations.

"There are a boatload of men downriver. Here to torture and kill us."

Spoken as a whisper, and she returned the same.

"How do you know this?"

A quick review of my perspective would prompt enquiries from her about teammates at base camp. Which opened too many emotional doors. Right now, this second, required intense focus. No mental distractions. This was going down, and people would die.

"You asked if I'd killed men. Yes. I'm not proud of it. But this is one of those situations." I let reality marinate for a couple of seconds. "I know what I'm doing. Do you understand?"

Kim stood motionless, with wide eyes and a bitten lower lip. She returned a tight nod.

"Do exactly as I say. No argument, no discussion. Understood?"

She gave another nod. I released her arms and took her hand, a finger to my lips as emphasis, and led her away from our current position and toward the river. She took a small footstep, and a ground twig snapped. I halted, pointed at the ground, and wagged a finger in her direction. No. No noise. The jungle became healthier as we progressed. We stopped alongside a thick collection of waist-high fronds.

"Crawl in there and wait." Spoken an inch from her ear.

"Wait for what?"

"I'll be back. Don't move. If this goes sideways, they'll walk past here a dozen times and not see you. As long as you don't move. Got it?"

Kim responded by sliding into the frond patch, using both hands to brush them aside. A final turn toward me, and she sank into the ground. Disappeared. There was something waiflike about her expression. Couldn't blame her. Helluva position to toss at a bio-prospecting scientist.

At the sound of their arrival, an immediate plan presented itself. Rough, but workable. I'd access our boat, retrieve the Colt assault rifle, and retrieve Kim. Dash along the riverbank toward the small creek we'd followed to Amsler's takeoff point. Hide Kim across the creek, return, and hunt these bastards down.

I pulled the Glock and leveraged years of silent movement through jungles. Approaching the rain forest edge, I dropped and crawled the last several yards. Eased my head through thick vegetation, kissed dirt. Emerged a dozen paces upriver from our boat. And a hundred yards upriver from theirs.

Three of them. Two still futzed with equipment. AK-47 assault rifles, ammo belts. MOIS thugs dressed in fatigues, playing soldier. The third, clearly irritated, shot them hard glances and spat quiet demands. Too far to hear his voice, but the guy was bent. Saddled with morons. His stance, movement, and demeanor spelled military experience. Iranian special forces, maybe.

I waited, watched. A couple of insects buzzed past; birds called from across the river. Life. I'd missed it. The two amateur soldiers finished prepping. Showtime. If they headed inland, pushed into the jungle, I'd carry out my plan.

They didn't. The lead guy, rifle ready, moved with determination and intent toward our boat. The two goons followed. So plan B was formed and soon tossed away. Make a mad dash toward our boat, pull the containerized Colt weapon, and cut loose high-velocity lead. While they did the same. They'd fire before I retrieved my weapon. I could hunker below our boat's hull, but the thin aluminum wouldn't stop their bullets. And if they winged me, standing thigh-deep in river water—well, dripping blood brought another element zipping onto the scene: freakin' piranhas.

So me and a pistol and a small Swiss scientist. Against three men armed with automatic weaponry. One with clear chalked-up experience under his belt. Time to get inventive. I still liked our chances. They might hold off with the automatic gunfire and plan on capturing Kim. She'd presented a vulnerable target when she stood and waved as their floatplane passed overhead. Plus, they had no concept of the dead zone waiting inland from us. None. Too bad for them. Plan C took shape.

I crawled backward, slipped into thick green. A silent hustle back for Kim. I parted fronds, whispered her name. She gathered and stood slowly, concern and fear on her face. She'd unsheathed the machete in her hiding spot. Good for her. A spark of fight.

My weapons case clanged against the inside of our boat. They'd handle my Colt, assess it as a weapon. Man, I hated scumbags groping my personal weaponry. I signaled for Kim to follow, and we retraced our steps, moving fast. As the path started downhill toward the small creek, we turned right. I stopped and whispered the battle plan.

"We'll circle the dead zone. Get situated on the other side."

"Have you seen them? The people from the boat?"

"Yeah. MOIS. They were in the plane yesterday and may think you're Amsler. Hard to say."

"Do they carry weapons?"

"Big time." Communication, Lee. Don't be an idiot. "Yes, they carry weapons."

Ball cap removed, head scratching commenced.

"Should we not make an effort to communicate with them?"

"No. We're at the point where this does the talking." I lifted the Glock.

She returned a hard stare with no evidence of incredulity or doubt or fear. But she required more input. More data. And I required from her a headspace where certainty prevailed.

"I've dealt with these types of men many times," I continued. "So trust me. This, right now, is a time to live or a time to die. There is no middle ground. My job is to make sure we live. I'll make it happen. Promise."

Statement absorbed, she situated her cap and clenched her jaw muscles. Shot me an eye lock and a tight nod. No ambiguity. She was all in.

"We have to hustle," I said. "But no movement noise. That's really important. You gotta focus on no noise."

She did. We worked our way toward the other side of the dead zone. Sidestepped obstructions, pushed aside foliage with our hands. I swiped at eyebrow sweat with my shirtsleeve, sought the right spot. The right place for an ambush. The right place for an encounter of the terminal variety.

A double impetus for their demise now loomed. Yeah, reason enough they wanted us captured, tortured, and killed. But these scum buckets would soon enough discover the dead zone. The location. The potential. For these MOIS agents, remaining alive wasn't an option.

A patch of less sick trees and bushes and vines, thick, fifty paces from the dead zone. It would do. I situated us near a small tree with ample near-ground limbs and leaves.

"Okay. Let's have a conversation. A loud conversation. Doesn't matter what it's about. As long as it's loud."

Eyes crinkled, finger shots, and a whispered response.

"You have been most insistent on silence. And now you wish to make noise?"

"Lots of noise."

"And let them know we are here. At this spot."

"Yes. It's a trap." I rested a reassuring hand on her shoulder. "It's time, Kim. Live or die."

I raised my voice to a near-yell. "I don't think you're right. Not at all."

"Be most assured I am correct!"

She spoke with insufficient volume. I indicated as much with a hand signal.

"Flat wrong. And don't give me any BS about being a scientist."

"But of course I am correct!"

Better. I signaled for more.

"I am correct about this thing, and I am correct about the other things, and I do not understand why you insist I am wrong!"

Well done, Kim. We kept it up for thirty seconds. Hand-signaled for her to stop. Whispered instructions—hide again, another thirty paces farther away. Toward healthy forest. Hunker down, wait. And no movement or noise until I came for her.

A resigned sigh from an out-of-her-element scientist. I wished there were appropriate words to calm her fear, the can't-be-happening coursing through her. I had nothing. She did.

One small hand against my right cheek, a kiss on the other, and "Bonne chance" whispered in my ear. Easing through greenery she paused once and turned, those amazing eyes locked with mine. No gestures, no words, but a brief moment of connection. A goodbye. She disappeared.

I shook my head at her departure, at her stoic courage. But game on, Lee, so get your mind right. A visitor called death floated through the door. A grim, final, and absolute visitor. A mantle of resolve blanketed me—Kim and I would walk away from this place. I became all fight.

I holstered the Glock and shot up the tree, pressed against the trunk, no noise. I intended to assess my enemies' positions, leverage the environment, use the tools at hand. Watch if they'd take the bait of our loud and emphatic argument. The two untrained thugs did. They crashed through brush, running, headed toward our voices. And dashed into the dead zone. I shifted a thin limb aside for a better view.

They broke through the ring of sick jungle and entered the dead zone a half-dozen paces. Slowed at the sight before them. And slowed as the horror of certain death filled their souls. I'd observed more than my fair share of bizarre deaths, horrid endings. But nothing like this. Two assault rifles dropped, clattered to the ground. They knew. Knew it was too late. Final expiration's iron grip clutched them, and release was a pipe dream.

One dropped to his knees, eyes bugging. His mouth opened and shut several times as one leg lifted, a last effort at standing. With a bright purple face and eyes rolled back into his head, he performed a folding collapse. And settled onto toxic ground, dead. The other completed a stumbling sidestep with mouth open as he fell. His arms flailed at an unseen harvester. He bounced once on the ground and gave a desperate yet futile attempt to push up. He rolled onto his back as one arm, one hand lifted toward the heavens and a boot heel kicked. Then, as a backstroke swimmer reaching, the now-purple arm lowered to the ground. Silent stillness followed. Oh, man.

The third MOIS hitter lurked. I couldn't see him, or his movement, on the dead zone's other side. I had high-ground visual advantage. And one large disadvantage. The remaining hitter showed signs of a military background. If he'd had Iranian Special Forces training, he'd wait, scope the area of our fake argument, and if he spotted me up the tree he'd take his time with the assault rifle, aim true, and *adios Case*.

Observed movement meant death. For us both. Movement would identify his position. While I couldn't chance a pistol shot across the long distance, his movement would reveal a route, an attack angle. And if I could pinpoint his route, I'd bushwhack the son of a bitch. Up close and personal.

Chapter 17

We waited. Still, silent, searching for the slightest movement: a frond or low limb or the tremble of a vine moved aside. I wondered if he'd watched his partners' deaths. Wondered if he cared. I'd never know. Five minutes passed, then fifteen. The battle area—hushed and centered on a terminal game of hide-and-seek. I prayed Kim remained hunkered, was quietly confident she would. No shots fired, so she'd comprehend the hunt remained active.

He moved first; a small tree limb jiggled, chest high. He'd either brushed it with his back ducking under, or lifted it with a hand. Either way, he might as well have shot a flare. I still couldn't see him, but no worries. The next foliage movement would ID his direction. Several more would nail his route. And his coffin. They came soon enough. He followed our initial path, toward the small creek. A right turn inevitable, a route toward our last known and heard position. He circled the dead zone, hunting us.

I eased down the tree trunk, keeping it between him and me. Slow, slow—one arm, one leg at a time. I gained grip, focused on acquiring the next silent hand- or foothold. As an oversized lethargic lizard, one soundless placement at a time. I sweated bullets—the exaggerated slow-motion strain ensured nothing out of place, no noise, no indicators. Made terra firma—my friend and hunting partner. Glock unsheathed, the killing floor accessed.

A silent stalk toward an ambush position. Away from our earlier sound signature, away from Kim. Toward my enemy. Thirty yards later, I found it. A cluster of thick shoulder-high bushes and spindly trees. But eighteen inches of bare shrub and tree trunks at ground level. Eighteen inches before leaves and limbs obscured visibility. The plan—press flat, wait, and watch along the ground. He'd pass within fifteen yards. And wouldn't be focusing his hunt on a stretched-out enemy. I'd watch his cautious boot steps pass. Then a silent rise to a standing position. Shoot the SOB in the back. Multiple times. To be sure. He wielded an automatic assault rifle. I held a pistol. All's fair in love and war, baby.

I crawled into my lair and waited, belly-hugged earth. Earth lacking the aroma of rich jungle decay that brought forth life. Sterile and struggling earth. Few insects worked the underbrush; a sickly leaf drifted down from above. Hyper-focus reigned. Ten minutes passed; the sweat flow abated. And his misstep sounded.

A ground twig crunched ahead. Not a crisp snap, but enough. He made his way toward a final resting spot. A glimpse, a full second's worth, of a booted foot. And another. He was angling away from the dead zone. And angling away from me. Left unmolested, he'd pass close to Kim's hiding spot.

Fifteen yards away and gaining distance through slow, cautious footsteps. He passed on my right, now an additional three or four paces away. I'd lose him in the jungle green if we separated much farther. My head reeled with options, possibilities, attack plans. Gotta do something, and do it right now. Right freakin' now.

Decision made, the luxury of time no longer on the table. A two-handed grip, arms pressed against the ground. Steady and stable and as good a pistol rest as a person could hope for. But a twenty-yard shot. At a foot. If successful, he'd collapse in shock and pain. And open the door for a headshot. Deep breath, let half out. I squeezed the trigger.

The Glock's massive boom acted as a starter pistol. To a messed-up situation and best-laid plans out the window. His foot jerked off the ground as the bullet slammed home. A guttural scream, a one-foot hop. But the bastard didn't go down. He remained upright and unleashed automatic fire toward my general location. The concussive blasts deafened me as a chain of bullets thwacked leaves and limbs and dirt across my general area. Joined with a chorus of angry bee buzzes as high-caliber lead whipped past. One of *my* feet jerked. He continued hopping away, his good foot more difficult to sight capture.

He stopped his one-footed dance, ejected an empty magazine, and slammed a fresh one home. Big mistake. I'm not fond of spraying lead toward the enemy. Damn unprofessional. But with his boot's position twenty-five yards away I had a better than good grip on his torso's location. Lots of green between us, but dead-aim options were off the table. Fresh ammo loaded, he slapped the trigger again. A wall of high-octane bullets ripped and snapped foliage inches away.

I returned the favor. Fifteen bullets were left in my .40 caliber, and I used them all. I assumed my target's body position, ripped shots through the jungle growth obscuring him. The immediate area filled with sharp, explosive cracks. They rolled and echoed and deafened. Discernible between barrel blasts were the wet thwack of body shots. Hollow-points hitting their target. Now a partial view of a fatigue-clad mass, his collapsed body. I continued firing, slowing the trigger pulls for better aim. I ejected the Glock's magazine, slammed a new one home, took dead aim and waited. Sixty seconds ticked off. Silence. Spooky silence from the dead zone behind me, the hush of finality from my enemy.

I stood and changed position. Circled behind him. A weird step pattern from my right foot. Closer inspection revealed part of my boot heel blown away. The quick inspection also highlighted the blood dribbling down my arm. A rapid check—grazed in the upper triceps. Both foot and arm were close calls. Too close.

I approached the still body. No movement, no sign of life. Stopping at seven paces away, I put a round in the back of his head. A coup de grâce and the final shot fired and a signal to gather Kim and get the hell away from this place.

"Kim!"

No response.

"Kim! It's alright. It's over."

"Here." Her voice soft, filled with trepidation. "I am here."

As I approached, she stood with eyes wide as saucers, mouth open.

"You are injured! And those other men? Are we safe?"

"I'm fine. The other men are dead. And we're not safe until we're downstream from this place."

I led us away from the dead zone and toward the small creek Amsler had used. I followed it to the intersection with the main tributary and hustled toward our boat, Kim trailing. Not a word was spoken. I shoved us off, started the motor, and scooted toward the other boat. Eased alongside, crawled onboard, and checked the contents. Nothing surprising, although three satellite-capable cell phones were left onboard and left on. Which dictated the next course of action.

I grabbed their boat's bowline and tied it off on our stern. We'd tow it. They'd tossed my Colt rifle across a seat. I checked its functionality, ensured it was good to go, and kept it by my side. Goosed the engine and tore downriver, the other boat surfing behind us.

"Why are we pulling their boat?" She straddled the middle cross-seat. "And give me the first aid kit you carry."

"You hurt?"

"No. You are. Hand it to me, please."

I did. And explained their phones were GPS-enabled with satellite feedback. The data fed to MOIS headquarters in Tehran would reveal they'd made a brief stop and were now headed back downriver. Once we hit the tributary fork, I'd hang a left and head upstream again for a few miles. A false trail. Ditch the boat at a riverbank, toss their phones into the river.

"I have no words. It is all so … so bizarre. Your world is a most peculiar place." She shifted position again. Squeezed alongside me and inspected the wound, adding, "This cannot be argued."

Yeah, Kim. No argument from me.

"I heard two weapons firing," she continued. "Yet you said there were three men."

She raised her eyes from her patching work, an explanation expected. And required.

"They went into the dead zone."

"And the effects of such an action?"

"Immediate. They were dead within seconds."

She focused again on my arm. No more questions regarding our attackers. But Kim delivered one large and terrible question regarding her fellow scientists.

"Did these men kill my team?" she asked, head still bent administering first aid.

Hoo-boy. I could hem and haw, dance around it. Claim uncertainty multiple times. Forestall the inevitable. Lie. But I owed her better.

"I'd be surprised if your teammates remain alive. I'm so sorry, Kim. And I could be wrong."

Her shoulders shook as she stopped her ministrations. Kept her head lowered.

"You are not wrong. You have not been wrong about anything regarding this effort."

Her tears fell. I tried lifting her chin to look into her face and express shared sorrow. She wouldn't allow it at first, determined to maintain her private grief. I cut the engine and stopped worrying about making headway. The lazy current pushed us downriver. Fresh air and fresh life surrounded us, and I'd never been so aware of its vibrancy, its importance. Birds called, wildlife scampered through nearby underbrush. Eons-old cycles of life and death and rebirth. But for the moment, inflicted death, cruel death, required addressing. I possessed no magic potion, no soothing words. Physical comfort was the lone salve, and inadequate at best. But it was all I had.

I pulled Kim Rochat from her locked, bent-over position into a head-on-my-chest hug. She resisted momentarily, then collapsed. Sobs and cries unleashed, she wrapped her arms around me as her small body shook. It shook me as well. I'd pulled a well-meaning Swiss scientist into a shitstorm; I hadn't prepped her for the realities of a dark and evil corner of life, a corner occupied by people who regarded life as a toss-away item. A corner I was shoved into too many times.

We drifted, two small boats floating within a vast wilderness. Pushed by a current headed for the Atlantic Ocean a thousand miles away. One distraught bio-prospector. And one emotion-roiled ex-Delta operator.

This entire job was drowning in a false narrative. The Manaus violence held no mystery: two blood-enemies. Israelis versus Iranians. An arena ancient and blood-drenched. Got it. But this level of violence from MOIS had other earmarks. Maybe they *had* picked up on an errant conversation in a Swiss coffee shop. A rumor filtered through channels, keen interest kicked off. MOIS's physical actions weren't unexpected—they'd always brought a rough sadism to the table. A pack of mad animals, unleashed. But another element lurked at the periphery. They had been guided, prompted.

Ana Amsler had opened other portals, other communications. She'd fed the beast. How and with which beast remained unknown, but her words or some release of information had triggered frenetic actions. And maybe signed her own death warrant. A gray and murky and ugly situation, fraught with death realized and death yet to come. And my scarred butt sat smack-dab in the middle of it.

Chapter 18

Kim wiped her eyes against my shirt front and pulled out the handkerchief she'd used to wet her head. She sat up, blew her nose, and allowed me access to those ice-blue eyes. Tears welled, and she struggled to maintain decorum. Enough emotion expressed, I supposed.

"What is next? After you drop this other boat?"

"Your base camp. I'll ask Bernie for a pickup. Fly us to Coari."

"Where I depart. Run away. I do not believe this is appropriate."

A touch of feistiness or Swiss hardheadedness or both. Either way, I admired it.

"Not running away. Travel toward safety. At the base camp, contact your company. Let them know what has happened."

She returned a desultory nod.

"Tell them you require evacuation."

"Run away."

"Look, Kim. At a minimum, MOIS might mistake you for Amsler. A probable death sentence. You can't hang around Amazonia, or Brazil for that matter. It's time for you to go home."

She shivered in response, signifying grief or anger or an effect of toxic exposure. Or all of the above. I wasn't feeling on top of the world either.

"And what will you do?" she asked.

Helluva good question. My mission remained. Find Amsler. Deliver her to Switzerland. But the job was crafted in terms of Amsler being located somewhere in the area. The Amazon wilderness or Manaus or Coari. As things stood, she could be anywhere. And I didn't have the wherewithal for global search missions.

Another pressing point remained. Knowledge of the location and potency and attributes of what could constitute the world's deadliest toxin resided with three people on this good earth. Amsler. Kim. Me. Amsler as the wild card. Kim much less so.

"I don't know what I'll do. Working on it," I said. "What will happen with you? Once you're back in Switzerland."

"There is a chance they will hide me for a period of time."

The *they* part included both her pharmaceutical company and the Swiss government.

"In the future, I would hope another endeavor awaits. Perhaps a remote coral reef on the other side of the world. The animal life around coral reefs has great potential."

"Good. I hope it happens."

"Or they may restrict me to nontravel status. I would not be allowed to leave Switzerland."

"I hope not. I really do. You're built for bio-prospecting work. I admire your efforts."

It wasn't BS. I did admire her tenacity and focus and educational background. A lot to like there.

"Kim, three people know the whereabouts and potential impact of Amsler's discovery," I continued. "I sure don't have any plans on revealing what I know."

She understood what I meant.

"I considered this. It was strange, but such consideration came when I climbed the tree and observed."

Not so strange—a mouth-opening experience, and a view into the pit of hell.

"My initial reaction was the potential for good," she continued. "A new and unique chemical compound. I must say, this view has changed."

"How so?" I tried not to press, but this was an important marker. Humans are a strange bunch, and I required perspective on how strange Kim Rochat could be.

"It is too dangerous. Oui. Too powerful. A receptacle of great death, and it should remain hidden."

"Yeah. Agreed."

"This attack on us is a reflection of its effects. Such a discovery deals in death. I fear more. And feel certain that more lies ahead for you." She paused and removed her hat to scratch her head. "You wish to know if I will reveal this secret. No. I will not. It shall remain with me until I die."

Good enough for me. Had to be. No other option. I fired the engine. Not far until the river split, where I'd head upstream along the right fork and stash the empty boat we towed behind. Kim shifted to the center seat. The sun blazed overhead, and I relished it. Away from death's hellhole, away from vicious MOIS killers, and away from this phase of the mission. Whether or not a next phase existed—a large TBD.

"How are you feeling?" I asked.

She lifted her head, a "How the hell do you think I feel?" expression on her face.

"I mean physically." I paused. "It's hitting me like the onset of the flu or something."

"Residual effects of the toxin. I also experience such symptoms."

"So what do we do?"

She turned her head, sighed, and gazed into the Big Lost. Man, I felt for her. But this was critical stuff.

"Look. You've been through an awful lot. No doubt. And you carry the strong possibility your team has been executed. I understand how you must feel. But we have to address immediate concerns. I'm sorry."

She sighed and held in another shiver or sob.

"We spent the morning around what might take top honors in toxic hotspots," I continued. "And not just around it. Breathed it. Down in the dirt and, in my case, bled while doing the voodoo bullet shuffle. So I'm thinking we're in danger from the exposure. What we do about it, and do about it right now, sits at the top of my priority list. And I'm looking to you for answers."

"Take us to an exposed riverbank," she said and lowered her head again.

I did. Kim explained that our best bet was to remove and discard all the clothing we'd worn at the dead zone. Footwear included.

"Do you have an extra pair of boots?" she asked. "And additional clothing?"

I did. As did she. A clothing pile formed, and an odd couple stood naked at the riverside. We dipped water with a plastic pitcher and poured cool Amazon River water over our heads. We lathered with soap, rinsed, repeated. I produced a bottle of rubbing alcohol—a godsend and standard treatment in fetid jungles around the world. A thorough alcohol rubdown was followed with clean attire. She insisted on repatching my wound.

"Okay. We washed away the exterior," I said. "Now what about the stuff we breathed?"

She shrugged, intent on taping gauze over the furrow on my upper arm.

"Could use a little more than a shrug, thank you. We breathed a small amount of the toxin. No doubt. Now what?"

"This is unknown. We should drink a great amount of water. Continue sweating. Perhaps this will flush it from our systems. I am not a medical doctor."

"Yeah, but a big chunk of your career dealt with nature's toxins. What if water and sweat don't do the trick?"

"We shall die, I suppose. Quickly or over several days. Again, this is an unknown."

Great. Freakin' great. She finished the first aid ministrations while I contemplated, for the umpteenth time, a career change. I'd accepted a simple search-and-rescue gig. Right up my alley. And walked into a Manaus spook shooting gallery. Plus a midnight ramble with restless natives. And another spook firefight while cozied up to one of the most toxic spots on earth. Case Lee Inc.'s business strategy, at this point, sucked.

I used an entire five-gallon tank of gasoline. Soaked the clothes and the immediate area. Kim assured me such a conflagration, such heat, would kill any residual toxins. I fired it off, heat blazed, and we moved on. Two hours later, having taken the right fork, I shoved the other boat far onto a riverbank. Tossed the three phones. We were miles and miles from the dead zone, up a different tributary and separated by dense rain forest. About all I could do. So I pointed us downriver and floor-boarded the throttle. It would be late in the day when we arrived at the Swiss base camp.

Boat-driven wind flapped our loose clothing. Rainbow-colored flocks of birds burst overhead, and violent swirls flashed near the bank as we flew past. I began feeling better. I think. Plenty of sweat and plenty of water. Kim turned and faced me.

"I am prepared," she stated. "My expectations remain quite low regarding my team. This would include the Brazilian laborers, who I am quite fond of. But I am prepared for what might greet us."

She shifted again and faced forward. Removed her ball cap. The wind blew and lifted and mussed her short hair. A brief pause and she faced me again with a fiery stare, her jaw set.

"I wish to arm myself with one of your weapons. If any evil men remain at our camp, I shall participate in this voodoo shuffle you spoke of. Be most assured."

She waited for an argument. When none came back, she faced front. Kim Rochat, Swiss scientist turned badass.

Chapter 19

They murdered Bernie. The SOBs whacked him at his small office on the floatplane docks. A discovery made when I called his phone for a pickup at the base camp. We were aiming to make a Coari hop, where I'd put Kim on a charter flight. But the bastards took him out.

His office manager Pablo answered Bernie's phone and, between crying jags, explained what had happened. Bernie had made a late-day flight and, after tying off at the floatplane dock and refueling, he'd squeezed into his desk space and ground through paperwork. My mind's eye could picture it. A MOIS agent—perhaps Kirmani—strode in. Bernie would have flashed his wide smile, pushed the thick glasses up his nose, and greeted the visitor. A visitor who pulled a pistol and put a bullet in his head.

The events leading to Bernie's murder were clear. The three MOIS agents had landed at the Swiss base camp and informed their boss they would head upriver and hunt us the following day. Kirmani ensured escape routes were shut down. No floatplane. No Bernie.

Kirmani was a dead man. He just didn't know it yet. I had the bastard's phone number. We'd meet again. Maybe over another table in a makeshift bar. Didn't matter. He was a dead man.

"Call your office, please," I said to Kim. "Arrange a charter flight, a private plane, from Coari to either Rio de Janeiro or São Paulo tomorrow morning. And tell them you require evacuation from Brazil. First flight available."

The sun lowered, and we were still an hour or so away from the Swiss base camp. Plenty of fuel and food for the required next steps. She stood and changed seating, facing me.

"Mr. Anderson is dead, is he not? I heard your side of the conversation."

"Yeah. Killed."

"The same organization? The Iranians?"

"Yeah. MOIS."

My jaw muscles wouldn't stop working, and my blood boiled. Perhaps I wouldn't snap his neck. Slice him a few times, let him bleed like a stuck pig. Then feed his ass to the piranhas. Kim removed her cap and lowered her Ray-Bans.

"I am so very sorry. Such a horrible thing. Mr. Anderson was a good man. A very good man."

"Yeah. He was."

Her eyes were soft with sorrow and sympathy. While I squinted back, unblinking. She extended her small hand and squeezed my knee. An act noticed in passing as I was filled stem to stern with ugly revenge. Those bastards.

"We'll travel by boat to Coari," I continued. "Make tracks until dark and finish the trip early a.m."

"Is it not possible, under the circumstances, to travel at night?"

"No. The Urucu River widens into a massive lake before it hits the main Amazon River. Bernie said pirates and drug runners call it home. If they come after us during daylight, well…" I lifted the Colt rifle. "But nighttime is another story. So make the call, please. You gotta get home."

She did. Her company jumped all over it and spared no expense. There would be a charter jet waiting in Coari. And another in Rio for the trans-Atlantic flight. They would wait for her report from the base camp, although she prepped them on the probable situation.

I cut the engine a half mile upstream from the Swiss base camp and signaled Kim with a finger to my lips. At a quarter mile, I beached the boat. Rifle locked and loaded, Glock on hip.

"Wait here," I whispered. "I'll check it out and report back."

Check it out and kill any lingering MOIS agents.

"No. Unacceptable." Kim delivered her statement with an unexpected vehemence. "Provide me the other gun. The pistol."

I was headed into potential battle. No time for this.

"I'll give it to you if it makes you feel better. But you're staying here. Until I get back."

I fished out the other Glock and chambered a round. Explained it was ready to go, and a trigger pull was all it required. It appeared huge in her small hands. But a safety blanket, a comforter—a sense of emphatic power at hand I well understood. Rifle at the ready, I worked through the foliage toward the camp. She followed. I turned and mouthed an emphatic, "No!" She continued forward until face-to-face. And unloaded on me. At least she did it with a whisper.

"I have listened to and accepted your directives this entire trip. This is no longer the case. I shall walk into my camp and if necessary fight those who would harm us. There will be no more discussion on this issue! Now, lead the way."

I remained stock-still.

"Go!" she said, the pistol held with a two-handed grip and pointed toward the ground. Jeez Louise. Not a lot I could do. So I opted for subterfuge.

"Okay. You stay ten paces behind me. Ten paces. Got that?"

"I shall do no such thing."

"We're headed into potential battle. A position ten paces back has a name. It's called covering my back."

She mulled it over, lips pursed, with a hard glare digging for BS. Not finding any, she returned a tight nod.

"And please don't shoot *me*," I added, leading the way.

It took a half hour to cover the short distance. We moved slow, deliberate, silent. And at the camp's edge, we hunkered down among deep green and observed. I could smell it. Carnage. Great amounts of blood don't soak in and disappear. Or quickly evaporate. A scent signature is left behind, and it takes only one such lifetime experience for etched-in-stone recognition. The buzz of fat flies joined the horror show, audible from a distance. Ten minutes later I moved in, Kim on my tail.

No bodies. It was a relief not to see their direct handiwork—for Kim's sake and mine. They'd dragged their victims into the river and let the piranhas and gators and slow current handle it. The blood trails, one after the other after the other, led toward the river from the mess hall. Inside was sufficient gore to paint an accurate picture. Each camp member tied to the mess hall's stout center pole, one at a time. Each tortured. The horrific screams and cries ghosted around me. The plywood around the center pole wet, sticky, blackish-red. Those inhuman bastards.

Kim stood at the tent's entrance and absorbed the scene. She'd figure it out, and if she didn't, all the better. She emitted harsh breaths, a slight tremor in one leg. Her blue eyes attempted comprehension, a reason or rationale. At some point—perhaps today, perhaps ten years from now—she'd understand. Evil. Pure evil.

"Let's check the other tents," I said with a gentle grip on her arm, turning her. "Collect what we can."

There was nothing left other than a few personal items. Laptops, phones, anything of potential intelligence value taken. Loaded onto a floatplane and sent back to Kirmani. I wondered about their pilot. He deserved a chunk of my ire. But he may have performed his duties with a pistol at his head. I'd never know. Kim spent a half hour collecting her personal items and those of her teammates. Remembrances. Their families would appreciate it. I grabbed a bedsheet, piled everything, and tied a tight bundle. Tossed it over my shoulder. Departure time. And time for experiencing the all-to-often hollowness of expressing sympathy for these situations. Words held no meaning, no magic. Time and reflection the solitary healer.

"I'm sorry, Kim. So, so sorry."

She handed back the pistol. A symbol of violence, or death, or a signifier of her potential participation. Hard to say. She turned and headed toward the boat, not having uttered a single word during the entire ordeal.

We headed downriver until near dark. A brief shoreline stop for personal matters and a boat-bound cold camp, anchored in an eddy. We ate energy bars and prepped the sleeping quarters. I had little compulsion to speak of tomorrow's plans and dangers, but such items formed an icebreaker with a still-silent Kim Rochat.

"We'll have to be careful in Coari. I'm expecting an enemy or three."

Dead eyes looked back in the Amazonia dusk.

"Why?"

Oh, man. A question wide as the sky. But I didn't tread outside operational bounds. Cold, I know, but Case Lee's personal counseling tank ran on empty.

"Because MOIS has declared war."

She struggled and brought my statement into current context.

"On who?"

"Me. And to a lesser degree, you. I'm sorry, Kim. Sorry for everything. It's a big freakin' mess."

She returned a long hollow stare.

"I should contact my office."

She did. The boat performed a languid dance as the eddy's currents shifted us to and fro. Flocks of birds roosted, their calls now muted, settled. Scuffles from the dense jungle, animals hunting or hunted. A bright night, cloudless. And while I couldn't understand the words she said, I welled with sympathy the times she broke down during the home office conversation. Just flat tore me up.

We settled for the night, the tarp draped over the boat's sides and us underneath. Dog tired, worn out, sick and tired of being sick and tired. I held

Kim, wrapped her in my arms. An embrace received with limp acceptance. Sleep came in short sprints. I was woken often by my bunkmate's shaking sobs. One helluva way to live.

Chapter 20

Morning—and much improved in mind and body, if not spirit. The flu-like effects were gone. Talk about a major relief—man oh man. Now to run the gauntlet—travel through drug-runner and pirate waters into Coari. Arrive at the airstrip unseen and unscathed. Put Kim on the charter flight. A mini-mission and one needed because I had no clue as to my next moves. I stood empty within the find-Amsler world. Enough. Enough of this crap. I itched for confrontation, for a fight, for righteous justice. Stupid and irrational and unprofessional, sure. But it was an attitude I made zero effort to tamp down.

"Tell your company we'll arrive at the airstrip within three hours. Come hell or high water."

Kim called and was informed the plane had left Rio de Janeiro and would land in Coari within our arrival window. So far, so good. Kim looked better—no smiles, no eye crinkles of amusement, but with back straight and a hard set to her jaw it was evident she wasn't as torn apart inside. A cathartic experience during the night, maybe. Or she'd adopted a Swiss facade of reticence and lack of public emotion. Hard to say.

To mitigate the risks posed by pirates, drug-runners, and other motorcraft miscreants, I stood while piloting the boat. Stood bold as brass with the rifle slung over one shoulder and both Glocks holstered on my hips. Don't even think about it, boys. Don't even think about it. They didn't.

We arrived at the outskirts of Coari on the Amazon River and tied off alongside other small boats at a rickety pier overlooked by shanties. A Coari favela, or slum. Good. The weapon stayed slung across my back, visible to the residents of this out-of-the-way area. I was confident we'd be left alone. Until I initiated a conversation. The location also ensured that this wouldn't be an area MOIS agents covered. They'd stake the main docks. And the small airport. I'd deal with the latter when the time came.

"We'll take the rucksacks and a bundle of personal items from your base camp. Toss whatever else you want into your travel bag."

"And the other items? Our supplies? And this boat?"

"Currency for barter."

She didn't question or suggest alternatives. She stayed in her personal headspace with the drawbridge raised and the moat filled. Understandable and accepted. I wasn't a shrink, but I *was* capable of delivering her safe and unharmed to her own people. About all I could do at the moment.

"Fetch me the boss."

I tossed the statement toward a young teenage boy at the end of the slapdash pier. He'd watched our arrival. Each favela, or section of favela, had a syndicate. A criminal organization. This one wouldn't be any different. Dirt-poor, they'd steal and kidnap and kill—driven in no small part through competition with surrounding shanty neighborhoods. The kid nodded and took off among the plywood and plastic and tin shanties. We packed. I'd brought a small travel duffel bag of sufficient length to house the rifle. Added the extra Glock and a coil of nylon rope. The weapons had a specific purpose. The rope much less so, but it's never a bad idea to pack some.

Five minutes later the kid returned with three men. The lead guy was midthirties, open shirt, tats galore. Clothes tattered but his ball cap, with a Brazilian soccer team insignia, new and bright green. The two guys trailing were his posse, muscle.

"Just you," I said as they approached the pier. I wouldn't tolerate input and argument from the muscle. Me and the boss, a deal struck. Let him sort the divvying of the spoils. He gave a hand signal, and the entourage remained behind. The boss walked forward.

"I need a car and a driver. Take us to the airport. No problems, no hassles. Just get us to the airport."

He fired a cigarette, pointed a chin toward my waist, and said, "You are well prepared for problems."

He meant the holstered Glock.

"Yeah. I am."

He took a drag and exhaled. "What of your boat?"

"Payment. Boat, motor, and everything left in it."

He'd commandeer the boat. Dole out the rest. The plastic tarp would become a shack's new roof. Extra fuel tanks, food, camping sundries. Plenty of hard goods for trade. All for unhindered passage to the small airport. A large smile, white teeth flashed. His lucky day.

"I will provide you a ride. And guarantee a safe passage."

"Yeah. I know you will. Because you're driving. And I'm sitting behind you."

I patted the Glock. The smile disappeared, as well as any double-dealing plans he'd concocted in the last fifteen seconds. He took another drag, exhaled through his nostrils, and called for his men to produce a vehicle. Ten minutes later we loaded our stuff and slid into an old sedan's backseat, the boss behind the wheel and, for a brief interval, another gang member in the front passenger seat.

"Get out. Now."

The additional passenger twisted in the seat, started to address me. I lifted the unholstered pistol for emphasis. He slid out. His boss watched my part of the exchange in the rearview mirror.

During the drive I formulated the next steps once Kim was on board the Rio plane. I'd take a flight to Manaus. Kill Kirmani. The sole actionable step making any sense at the moment. Triggered in part through interactions with the favela boss and his minions. Neck-deep in the world of hitters, thugs, crime, cheap life. Well, Kirmani wanted my head on a stake. Happy to oblige, asshole. Except you get the whole Case Lee package.

An uneventful drive through town and four isolated miles to the rudimentary airport: a decent-sized tin-walled hangar with a couple of prop planes parked. A cinder-block building, small, like the terminal. A private jet sat nearby. Kim's ride. A locked gate prevented us from driving to it, so we bailed at the terminal and collected our stuff.

"Are we good?" the young favela boss asked.

"Yeah. We're good."

He smiled, waved, and drove away. He'd cogitate usage of the small boat and new engine. Pirating or running drugs or selling the whole kit and caboodle for quick cash. Decisions, decisions.

"I'll see you onto the plane after checking with the pilot."

Kim nodded and hefted her gear. I had logistical concerns with the pilot and would attempt to ensure his personal oversight of her Rio charter jet transfer. A jet prepared to whisk her out of Brazil. MOIS agents could be present, and the pilot's escort mitigated risks. As crazed as they were, I couldn't envision them running onto the tarmac in Rio, guns blazing.

We entered the terminal's small back door. The aroma of fresh-brewed coffee filled the room, along with three male airport employees draped across two couches. Kim's two pilots stood with elbows on a counter, chatting with a pretty young female employee. All good. Until the bathroom door creaked open and a MOIS agent wandered into the room, checking his fly. The dumb bastard never had a chance.

He had the same look and feel as the other MOIS thugs. As he fooled with his fly, he exposed the semiauto pistol slid into his waistband. I dropped everything and launched. He looked up as my boot detonated into his solar plexus. He flew backward through the bathroom door, airborne. Performed a desperate backward roll and ended on his feet. On him in an instant, I slammed the door behind me. He made a desperate grab for his pistol, terminated when I took his wrist, twisted, and dealt an elbow hammer blow. Bones shattered, and he screamed. I ripped the pistol from his pants and tossed it into the bathroom sink. He cradled his broken elbow and exposed both sides of his body. I pounded him with two consecutive left hooks——one rib-breaking punch mid-body followed with a vicious kidney shot. He went down again, poleaxed, head bouncing off the tile floor.

I should have questioned him. Found a common language. But I'd had it up to here with these sadistic bastards. Filled with controlled fury, I wasn't in the mood to converse. I slammed a boot toe into his testicles. He screamed again, curled into a ball, and puked. I dragged him upright and applied the sleeper hold. Pressed both arms against the carotid arteries on either side of his neck. He rag-dolled, unconscious within three seconds. I let him drop like a heap of laundry. Removed his belt and ripped off a portion of his shirt. Hog-tied him with hands behind back and feet tied to hands. Trussed the bastard. Left him unconscious on the floor. Pocketing his cell phone and plucking the pistol from the sink, I exited and shut the door behind me.

Dead quiet, eyes on Case Lee Esq., several mouths open. I strode toward and addressed the two pilots.

"She's your passenger," I said, nodding toward Kim. "When you land in Rio, she transfers to another private charter. I want the transfer coordinated and quick. Understood?"

"Yes. Of course. Understood," one of the pilots said. "It shouldn't take long to pass through immigration."

"You're not listening to me. I want it coordinated. And quick."

The pilots looked at each other. A long agonized groan emanated from the bathroom.

"I know an excellent despachante," the second pilot said. "But there is the question of payment."

"Her company will pay. Coordinate with your passenger after takeoff. Make it happen."

Another shared look between the pilots, followed with two nods in my direction. The room's other occupants remained still and quiet.

"Go fire the engines," I said. "You're leaving."

Both pilots made a hasty exit onto the tarmac. I helped Kim collect her things. Her expression was deadpan except for the slightest eyebrow lift. This was our goodbye. It rang hollow, inadequate as hell. Moving her to safety, but without shared panning for personal gold, common threads, joined sentiments. Neither of our heads were in the right space.

Then it came from left field, an afterthought, a tossed Hail Mary. I pulled a folded photo of Ana Amsler from my rucksack and displayed it to the room's other occupants, one at a time, as a lawyer would address individual members of the jury. The first one denied having ever seen her. The second one expressed a maybe, diverted his eyes. He held back information. Threatened? Paid off? I prepared to plumb his drainpipe, no holds barred. But my questions and photo display prompted the young lady to sidle over. She took the photo from my hands.

"Yes. I've seen her. Maybe four or five days ago," she said.

Out of the blue, unexpected, and borderline surreal. Everything changed. A trail, a lead, and the find-Amsler radar cranked right back up. I'd imitated a birddog on scent, nose working the air. Blind luck played a part, no doubt, but I'd take what I could get.

"Did she charter an airplane?" I asked.

"Yes. A small one." She tilted her head toward the hangar. "Similar to those. It was the only one available, and she wished an immediate departure."

Kim arrived at my elbow and asked, "Are you certain?"

"I explained such a small plane would make at least two stops for fuel. The trip would take the entire day. She did not care. Yes, I am certain."

"Where was she going?" I asked. "Her destination? And how did she pay?"

"Rio de Janeiro. She paid with cash. Euros."

Possibilities floated, the scent thin. But a scent. And I was on it.

"Did she arrive in Rio?"

A couple of fuel stops provided ample opportunity for the wingnut to go on walkabout. Land in a smaller Brazilian city and decide it was a grand hideout location. With her lethal little red box.

"Oh, yes. I talked with the pilot only yesterday."

An attractive young lady, stationed at an obscure airport. Yeah, I could see the pilot holding a conversation with her. Chatting about recent events and passengers. Same as the two guys now waiting for Kim to climb on board. Oh, man. A trail. A few days old, but a trail.

"I'm hitching a ride with you, Kim. Going to Rio."

"But of course. As you should."

Delivered with a half-smile, and a half-smile returned. Signs of life and a touch of fire emerged behind those iceberg eyes. Good and fine. But a loose end remained.

"Does that guy know about this?" I asked the young lady, a thumb pointed toward the bathroom. "About the charter flight with this person?" I held up Amsler's photo.

"Oh, yes," she said. "He arrived yesterday and asked the same questions about her. And he's been here ever since."

Two realities were highlighted by her answer. Both jaw-clenchers. Kirmani would have shifted his base of operations to Rio by now. He and his henchmen were on Amsler's trail. The lone upside—a Manaus trip wasn't required to whack him.

And her answer shone a spotlight on why the MOIS agent had hung around this middle-of-nowhere airstrip. He'd been ordered to. After relaying the Amsler flight information, he was ordered to stay, and stay for one reason. Watch for us: Kim and me. A fallback plan in case the three MOIS agents failed with their upriver mission. Watch, wait, capture us at gunpoint. Or shoot us on sight. The urge to revisit my bathroom-floor buddy pulled like a mule. Nostrils flared, I turned for a final tile-floor visit.

Kim stopped me. She grasped the frustration and anger and the immediate object of my intent. She stepped in front of me and pressed her small palms against my waist.

"No. Please do not."

"Kim. He's a killer."

"Oui. He is. But you are not."

"Recent events would argue otherwise."

No point skirting the obvious.

"Those were actions based upon events and circumstances." She shifted closer, spoke with a near-whisper. "And this is a different circumstance. Prove me right. Please."

No more killing and death and horror related to her. Understood. But still. The SOB hog-tied on the bathroom floor would kill us both given the chance. No doubt. None.

Kim squeezed my sides, eyes crinkling. "Please. For me."

Sometimes you've gotta let it go. At least the bastard wouldn't draw a pistol with a broken elbow anytime soon. And killing him would involve the Brazilian national police—unlike a severe ass-kicking delivered in an obscure Amazon basin town. Yeah, I'd walk. For Kim. But cold reality pointed toward unfinished business on a bathroom floor.

"Okay. Enough. I get it."

She guided me away from the bathroom door.

"And so," she said, a side-pat delivered. "I shall remember you as a special man. An explorateur extraordinaire. As it should be."

I thanked the young Brazilian for her help, collected my possessions, and held open the door. The jet's engines whined, warming up.

"Let's get you home, Kim."

THE AMAZON JOB

Chapter 21

The first order of business was to make arrangements for a Rio de Janeiro immigration official, who would greet us upon arrival, provide a perfunctory passport stamp, and Kim would board a private flight and head home. If MOIS was present, I'd handle it. Odds were high such actions wouldn't be necessary, but fanatics could be, well, fanatical.

The second order of business was a cocktail. I wasn't jonesing for a drink, but small victories realized and a several-day dry spell prompted the request from the plane's steward. Grey Goose on the rocks. Kim declined the steward's initial offer but changed her mind after I ordered and asked for the same.

We chatted. Casual, personal, relaxed—the first and last time. I came to like her even more. She talked about growing up in her neck of the woods. Mom and Dad owned and operated a bakery in a smallish Swiss town. A family tradition, several generations deep. Married for a short while, then divorced. "I suppose I am married to my job," she said. A passion for microbial life forms—exploration at the cellular and chemical-compound level. A Grand Prix racing fan and a reader of obscure biographies—fellow scientists more often than not. Plus a strong fondness for Mexican food. I sorely regretted her not opening the personal-life kimono during our search. But at the end of the day she was Swiss, and perhaps it took time and trauma and shared experiences before such a personal conversation could unfold.

She asked about my background. I kept it benign and shaded and obscure. She flashed a wry smile often—"Yeah, right" was my best interpretation of her feedback. But she also responded with humor and understanding. All good, a bond forged through a once-in-a-lifetime series of events. Two of the three people on earth who knew the dead zone's location and fatal reality. A bond solidified through discovery and horror and death. A rare bond, and one we both recognized.

"So how did you pick your team?" I asked. "For this Amazon project?"

"There is a volunteer element, of course. Compatibility is also a consideration." She sipped her drink. "A balancing of skill sets as well."

"It doesn't sound like Amsler was all that compatible. Taking off on her own, disregarding directives."

"She is the most brilliant scientist I have ever met. Such an attribute overcomes many peculiar behaviors."

Given the nature of the discovery, Kim and I might disagree on such a trade-off, so I didn't go there, and instead eased toward Amsler's lifestyle characteristics.

"You mentioned Grand Prix racing and biographies. And Mexican food. What about Amsler's interests? Bungee jumping? Falconry?"

She laughed. "Very little in such regard. She has a complete work focus. I must assume she had other interests growing up. The Amsler family is quite wealthy." She took a sip, closed her eyes for a moment, and continued. "She would often read at night, but otherwise Dr. Amsler is absorbed with her profession."

The steward served us cheese and pâté with toast. Offered wine, which Kim accepted.

"What kind of stuff did she read?"

"This is quite good," Kim said, crunching into toast topped with pâté. She chewed and stared out the plane's small window. "Strange books. Apparently we are all part of a vast conspiracy."

"Including you and me?"

"In particular you, I am afraid. She is not fond of your country."

"What's her issue with the US?"

Kim wore a smile as she prepped another slice of toast. A slug of wine followed a hearty bite. Her eyes sparkled, humor lines at the edges.

"Your country is to blame for everything, it would seem. You see, the US leads the global conspiracy. Although you have kept your role in the conspiracy well-hidden during our time together."

"It's what they've trained me to do. That, and maintain communication with the alien spaceship orbiting overhead."

"Then you shall have most interesting conversations with Dr. Amsler if you find her."

We both chuckled. I raised my Grey Goose as salute to the proposed encounter. And added more information to the Amsler data bank.

"Okay. So she holds a grudge against the US. Does she have friends? Lovers? Space alien escorts?"

"This word grudge. No. It is most inadequate for describing her feeling. She hates your country. And is quite passionate about it." Another swallow of wine. "Which is peculiar given her relationship—her lover, one might suppose—is also Américain."

"You know this guy?"

Why she'd waited until the last minute to reveal such pertinent information would remain unknown. Didn't she understand this was vital stuff? Maybe not. My expectations regarding valid intel were seldom matched when dealing with folks who lived within a more sedate world. A normal world. Still, it grated, but at least the faucet had opened.

"To be sure. We have met. At a Berlin conference. He holds a doctorate in organic chemistry."

"So the original odd couple met at a conference?"

"So it would seem. He, too, is peculiar. I do so remember him staring into my eyes. There was something behind his look. Quite strange. Of course, this is my interpretation."

And high odds a valid one. This guy and Amsler—two wackadoos hooked up. Great.

"Do you remember his name?"

"But of course. Dr. Archer. Dr. William Archer."

A side trail, maybe. Or not. Still, intel gathered and added to the pile.

"Where does he live?"

"I have told you. The US."

"Big country."

"California, I believe. Los Angeles, perhaps. May I have your toast and pâté? It does not appear you are hungry."

I handed it over with a smile while wheels turned in my head. Kim opted to end our conversation and focus on the scenery outside the window while finishing off my food. So I leaned back, sipped, and thought about Amsler. One ballsy scientist. Collected the toxic sample, formulated a plan. And carried it out. Waited to travel at night, killed her boat's engine at the appropriate time. Floated past her base camp, silent and aware and conniving. Continued down the Urucu River. Past pirates, drug runners, and men who'd kill for a laugh. Done with a strange Amsler insouciance. Maybe it was the tinfoil hat. Shiny mojo. Chartered a small prop plane and flew to Rio. Then what?

There are six million folks in Rio de Janeiro. It's not a challenge hiding out. But why hang around? Indecision, maybe. I'd seen it more than a few times. Pull off a phase one of a grand plan. Reconnoiter before next steps. Possible. Or she'd moved on. To where?

Gotta assume she kept her phone off. Otherwise tracking her was possible. Unless she owned a satellite phone like mine with 256-bit encryption. Even with this precaution, the NSA might crack the algorithm and track her, listen in. If they cared. Or she could be tracked through credit card purchases. Even MOIS—not a top-line espionage outfit—would have the ability to backdoor credit card systems and follow her. Mossad, and Uri Hirsch, for certain had the capability. So I would remain behind the curve regarding electronic sniffers. But Amsler came from wealth, according to Kim. Access to cash. Lots of cash. Her Rio charter flight as an example. And cash fostered anonymity. Hotels, restaurants, sundries. So yeah, she could have slipped away with her prize to anywhere. Bolivia, Botswana, Bangladesh.

The lurking vibe of Amsler having talked with someone about her discovery—someone outside the Swiss coffee house—made me itch. One I couldn't quite scratch. I couldn't connect those dots. I couldn't even identify the dots to connect.

"I'll miss you. Do you know this?" Kim asked. She lolled in her seat, a decent buzz evident.

"I'll miss you, too."

I meant it. But seeing her safe, tucked onto an international flight back home, was a cause for celebration. A small chunk of this gig with rock-solid satisfaction.

"I suppose we shall never meet again." She giggled. "I sound as if we were in a Hollywood movie. We shall *never* meet again."

More than a decent buzz. "Probably not. But you never know."

"One never knows. So true." She returned to staring at the passing landscape below. A sea of green.

Amsler hated the US. Worrisome. I wouldn't give a rat's rear end under normal circumstances. This was anything but. She and MOIS had common cause. If those two teamed, then "Katy, bar the door." And MOIS was hell-bent on them hooking up.

"Kim, does Amsler have the ability to synthesize her discovery? Produce a quantity of it? By herself?"

She had lowered the seat back and now faded toward a nap. She raised a hand and waggled it back and forth. Added a shrug.

"Does that mean maybe?" I asked.

"Oui."

Alrighty then. A potential Wingnut Central chemical company. A small operation, granted, but *filled* with potential. If she did synthesize the toxin, create substantial amounts, a terrorist tool second to none became a reality. More than enough impetus for finding her.

Now with the soon-to-be-added distraction of spookville's major leaguers engaging. Bound to happen. The violent Manaus activities between Mossad and MOIS and me. The Swiss base camp slaughter. Word would filter out. Out into the gray fog where the shadow players lurked. Guaranteed to rattle a few major clandestine cages. The big boys wouldn't sit on the sidelines long. Nope. I understood all too well how it worked. Whiteboard sessions at headquarters, apocalyptic scenarios presented, budgets spent. A major difference this time around—the apocalyptic possibility held water. So they'd assign assets, wondering what had gone down in Brazil. The CIA, Russians, Chinese, Brits, French—you name it, they'd sniff around. Great. Freakin' great.

Along with their involvement was the little matter of my scarred-up hide. I'd been cannon fodder for the CIA, target practice for the Russians. The Chinese had attempted my birth certificate's cancellation through proxies—several times. So this gig now featured the additional angle of Case Lee gallivanting through a sea of spooks. I'd rather lick a rodeo parking lot clean.

Toss the whole bloody thing into the pot, and another big question loomed. If I was successful—long odds at the moment—and found Amsler, who kept the football? Not yours truly. I couldn't see the little red container stowed safely on the *Ace of Spades*. The CIA? I didn't trust them as far as I could toss a sumo wrestler. The Swiss were the probable candidates. They'd bury it under one of their mountains and never speak of it again. Maybe.

I catnapped the flight's final hour. Faded in and out of mission focus, anger, and futility. The Clubhouse aside, I didn't own the technical necessities for electronic tracking—flight manifests, GPS, credit cards, phone call interceptions. What I *did* own was a thin trail. Inside a city of six million.

I would miss her. Kim. We shall never meet again. A poignant and pulling statement. True and nothing funny about it. I'd miss her, plain and simple. A solid teammate with backbone and fire and smarts. Lots to offer there. Yeah, I'd get her on the Switzerland charter flight and chalk up a small victory. But still, I'd miss her.

Flaps and landing gear lowered, waking us both. Rio de Janeiro. I untucked my shirt and slid the Glock into the waistband. A casual exit from our plane and into the private terminal lounge. Leather seating, vacuumed carpet, and the aroma of pilot's fuel—brewed coffee. Two dozen folks lingered about, conversed, read emails or chat messages. No MOIS agents present. A signal their Coari agent was still kissing tile. Or the kidney shot had killed him. Either way, all quiet on the Rio front.

A well-attired European pilot addressed us, followed by a Brazilian immigration official. The pilot introduced himself and pointed out the Gulfstream hired to whisk Kim home. Two airport employees hoisted her luggage—the sheet-wrapped artifacts from the base camp included. The official stamped her passport. The pilot held open a glass door leading to the tarmac and her jet. Done and done.

I expected a hug of goodbye and Godspeed. I did *not* expect the arms-around-neck passion of a full body-on-body deep kiss. I reciprocated without hesitation. For all too brief a time we stood embraced within our own bubble of reality. Without a second's consideration what others saw or said or thought. We'd run the gauntlet and been put through the wringer. Together. And she'd walked with me step by step.

The embrace ended and tore a small rip in my heart. Our bodies separated first, lips last. The kiss's final release slow, lingering, absolute. A final lock with those ice-blue eyes, no words, and she turned. Gone. Oh, man.

"Marvelous stuff, Mr. Lee. I mean that with sincerity and more than a touch of envy."

The voice, American. Delivered from a man in his midfifties, gray hair, slouched nearby in a padded leather chair. Rumpled, he wore a brown blazer and a sincere smile.

"Bogart and Bergman have nothing on you two. Well done, sir. Well done."

Spookville had announced its presence and the CIA entered the hunt.

Chapter 22

"Let's get a cup of coffee," he said and groaned as he pushed from the comfortable lounger. "I have found a good cup of coffee a solid starting point."

We did. No point avoiding the reality of the Company's presence with the Amsler chase. Bound to happen. Too much information plucked from the shadows. A Manaus shoot-out. Possible communiqués between the CIA and Mossad. Intercepted calls—the conversations between Kim Rochat and her home office sufficient for NSA's algorithms to blink a few red lights. This guy would attempt a subtle wringing of information from me. I would reciprocate, albeit with less nuance. We both ordered cafezinhos from the coffee bar while I wrapped my head around the reality of a major clandestine player brushing against my gig. One upside—the Company might provide useful information for the chase. And it *was* a chase, with rescue no longer on the table.

"I should start with introductions." He patted a few pockets, rummaged about his attire, and found a small and well-used leather business-card case. He fumbled with the extraction but got around to handing me one.

"My card. And I go by Ski. Always have."

Jack Kowalewski. Operations Officer. US Embassy. Brazil. Everything but the CIA designation spelled out. At least the card didn't claim Agricultural Liaison or other such rubbish. We sat at a small corner table, isolated.

"I would appreciate it if you entered my number into your phone," he said. "A best practices sort of thing. So you know who is trying to reach you."

Ski wore a Cheshire cat smile and bushy gray eyebrows raised with expectation. His buzz cut poked upward like short bristles on an inverted hairbrush. And his statement carried the usual Company BS. He didn't ask for my number. He already had it. A know-all, see-all opening gambit right out of the chute.

I slid his card into a cargo pocket. Yeah, I'd enter the number later. But not in front of this guy—I wouldn't play trained monkey. He knew my phone number—encrypted and privy to only a handful of people—because of one reason. Marilyn Townsend. The director of clandestine services within the CIA. We knew her from Delta Force days. Myself and my blood brothers: Catch, Marcus, Bo. Townsend had been a CIA field agent years ago, and a damn good one. Delta acted as hammer for her pointed-out nails. We separated for years, although we knew she'd climb high. I reengaged with her during a New Guinea job, where we'd exchanged private contact information. She'd used me a couple of times since. Used wasn't the right word. Played me like a Steinway. The world's top spook. Her identity known to few people. I could guarantee this guy sitting across from me didn't know her. Four or five levels above his head where shadows become pitch-black. Congress critters didn't know her name, and I wasn't sure the president did either. It allowed for a separation of knowledge. Plausible deniability.

"So how is the director?"

No pronouns. No clues. Man or woman, this guy wouldn't know. But it laid an insider-information card on the table, evened things up. Childish, I know, on both our parts. But games were played, promises made, and few if any gifts exchanged. The ledger entries with the Company showed a large deficit regarding the Case Lee account, and they owed more than a shovelful or two of help. Hell, they owed a dump truck or two, the way I saw it. High odds Marilyn Townsend would disagree.

"Fine."

As if you'd know, bud. A passing thought how he'd known that I'd land here, at this time. I flew commercial into Manaus. They'd know I was in Brazil. But the timing of this meeting could have been driven through several avenues. A big bird positioned over Coari, perhaps. High-resolution photos of me and Kim captured. Or my photo faxed or emailed to the Coari airport manager with a phone number and price tag. If you spot this man, call the below number immediately, $1000 US reward. However it happened, here sat Ski, doing his hail-fellow-well-met Company routine.

"And you should know," he continued, changing the subject. "I read your dossier. It is very impressive, and I'd like to offer a personal note of gratitude for your service."

"Thanks."

He grimaced and flexed his right knee. His trouser leg cuff flopped down. It required a few tailored stitches. I didn't think he'd get around to it anytime soon.

"I should have this knee replaced. I'm thinking about doing it once I return stateside. This is my last assignment, and it's a fine place to end a career." He stopped the leg extensions and resituated again, slouched and smiling. "It's quiet here, and I like Brazilians."

"Okay."

"Because of your service and sacrifice, I want to be frank with you."

"I like frank. I like honesty better, but I'll take what I can get."

I lifted the tiny cafezinho cup as mock salute and drained it. He chuckled.

"You do have an Indiana Jones thing going. Your appearance. It fits you, but you may consider a shower and shave in the near future."

Another chuckle. My bosom buddy, Ski. Man, I missed the clarity, the no-white-noise focus of a jungle search. And I already missed Kim. But hard reality smiled at me from across the table. Accept it and plow ahead.

"Tell me about MOIS. Here in Rio," I said.

"Straight to the point. You can take the man out of Delta, but you can't take Delta out of the man."

"MOIS."

A lounge employee wandered over and asked if we'd like another. I declined. Ski replied in the affirmative and ordered a brandy on the side. He draped his forearms along the table, the genial countenance still pasted in place.

"The first we heard of them was a report from Manaus," he said. "Apparently there was quite the kerfuffle at the opera house."

"Oh, yeah? The tenor have a bad night? People rioted?"

My gut said he'd heard from Mossad before it made the Brazilian news. Uri Hirsch. It wouldn't bowl me over if the Company worked the Amsler rumor with Mossad. But the Israelis weren't chumps. They'd work the Company as hard or harder than they were worked.

"A bit more severe than the poor delivery of an aria, I'm afraid. A touch of the Wild West deep in Amazonia. Can you tell me about that?"

"Nope."

He sat back and stretched his leg again. The Company weren't cops. Information gatherers, they focused on the obtainable and manipulation and, when needed, hard action.

"I'm telling you, this knee is a pain. So how's the Dr. Amsler pursuit going?"

"She came here. Rio."

Tossed out as an operational truth card, joined with a vague hope of reciprocity. A credit entry in the ledger.

"Did she? I'm sorry we didn't know about it."

Translation—he wouldn't share what he knew about her location, if anything. The usual malaise settled. Similar to a bad cold's onset. Cotton brain. Playing three-dimensional mental chess with spooks always triggered it. Nothing as it seemed. Straight answers sprinkled across the conversation, adding validity to the lies. Man, it flat wore me out. An internal sigh, situational acceptance. Push through this, Lee. You have a horror-packing crazy Swiss scientist to catch.

"Where do you work, Ski?"

I required clarity on the Company's Rio assets. Strong odds they were minimal.

"Why, the embassy is in Brasilia."

A non-answer. Brasilia was the capital, fair enough. Hacked from scrub and savannah in the 1960s. Built with the sole purpose of establishing a new capital and opening up the interior. Two-and-a-half-million folks lived there. Sure, he'd sniff around when the Brazilian congress was in session. No doubt. But the seat of Brazilian power nested in São Paulo, an industrial city of twelve million and Brazil's source of influence, money, and string-pulling. Dollars to doughnuts he lived there. And traveled to Rio de Janeiro when required. His coffee and brandy arrived. A slurp, a sip, and back to business.

"Were you able to confirm the rumor of Amsler's discovery?" he continued. Another lane change performed without the blinker.

The inevitable question. I'd prepped for it long before Rio. Developed a fallback position if and when things spun well outside my purview, my control. At such a point, I'd reveal the reality. Not the dead zone location, but the potential of Amsler's package. And Amsler's hatred of the US. But not now. Not with the fresh scent of a trail.

Chapter 23

I walked a fine line, settling on giving this guy a heads-up and leave it at that. For now.

"Yeah. I can confirm the rumor. She discovered some nasty stuff."

"An organic compound, obviously."

His tone was borderline dismissive, although the pleasant smile remained. Well, here's the deal, Ski, old buddy. Whatever "double, double toil and trouble" you've got cooking in Company labs can't hold a candle to this stuff. Nossir.

"Yeah. Organic compound."

"Did you find the source?"

"No. But I have a strong inkling Amsler is toting around a sample."

"Ah."

Yeah. Ah. Company Man wheels turned, played the odds. And played cat versus mouse. A newbie with such affairs, to sit-downs like this, wouldn't notice. But get shoved through the Company's wash-and-spin cycle a few times, and it became beyond obvious.

"What have you got on Amsler?" I asked, testing the waters for a whiff of quid pro quo.

He returned a slow blink, his facial expression pleasant as could be.

"This situation would make a good movie. Something with a noir feel, I would think. A brilliant Swiss scientist. A mysterious organic poison. And, of course, our intrepid sleuth on her trail. Although the love interest would appear to be finished halfway through the tale. That was Dr. Rochat, I assume."

"Yeah. So what does the Company have on Amsler, Ski?"

"Dr. Rochat is quite attractive. And I'm not kidding about the kiss. It was borderline epic."

"Ski."

A shrug. "Not much, I'm afraid."

"How about a few dots? I'll do the connecting."

His smile widened until he shifted position and emitted a light groan. A sip of brandy followed.

"We owe you, Case. Your past service with Special Forces. And your more recent endeavors with the Company, although I'm not privy to those activities. Whatever they were, activities and actions of a sufficient nature to prompt this gathering."

Translation—word had filtered to Marilyn Townsend. Case Lee is mucking about in Brazil, chasing the Swiss rumor. As is MOIS and Mossad. Orders issued. Go talk with him.

Time for my own quick lane change. "Should I call Mossad? Maybe they could fill me in."

A bluff. Tactical details aside, my statement threatened loss of Company control. Control of me. Wouldn't look good on Ski's ops report.

"We heard about the rumor in Basel." As expected, he ignored the Mossad reference. "As did every other Tom, Dick, and Harry. It piqued a mild interest. You know, borderline white noise."

"Okay."

"Now, I don't wish to be too obtuse, my friend. But there is something else. A dot or two, as you call them."

My friend. Another bosom buddy. I was collecting them like rare stamps. But the "something else" put me on high alert.

"As I'm sure you know," he continued, "she spent several weeks in Basel before her Brazil return. But she did make a little side trip while home."

He was as pleasant as the Uncle Phil you saw every Thanksgiving. The one from Des Moines. I waited for Ski's grand reveal.

"Amsler visited the Russian embassy in Bern, the Swiss capital. A quick sixty-mile trip from Basel."

It didn't come as a blinding light of clarity, no mountaintop epiphany with a crescendo soundtrack. More of a "sit back and consider the hazy picture presented." Spookville's own Ski flung paint across a canvas. Called it a picture. A Jackson Pollock delivery—interpretation dependent upon the viewer, the recipient.

If you bought into my jaundiced view of the world, the interpretation was evident. It was confirmation of my suspicion that Amsler used a back door. A conduit of information that triggered the frenetic Iranian actions. The Russian embassy in Bern greeted Amsler as it would any other wingnut. Polite nods as she explained her discovery's vast potential. Loony sprinkles on top as she no doubt detailed the vast US conspiracy. She perceived Russia as the offset to the evil US plans. A counterweight.

The Russians, having heard her tale, fired up the street organ. Handed the speculative information off to their proxy and quasi-ally, Iran. And inferred, "Chase it, monkey." The Iranians, with visions of a grand terrorist tool in-hand, headed toward Brazil.

While the Russians smiled. A solid move and a safe bet on their part. They'd dangle assistance with the synthesis of Amsler's find if it proved valuable. The Iranians might not have the capability. The Russians would track, at a distance, MOIS. Let the Iranians get their hands dirty, expend the requisite effort. And watch, wait. I wondered if they were watching now.

"The Russians triggered MOIS," I said.

Ski shrugged. As close to an affirmation as I'd get.

"Mossad followed," I continued. "And now, the Company. Any other players I should know about?"

"An organic toxin—as yet undefined—isn't enough stink to draw many flies," Ski said. "But I will tell you we're not burning a great deal of calories on it. But then again, that's *your* job."

He chuckled, sipped brandy. Funny guy. With a point. It *was* my job, and the Company knew it.

"She blew in here a couple of days ago. Did she visit the Russian consulate?"

"I have no idea. It's not much of a consulate. The Russians opened it for the 2016 Olympic Games and have kept it open since."

He had no idea. I believed him.

"Do the Russians know I'm here?"

Important question—the Russian version of the CIA, the FSB, would kill me on sight. Or try to. The last time they attempted such an action in New Guinea, they came out on the short end of the stick. Big time. It was a long shot that the Russians would unleash assets to Manaus or Coari or the jungle merely to settle a score. But hanging out where they had a consulate, a presence, was another dance floor. And if given the chance they'd dance with me in Rio.

"Again, I have no idea. My apologies, Case."

I halfway bought it. He might not know. It was possible this whole sit-down with Ski constituted a Company finger-snap in the air accompanied with "Go fetch" directed my way. Do their bidding, find Amsler, and keep them informed. Man, I hated dealing with spookville.

My next steps were clear. My lone viable escape from shadowland would be to focus on the mission. Track Amsler. Don't sweat the smoke and mirrors. Start with the Russian consulate. Work the exterior players. Street vendors, taxis, nearby shops. The few Amsler photos in her dossier revealed a storklike appearance. Tall, thin, angular, blond. The still photos of her in motion lacked grace. Symmetry. All elbows and knees and hunched-over focus. A street vendor or shopkeeper in Rio would recall her.

"So what are your next steps?" Ski asked. He again flexed his leg, rubbed the knee.

"Find Amsler."

"Good, good." His smile increased. "Please call me if I can help. I mean it."

BS. Please call him if I found her or discovered any salient info he could feed the beast. He signaled for the check.

"Let me give you a ride into town."

"No, thanks. Appreciate the offer."

We shook hands and he departed. Back to the hunt, the chase. A city of six million. One crazy scientist. Yeah, you've been good at running, Amsler. But the running is over. And you can't hide. Because there's one fed up former Delta operator on your butt.

Chapter 24

As Ski drove away I considered immediate plans. A room in Leblon waited. A hot shower, shave, and clean clothes the first order of business. The Company confab could have gone worse. I'd learned a truth nugget or two, gotten a feel for the playing field. Not bad. The Russian reveal had promise. While the Iranians and Israelis owned the immediate sharp elbows, they were now a borderline sideshow. Ski's information constituted a search anchor, a starting point. This was down to me and Amsler. Yeah, I'd watch my back. But the intrigue and shadow dance remained outside the job. The mission.

I caught a cab and headed for the hotel. Three prime beach/promenade areas define Rio. Copacabana stretches south for two miles until a rocky point of land. Around this point and running east to west lies the mile-long Ipanema beach followed by the smaller Leblon beach area, a quieter section of Rio with tree-lined streets and distanced from Copacabana's hustle and bustle.

Deadbolt thrown, chair under the door handle, Glock placed near the sink. Hot water pounded, cascaded. I kept the shower curtain half-open. An old and solid habit. The Russian consulate was priority one. Amsler may or may not have been given a contact number when she visited the Russian embassy in Bern. A Russian contact in Brazil or a MOIS contact. I doubted either one occurred—it would have dirtied Russian hands. The Russians would have given MOIS her contact information, but the virulent reaction from MOIS the last several days indicated no contact between the Iranians and Amsler. No peace and love fostered.

Amsler was clever enough to have kept her phone off the last week. She'd focus on face-to-face, with another Russian visit the likely port in the storm. Her perceived ally for combating the US-led global conspiracy to, well, control the world or foster hemorrhoids or promote tooth decay. Who knew? One item stood clear—she had crossed the Rubicon. Carried ill and evil intent. She wouldn't see it that way, but crazies never do.

A chorus of disconcerting thoughts accompanied my shower. If the Russian consulate proved a dead-end—and it well might—then the next steps were long shots. I could walk the wide sidewalks of Copacabana, Ipanema, and Leblon beaches. Those sidewalks had miles of outdoor tables and chairs, grouped to associate with their respective hotel or bar or restaurant. Amsler might hang among the crowds. A daunting search, and likely fruitless. I could check hotel registries, but with her paying cash a false registration name bordered on the guaranteed. Check university libraries in Rio, places she'd utilize to access the internet if uncomfortable using her laptop. Places where she'd dive the dark web and communicate with others of her ilk. I knew the dark web well enough—used it myself for communiqués with the Clubhouse and my client, Global Resolutions. A deep and murky place where electronic sniffers from clandestine agencies were thwarted and frustrated due to false IP addresses and packet encryptions. A place where arms deals, drug deals, sex traffickers, and scum from every corner of the earth dwelled. Including terrorists and flavor-of-the-month revolutionary groups. The fact I also hung there wasn't lost on me.

Chasing Amsler would head downhill quickly if the consulate gambit failed. A stone-cold reality. I'd been hired to find Amsler among Amazonia environs. She'd left those. But Global Resolutions offered consistent contracts due to my track record. Case Lee went the extra mile. Stayed on point. Maintained dogged pursuit. I'd deliver the same here. At least for a couple of days.

The Amazon presented an operational arena where experience, learned and inherent skill sets, and wilderness environments held court. Accompanied by a bio-prospector who'd turned out a stellar teammate—solid, reliable. I missed her in more ways than one. And yeah, the kiss bordered on epic. Mercy.

Now into an urban area with a wisp of a trail. Iranians, Mossad, Russians, and the Company shifted at the periphery. Behind the yellow tape. I erected a mental barrier, all energies focused on Amsler. If I was able to capture her and the malignant container—and *capture* was the correct term at this point—I still leaned toward a Switzerland delivery of the toxic sample. Neutral turf. If I came up empty, I'd inform someone besides my client. I couldn't leave Amsler to roam without some form of pursuit. The trigger point for contacting US law enforcement also signaled a big fat undeniable fact—Case Lee had failed. Tracked Amsler to the dead zone, and Coari, and Rio. Big whoop. She escaped and I failed.

I could wallow among the *what-if*s and wishful thinking or get my butt in gear. Chose the latter. Jeans, running shoes, loose dark button-up shirt. I slid a Glock into the waistband and, hand on doorknob, returned to the weapons duffel and stuffed two additional loaded ammo magazines into a front pocket. Okay. Good to go.

As expected, a sprinkling of consulates populated Leblon's back streets. A quiet, upscale area with shaded streets and quiet neighborhoods. The Russian consulate nestled within one such neighborhood. Unlike embassies that teemed with the hustle and bustle of daily business, consulates tended to be the quiet and obscure cousins of the diplomatic family. Visits through scheduled appointment the norm.

I had little doubt that Amsler would have contacted them, to crow about her success and ask about her next steps. It may have taken a day or two for communications to line up, but they would have connected her with MOIS. Maybe arranged the meeting, given the fact that her phone remained off. But the consulate was a starting point, and it helped shove the whole grasping-at-straws element aside.

I cut away from the beach promenade and into sedate neighborhoods, aware of my back trail, aware that MOIS and perhaps the Russians occupied space within this section of Rio. I performed the usual trail-checking maneuvers, paused at upscale shop windows, checked reflections. Crossed quiet streets often. Reversed course twice. No alarm bells, no sign of a hunter.

The Russian consulate was tucked down a small side street, shaded and quiet and lined with stone-and-concrete walls. Insular living for the well-to-do. The Russian address was no exception. Well, a few exceptions and expected. Broken glass bottles cement-embedded along the wall's top as a don't-even-try barrier. Discreet brass plaques announced Russian diplomatic turf. The plaques were positioned on either side of a gray steel door that matched the wall's color. There was a small call box, the speaker set at shoulder level.

Amsler would have pressed the call button and stood, waiting. Stated her case. "I met with your people in Bern." Another and much longer wait. Then an electronic buzz, entry allowed. Dollars to doughnuts she carried the surprise package with her. If only those poor bastards inside knew. But the overriding point was she stood and waited, exposed. Seen by others. So I worked the small shops and bistros a half-block away. Endeavored to enlist my own agents of sorts. A short time frame, limited options, and a tinge of desperation drove this ad hoc recruitment. I relied upon an old standby, and subtlety be damned. I waved Benjamins.

A US hundred-dollar bill represented many things in countries with high, and sometimes runaway, inflation. A Benjamin was good as gold. Better than gold. Convertible in an instant, but often stashed as a solid savings investment, stuck under a mattress. A hedge against hard times and, more often than we'd like to think, a life raft.

Two high-end shopkeepers—owners of small couture establishments—took a gander at Amsler's photo with no sign of recognition. The proprietor of a tiny bar/coffee shop displayed interest and signs of acknowledgement. I handed over a Benjamin and my phone number and told him four more bills were his if he provided clarifying information. Such as when and how she'd arrived and left.

I approached a tiny corner kiosk selling smokes and newspapers. The man there gave a tight nod and a "Perhaps so" after a long stare at Amsler's photo. Another Benjamin dispensed. Several taxis were parked, waiting for a rider, wealthy families and consulate patrons their bread and butter. The first two displayed utter indifference when shown her photo. The third eyeballed Amsler's likeness, eyeballed me, and glommed onto opportunity. Fine by me.

"I cannot say I have seen this woman," he said and turned down the soccer game that aired over his vehicle's radio. "But I do know my fellow drivers who work this area. I could enquire, if you like. And if worth my time."

I unrolled another bill. "Does this make it worth your time?"

"It most certainly does." To his credit, he didn't attempt to snatch the bill, preferring to play the long game. "And if I could connect you with a driver who knows of this woman? What would that be worth?"

I produced four more bills and spread them as a poker hand. His response was also nonverbal. A frown of concentration, a single tight nod, and the gentle removal of the first bill from my other hand. I scribbled my phone number on a receipt book he carried.

"Day or night. Call me."

Done and done. He pulled a cell phone and began dialing for dollars. Three hasty recruits, my assets, now worked the immediate area. I considered going as far as ringing the Russian embassy's buzzer myself, but stopped short. They did want me dead, after all.

I strode back toward Leblon's promenade, intent on a long stroll while my newly acquired agents wracked memories and worked contacts. It was late afternoon, the atmosphere muted, at ease, before the evening parties cranked up.

I'd visited Rio de Janeiro at other times. Relaxing times. The setting, stunning. The people, even better. Cariocas. Rio residents. Cariocas were often an object of derision within Brazil. Driven in part, I suspected, by envy. Paulistanos—São Paulo locals—were hand-wave-dismissive of the Rio lifestyle. The hard-working commerce center two hundred fifty miles south of Rio—and the largest South American city—viewed Cariocas as frivolous, base. They had a point. The residents of this gorgeous city had a let-the-good-times-roll attitude with more than a dash or three of self-indulgence tossed in. The Cariocas lifestyle peaked each year at Carnival—a bacchanal with no-holds-barred hedonism.

The walk was a leg-stretch exercise as much as a search. The odds were poor that Amsler sat among the hundreds of outdoor bistros lining Leblon, Ipanema, and Copacabana. But you never knew. I checked often for tails. MOIS, Mossad, the Russians. Or the CIA. Nothing. Just ol' Case on a fast stroll along Leblon and Ipanema with irregular stops, checking my back trail. I was preparing for a cut-through toward Copacabana when the phone buzzed.

"This the Americano?" the voice asked. I recognized it as the taxi driver who'd called his friends, seeking information on Amsler.

"Yes."

"I believe my friend knows your lady."

"Where is your friend?"

"He will arrive in ten minutes."

"Me too."

I jogged, cutting through neighborhoods, bee-lining toward the Russian consulate area, and well aware I might be heading into a money-draining operation, a scam. Hell, it was a high probability. But it was something, a pinpoint of light, hope kept alive. Shadows lengthened; dusk approached. I arrived and found my taxi driver outside his vehicle, speaking with another driver, his taxi parked nearby. We shook hands.

"Can you tell me what she looked like?" I asked, keeping Amsler's photo pocketed.

"Blond. Thin. European. How much money does this involve?"

"Four more for him," I said and pointed toward my initial contact. "And five fresh ones for you. If you convince me."

"Let me see her photo."

"Not yet. What else can you tell me about her?"

"Her face was somewhat hidden. She wore a large, loose sun hat."

"Okay."

Silence. Was this guy playing me or wracking his brain to pull more detail?

"A woman quite thin. But tall."

"What bird did she remind you of?"

"Bird?"

"Yeah. Bird."

More brain-wracking as he squeezed his chin with thumb and forefinger. "Uma garça," he said toward the ground." Head lifted, we locked eyes. "Sim, uma garça." A heron.

My blood rushed, and my nostrils flared. A heron or stork or egret—the same descriptive I'd use. Bay at the moon, the trail was hot.

"Did you deliver her here or pick her up?"

"A pickup."

"When?"

"Two days ago."

"How do you know she was European?"

"Her Portuguese was quite good, although with a European accent. Unlike yours. You are clearly an American, although your Portuguese is quite good as well."

A bit of stroking on his part, but legit intel delivered.

"Give me more. What else do you remember?"

"She carried a large straw bag. Nothing unusual."

Other than it carried the potential to kill everyone in Rio.

"What else?"

He pressed his chin once again. Seconds ticked by.

"She smoked."

The trail's scent increased. I struggled to maintain a calm demeanor.

"What kind of cigarettes?"

He shrugged. Okay—a detail too far.

"Where did you take her?"

"A most peculiar destination. And one I would only perform during the day."

"Where?"

148

"A person with money. A wealthy person. A European. It was most unusual."

Chill, Case. A Brazilian, telling a tale. Let it stretch.

"Unusual?"

"Very unusual. She asked me to drop her off in Rocinha. I would not enter, of course, but did drop her off at its boundary."

Rocinha. Over a thousand favelas perched on the hillsides around Rio, their borders understood and defined and defended by the local residents. A million people strewn high above the city. Living with abject poverty, drugs, crime, and one of the highest murder rates in the world.

Rocinha was Rio's most infamous favela. A slum where the cops didn't dare enter. And it made sense. Well, it made sense if you waded the hellish waters I kept finding myself in. She'd contacted fellow revolutionaries on the dark web. Where global authorities couldn't snoop. Arranged a haven, a sanctuary where she was untouchable. She understood she'd be pursued. Pursued by someone like me.

I pulled her face shot photo and handed it, folded, to the taxi driver. Focused on his face. As he unfolded it, I saw clear indications: raised eyebrows, a tight smile. His passenger.

"Yes, this is her." We locked eyes again. "I have no doubt."

"Take me. Take me where you dropped her off."

"Perhaps tomorrow. In the morning." He lifted a hand and eyes toward the approaching night skies.

I unfurled five Benjamins and placed them inside my shirt pocket.

"Now. Payment upon delivery."

He shared a shrug with his fellow taxi driver. "Why is my life filled with crazy people?" he asked his friend, who responded with a few sympathetic clucks. "Fine. Get in. But I will not stop. Only a pause. A pause long enough for you to pay me and get out."

The hunt—full force on a hot trail. The quarry—treed. Up one helluva tree, no doubt. But I was on her. No hiding, Amsler. Not from Case Lee.

Chapter 25

A gunshot echoed a half-mile away, followed by a second one closer and farther uphill. The evening festivities within Rio's favelas had kicked off. The taxi drop-off point was at the foot of a narrow hemmed-in passageway, headed upward. The driver scooted away, downhill, toward civilization and safety. No point standing around. The end game waited. I entered a different and deadlier jungle.

A sight to see during daylight. Housing stacked on the hillsides, one or two or three stories. Each appeared on top of the other, Lego pieces supporting one another. Brick, stone, tin, wood—a wash of colors ascended. Few roads traversed the favelas. The few that did were layered with local-built concrete speed bumps. Not for safety. An impediment for the rare cop car. A forced slow-down, which allowed locals a view, an assessment, and an easier shot if needed. The lion's share of access within the favelas was provided through narrow passages and sidewalks and alleys—veins and capillaries spread among the neighborhoods acting as turf demarcations. Gang boundaries.

At night, tens of thousands of lights shone through open windows and doorways. Music blared, faded, blared again as I climbed. Kids dashed past, and women gathered in doorways, their chats stopped long enough to eyeball the intruder. Babies cried, and young men yelled. Old men, survivors, sat grouped on recycled chairs. Collected around tiny corner bodegas, a beer or glass of cachaça in hand. They acknowledged my passage with a chin lift, a one-sided smile. Impossible to interpret—good luck or you're an idiot or welcome to a nightmare.

My concerns were with the young men, teenagers included. Concern coupled with the acknowledgement that they were my conduit, my sole informational source regarding Amsler. The women and old men, if approached, would become mute on the subject. But I had a plan. Loose, fluid, immediate adaptations expected. But a plan. It first required a statement. A message.

Overhead, electrical wiring collected as rats' nests, running throughout the neighborhood. The locals tapped into free electricity with wires strung across alleyways and rooftops. Satellite dishes were scattered here and there, unseen voices chatted, meager suppers were prepared. The place smelled of sewage and sweat and despair.

"Hey. Americano. How much money you got?"

A young man's voice emanated from the shadows. I'd cut across another passageway, a side-hill direction, the footing dirt instead of stone or concrete. I'd meandered with anticipation of a particular moment, a specific vignette. It had arrived.

"Enough for your hospital bills when I'm finished."

High odds this notorious favela was controlled through several drug gangs. Affiliated gangs, perhaps. Or not. Dog-eat-dog within these near-vertical slums, and a head dog housed Amsler. But dogs barked, communicated. And the first communiqué stood on the cusp of delivery. Another gunshot popped—low caliber, a pistol, from far up the hillside.

The voice emerged from the deep shadows. Shirtless and fit, he smiled and worked a stiletto knife like a baton twirler. His fingers danced, and the blade flashed under light from an open window overhead. His two companions emerged as well. They lined my left side along the narrow passageway, the drum major closest. The Glock nested in my right pocket and remained hidden.

"This one must be dangerous," knife-boy said with sarcastic humor. "Are you dangerous, gringo?"

The chubby young man alongside him crossed his arms above his gut, an old revolver in his right hand pointed skyward. I glimpsed electrical tape along the pistol's grip and a wire wrapping near the cylinder. The kid appeared as a Pancho Villa poster imitation, albeit one with less reliable weaponry. All he lacked was a bandolier across his chest. The third kid—the youngest of the lot—displayed no weapons.

"Only dangerous to little cockroaches." A baby cried through a nearby open window. Someone cranked up the stereo thirty yards down the passageway. Music poured from the hovel's front door. "I'm looking for my friend. A tall, thin European woman. Blond. Have you little cockroaches seen her?"

Pancho took umbrage at the remark, stepped forward, and swung his gun in my direction. I performed a lightning slide toward him before he could complete the gun hand arc. Gripped his wrist, twisted, and continued positioning behind his back. Took the now-empty gun hand with me. The pistol plopped in the alleyway's dirt and grime and filth. He yelped at the pain. A blistering kidney punch removed the little fight he had left.

I glanced at the youngest kid now behind me. He leapt forward, although the look in his eyes told a tale of action through compulsion rather than true intent. He received a backward thrust kick to the solar plexus. A harsh grunt and explosive exhale resulted. He tumbled down and away.

Drum major became desperate for engagement with the stiletto, but Pancho now acted as a blockade. The kid with the knife shot short violent thrusts around his companion's sides, ineffective and borderline comical.

I shoved Pancho forward, toward the drum major. Pulled the Glock. Checked my rear. The young kid I'd kicked pulled himself up, took a few ragged breaths, and viewed a modern semiautomatic pistol pointed toward his buddies. One or two more quick catch-up breaths and he turned, hauled ass. Excellent. The message was on its way.

"This would be a good time for you two to leave," I said and indicated with the pistol a direction down the alley. "If you stay, I'll get upset. You don't want that."

Perhaps life was so cheap it had drained his preservation instinct. Or he possessed outlandish, and stupid, courage. I'd never know. But Mr. Stiletto took a step *toward* me. I thought the crazy little bastard would make an attacking leap with his knife, so I added to the explosive nighttime gunshots symphony. Zipped a bullet alongside his head. May have nipped his ear. The bullet splatted against a cinder-block wall ten paces away.

He halted. With dignified machismo, he slowly folded the blade and spit toward my feet. Gripped his remaining companion's upper arm and led him away.

Alrighty, then. Welcome to the neighborhood, Case. But the messenger had been dispatched, the message soon delivered. A crazy American sought the European woman. Claimed they were friends. He's armed. And dangerous.

I tucked in my shirttail so the Glock would remain exposed, protruding from the front pocket of my jeans. I took the first cut-through available, climbed several steps, and headed along another tight-packed concrete path. Favela life continued, unperturbed by the recent nearby gunshot. Glimpses of stars shimmered overhead, between the stacked apartments and past the electric line tangles. A man and woman yelled at each other within a passed abode, more music played, someone tossed a basin of dirty water and heaven-knows-what-else from an upper window onto the now stone-paved passageway.

A tiny shop—no more than five-by-three paces—where several warren paths intersected held a collection of older men, sharing drinks and smoking. They lounged on beer bottle crates, several rickety chairs, and a stone retaining wall three feet high with no purpose other than a place to sit. I joined them. Conversation stopped. I stuck my head into the shop and purchased bottled water, then leaned against the exterior wall and waited. They'd retrieve me at some point. Their identity was an unknown, but introductions weren't far distant. Another gunshot echoed across the hillsides as a million packed people settled in for another evening in Rio's favelas.

"Are you lost?" one of the men asked. All eyes focused my way.

"No. Waiting for a friend."

My wingnut scientist deserved credit. If you wanted to hide, this was the place. No conventional law, no prying ears or eyes from authorities. Whether she was housed within this section of the Rocinha favela or hid under another section boss's auspices would soon enough become clear. If another section, she'd been issued a Get Out of Jail Free card for safe passage. A deal struck between two bosses.

"Who is this friend? Perhaps we know this person."

"A European woman. Tall, thin, blond."

Knowing glances among the men. They'd spotted her.

"I believe I may have seen her," another man said. "Only yesterday."

Cymbals might as well have crashed. Oh, man. The trail hot, my quarry near. Confirmation, affirmation, and I could smell the finish line.

"Where did she stay? Nearby?"

"This will require discussion with Vampire."

Fine. My boiling anger remained tamped down, controlled. The Manaus opera house shoot-out. The dead zone discovery. A jungle attack with MOIS agents intent on killing. Bernie murdered. The Swiss scientists at the base camp tortured and slaughtered. And now some dude called Vampire stood in my way. Whoever he was, he held the sanctuary door key. I'd meet with him. And with Amsler, hidden somewhere inside this labyrinth. Then I'd take her at gunpoint back down the hill. End of story.

Vampire's posse arrived. Five young men, armed, emerged from a narrow walkway. They halted and eyeballed me. I returned the favor. Three with sidearms, semiautomatic pistols. Two with full automatic rifles—one Romanian, the other an AK-47 knockoff, of Chinese or Eastern European origin. The size of the posse and their collection of weaponry told me this wasn't Vampire's turf. They'd come to collect a gringo, deliver him for their boss. Safe passage assured through negotiation, buttressed with firepower. Fine. One of them head-signaled for me to join them.

I did. Kept five paces away. Pulled the Glock when two of them attempted to slide past me. A frozen and gnarly moment, but I wouldn't tolerate these thugs at my back. A nearby motor scooter maneuvered through the maze, children called, second- and third-story conversations held across narrow alleys. And a Mexican standoff smack dab in the middle of the entire mess.

I had zero tolerance for argument. Too much carnage, too many innocents killed to get me here. Willing to shoot first, I scanned eyes, weapons, trigger fingers. Interpreted intent within hostile stares. I could take all five if needed. I might catch a bullet in the process, but five dead bodies added to the night's favela count would be assured if it hit the fan. I was fine with that.

"It is protection, gringo. Men at your back," said the one who'd head-signaled me.

"Not going to happen."

He considered his options. His boss had sent him to fetch me, and a shootout was not an ordered outcome. He muttered under his breath and arranged his men in a phalanx with him in the lead. He glanced over his shoulder, snarled, and gave another head signal to follow. I did.

We climbed. Our own little mini-Roman legion, formation tight, winding through packed and stacked abodes along narrow walkways. Five minutes later we crossed an actual roadway—a lane-and-a-half wide. Entered Vampire's turf, evidenced though the newly relaxed postures of my escort troops. We continued climbing until a mini-square appeared. A five-alleyway intersection, houses crammed together, a street bar set outside a hole-in-the-wall beer and liquor dispensary. And a two-story reclaimed brick and concrete flat-roofed house, lower windows shuttered, door open. Our destination.

Several of Vampire's soldiers hung at makeshift tables, drinking. Others lingered along each intersecting path. All were armed. My escort led me toward the drug lord's home and place of business. Concrete stairs led upward. Three entered. The other two moved away, wandered over and chatted with fellow gang members. I waited outside the door, framed by the interior light. The three who'd entered blocked my view of the head honcho as they talked. But an assessment of the room's layout was available. A makeshift kitchen toward the back. Hand-plastered walls, the red brick exposed in large patches.

The wall decor consisted of revolutionary depictions—posters taped or representations hand-painted. Old Soviet iconography, fists thrust upward, red flags fluttering, the hammer and sickle as savior. Two circle-A anarchist symbols—one in blood red, the other black. Plus the ubiquitous Che Guevara poster. I'd come to the right place.

I assessed the outside situation. Fifteen, maybe twenty, armed minions. Women stood and chatted in lit doorways, watching. A few kids scampered past. Somewhere nearby, meat grilled. One of the men at a table tossed his beer bottle into a beat-up steel drum. The bottle broke, joining dozens of others. Welcome to Vampire's drugs, death, and revolution World Headquarters.

While scoping the area, I sighted a small cigarette butt pile alongside the two concrete steps outside Vampire's castle. Bright white butts. Closer inspection revealed each had been puffed on two or three times, then ground out. I retrieved one. Davidoff. A Swiss cigarette.

Chapter 26

His men made way, and Vampire approached the open door. Shaved head, sharp triangle tattoos both above and below his lips. A coiled snake centered across his forehead. Weird random images on each cheek—a set of lips, knives, lightning bolts, circular patterns. Each tat done with indigo blue against mocha skin. The look wouldn't age well, but I doubted Vampire planned a long life. A Brazilian semiauto pistol protruded from his waistband. Hands gripped the doorframe above me, a hooded stare, and an open shirt exposing more tats.

"How do you know your friend?"

"Fellow scientists, mutual friends. We're worried about her. She disappeared."

It wouldn't jibe with me holding a gun to her head while headed downhill, but start with a semblance of the truth and build from there. It kept things simpler.

"She did not disappear."

He leaned through the doorway, arms supporting his position. Performed mini-pushups against the doorframe and scanned his troops. High as a kite—rapid involuntary eye movement, faltering balance. A consideration for subsequent actions.

"Okay. Maybe she didn't disappear. Maybe she's lost. But I have to talk with her. We're worried."

One of the men at his back clanged pots in the kitchen area. My conversation with Vampire—at this point, benign—lowered the crowd's on-edge vibe. A vibe prone to a rapid one-eighty change if this drug-addled clown decided to prevent me from seeing Amsler.

"You are worried. Yes. You should be worried."

His body wavered as he spoke. One of the inside men strolled forward and patted his boss on the ribs. Please move aside. Vampire removed an arm from the doorjamb. The guy edged past, descended the two steps, and delivered me a hard shoulder bump before calling to his friends at the outdoor tables. My had-enough-of-this-shit meter redlined. Amsler occupied the upper floor. I wasn't leaving this favela without her. So here's the deal, Vampire, old buddy. Buckle up. It's a guaranteed ugly ride.

I gave a quick thought to actions once I had Amsler. It required a plan, however fragile. I came up empty, but within a very short time things would become a frenzy of wild activity. Opportunity would arrive amid the mayhem and chaos. Always did.

"You do not look like a member of our cause. Our efforts," Vampire continued. He called toward his troops spread across the small square. "Does he look like one of us, meus soldados?"

His men returned insulting remarks, laughed. One made squealing pig noises. Vampire's chin flopped onto his chest, wild eyes focused my way.

"No. I do not think you are one of us. And I do not think you are her friend."

He'd try and kill me soon. A dozen armed men scattered among the outdoor bar tables. More leaned against the walls within the five dark warren-ways culminating at this semi-open patch of space. Back exposed, a sky-high drug lord at my front revved up about my uninvited appearance. Not the best situation. The weird part—I didn't give a damn. I'd come too far, been through too much. I'd play the cards as they were dealt, and I held a .40 caliber joker or two of my own.

Vampire angled far forward, arms straining, balance handicapped. "I believe you work for someone else. Someone who declares war against our efforts."

"Who would that be, Vampire?"

"You are an Americano. The CIA. You are CIA."

Sure, why not? As good a trigger point as any, and enough of this crap and let's get the party started.

"Yeah. That's me. CIA."

The confession froze him, facial expression washed with rage. He clutched his pistol grip—a clear signal for his men as well. It also signaled his last act on this earth. My Glock spoke first and sent a bullet through Vampire's forehead snake. I followed it. Leapt upward through the door, attacked. Rapid concussive booms as I double tapped the nearest inside thug. Two chest shots in quick succession. I slid right, back against the brick wall. Plaster and brick dust exploded near my head as the final inside guy managed a halfway decent shot. I returned the favor. Another double tap, indoor enemies eliminated. Game on.

Gunfire from the crowd outside popped against brick and through the open door—impotent, wasted shots. I sprinted up the stairs, pistol at the ready. Aware that Amsler's revolutionary fervor, her gun blazing, might greet me. I entered an empty room.

Two wooden desks, with desktop computers. Wiring strewn along the walls, held with adhesive tape. A five-foot-high stack of duct-taped, bundled packages. Meth or coke or heroin. A lone mattress occupied the floor, sheets disheveled. Amsler had taken one for the team. The funk of unwashed bodies and chemical drugs and remnant tobacco smoke filled the space. I scoured the desks—nothing other than more cigarette butts collected in a tin can. Oh, man. Gone.

A plywood divider separated the crude bathroom. I cut across the stairway entrance, pistol aimed downstairs. No activity yet, although the calls and cries outside indicated a semi-coordinated attack was forming. The toilet lid seat up, a few blond hairs in the sink. Otherwise, nothing. Gone, gone.

I killed the room's light and collected myself for a moment, absorbing the fact she'd fled. I flashed to the old man in the adjacent favela who mentioned he'd seen her yesterday. It would have been damn nice if he'd mentioned that she'd been dragging a suitcase behind her. And a large straw tote bag over one shoulder.

Snap out of it, Lee. Gotta move. Gotta get the hell out of here. Downstairs—nothing but screwed, blued, and tattooed as the sound of scuffling feet and cries filled the lower room. I considered a bedroom window exit. A tactic eliminated when automatic gunfire exploded below and sent a bullet string through the window, driving holes in the ceiling plaster. Gone, gone, she's gone. All of it, the whole kit and caboodle, dead-ended here and now. Oh, man. Another pointless rip of gunfire across the ceiling from the alleyway below. It began sounding like Armageddon around the building. Alright, Lee. Snap out of it. Gotta move, gotta haul it.

The bathroom's small window presented the lone option. It faced, three feet away, another shack's corrugated tin wall. Below, a one-person passageway. A passageway soon stacked with wild-eyed thugs seeking revenge. Back—gotta watch my back. The room lights below funneled up the stairs, an illuminated rectangle on the wall opposite the stairway entrance. Framed shadows moved and shifted within the rectangle. Bogies climbed stairs, headed my way. Gotta move, gotta get the hell out of here. But I wasn't leaving armed killers at my back.

I plopped on the floor near the stairway entrance, back hunched, knees drawn. A forward thrust, floor level, and I exposed head and upper shoulders to the encroaching enemy. And also exposed a two-handed grip on the Glock. The lead bogie caught it first, the one pressed behind him next. The third, at the foot of the stairs, ripped shots my way, striking the cement stair entrance near my face. The contained thunderclaps echoed, rattled. A headshot ended it. A piercing sting high on my cheek, blood dripping. I scrambled up and darted into the bathroom. A quick glance below at the alley—still empty for the moment. And a moment was all I needed. I dropped a near-spent magazine on the floor, slammed a full-load one home. Shoved the Glock into my pocket. Felt my cheek and removed a concrete shard. Gotta move.

Hated this part. Momentary exposure, weapon unavailable. No option. I shinnied through the tight window, strained for a handhold, stood on the windowsill. Gripped the rooftop, pulled myself up and over. Objective achieved—get on the roof. And just in time. One of them cut down the alley below and viewed my final rooftop lurch. He screamed his discovery and fired several shots toward my half-second-ago position.

My near-term tactic was clear—remain rooftop bound. The direction set—downhill. A leap across an alleyway onto a neighboring roof. Then another. Some roofs were planked and tarpaper-covered, others tin. I aimed for discernible rafters under the tin, prayed they would hold my weight. But I couldn't disguise the clatter of each landing. Another leap, shots fired. They zipped past, too close for comfort. Another rooftop. Estimating my traverse, one of the enemy scaled a two-story shack and laid in wait on a rooftop. Hoped I'd land there. Missed me by one house. He cut loose as I hauled across tin-rattling rafters, striding toward me as he fired. These cats required immediate negative feedback. Feedback delivered when I paused, aimed, and took care of business. His body, in motion toward the roof's edge, tumbled down. More cries, shouts, gunshots. Deep shit city, Lee. Gotta move, gotta haul it.

Another fired his assault rifle from a second-floor window. His backlit position provided a perfect frame. Paused, aimed, toppled him. They tracked me, anticipated my direction, dashed ahead. A tactic confirmed at the next rooftop. As I landed and sprinted accompanied with tin clatters, shots exploded from the room below and punched through the metal roof. The holes, room light below shining through, followed my pounding steps. I didn't return blind fire—didn't know who else filled the space under my feet.

Five loud foot-pounds and airborne again. The next roof was wood and tarpaper. Thank God. It allowed for an altered direction, ninety degrees, with much less noise. Three more rooftops. An unseen clothesline caught me across the chest and caused me to stumble. Far below, the lights of Rio. Their reflection rippled across still ocean. I changed direction again. Head for the big city lights. Relative safety. Gotta move, gotta fly.

Four rooftops later, my luck ran out. I hit a rafter while landing, but it gave way. Sharp-edged tin raked my flesh as I tumbled into someone's second-floor home. I crash-landed with a hard thump and an even harder out-breath. The residents—a woman and a young child—screamed. Understandable. I scrambled up, tested my twisted ankle. A window stood open and I made a decision. Enough of this crap. Enough rooftops. Hit the ground, return fire, run like hell. Make constant cuts through warren-holes. A quick "Sorry" toward the mom and no hesitation—I leapt through the second-floor window.

Two of them, alerted by the screams, dashed around a nearby corner as I hit air. They slammed on the brakes, rifles raised. I sent a wall of lead in their direction, rapid fire. A desperate move, firing shots with no great accuracy, focused on delivering volume in their general direction. But hell's bells, I was airborne, descending fast. I hit the ground with an "oomph," rolled, remained flat. Bullets ricocheted off the stone wall above my head. Our collective fire boomed, echoed along the narrow alley, deafened and lifted and rolled across the hills.

I was more than a little tired of this crap. A half-second aim, two double taps delivered, two bodies crumpled. I hustled upright, ankle screaming, and ejected the magazine. Slammed the last load of ammo home. Hauled ass again, downhill bound.

I ignored the twisted ankle, the blood-wet shirt along my right side where the tin had slashed. I was only partly aware of the sticky rivulets running down my cheek. Gotta move, gotta fly. As I approached another alleyway intersection, buzzing whines from two bullets ripped past me. Cut right, no stopping, the gang boundary road somewhere close. Another quick cut left, and I'd made it. I flew across the road, entered new turf. Whether I'd be followed—a large unknown. Whether the rival gang would attempt to kill me a soon-to-find-out. I kept running, a slight slow-down to accommodate both my ankle and this new playground.

I followed a long warren-path as people leaned from windows, stood in doorways. Food cooked, music played, kids called. I kept going. Sharp left and then right, downhill again. Thirty yards later, I slammed the brakes. My passage opened onto another mini-square. Filled with armed gang members.

The boss yelled orders as his men scrambled, prepared. The incessant thunderous gunshots moving his way drove the gang's actions.

They were prepped for either an incursion from the uphill gang or a headhunt for me. I'd stopped inside the narrow alleyway and stood in shadow. One of the young men pointed my way and yelled toward the boss. Over a dozen men gathered, the number growing as seconds ticked. Rock. Hard place. I could make it through, fight toward safety—but I'd need a careful aim, the judicious use of my remaining ammo, and a large dash of luck. A helluva gauntlet to run with the finish line so close. Harsh breaths bellowed—mine. I kept the pistol pointed at the ground and exhibited no overt sign of hostility.

"What happened up there?" the boss demanded, our eyes locked. Young, shirtless, wearing a sheen of sweat. His pistol was holstered, and he held his Brazilian assault rifle in a neutral two-handed grip.

Sometimes you gotta roll the dice. I stepped forward, left deep shadow, and stood within the relative light of the open space.

"I killed Vampire." My voice croaked as my freight train breaths slowed. "And many of his men."

Bright white teeth flashed back, a wolf's grin. More orders were barked, a new goal created, an attack plan formulated. He'd lead his men uphill. A hole in the neighboring gang's leadership required immediate exploitation. Turf and market-share expansion. No honor among thieves, baby. Or drug-dealing killers.

I remained still. I hoped, prayed, that the "enemy of my enemy" adage was more than a simple platitude. The gang boss, his troops now assembled, initiated the uphill advance. Toward Vampire's turf. He delivered another barked order toward the men on his left.

"Let him through." A final glance my way. "Leave, gringo. It would be best if you did not return."

No worries, bud—you're not in my vacation plans. I nodded slowly, eased past his men, and jogged toward city lights.

Chapter 27

The first order of business: lick my wounds. I was a mess. I waved down several taxis. They slowed, took a gander at the potential passenger, and floored it. So I pulled the Glock when the next one slowed to a crawl, stepped in front of the vehicle, and ensured he was accepting rides.

"A good Copacabana pharmacy," I said, sliding in. "One that performs repairs." I pulled a Benjamin and passed it forward. "This is for forgetting you ever saw me."

He flicked on the interior light and inspected the bill. "I understand. And it is good you do not plan to shoot me. But do not bleed in my vehicle." He rummaged around the pile of stuff on the front passenger seat and tossed a roll of cheap paper towels my way. "Use these."

Rio pharmacies came in all shapes and sizes. Pretty much anything you could want over the counter—no prescription required. B12 shots offered every morning for the hangover crowd. Oxygen fed from a large tank also available, and for the same reason. And minor "repairs" performed at select establishments, cash on the barrelhead. Copacabana had the highest odds of a discreet proprietor. They'd seen it all.

The driver dropped me at a back-street establishment, a well-lit sign declaring fulfillment of all your needs. A handy one-stop shop. Two young people were behind the counter, which was otherwise empty. The man averted his eyes as I entered. The woman raised one eyebrow, disapproving.

"I require a cleanup and stitches."

"There is a hospital not far away."

A hospital meant paperwork. Not happening.

"Clean up. Stitches. Repair. And one of those shirts you're wearing. In my size."

She and her coworker were dressed in jeans and blue-green hospital scrub tops.

"Yes. I can help, but it is quite expensive."

Five hundred bucks sealed the deal. She led me into a back room and slid the curtain divider shut.

"Remove your shirt. You are American?"

"Yes." I wadded what was left of the shirt, tossed it in the garbage. I took a quick glance into a nearby mirror. My upper left cheek would require three or four stitches. My side a dozen or two, applied across multiple gashes. Ragged tin had performed a number along my right side, big time.

"So you decided to visit our city and fight." She began swabbing me with medical disinfectant. "I am certain you could find such activities in America. It would save you the flight down here."

Pretty, young, sure of herself, and—it turned out—quite adept at stitching. And adept at a running commentary on the foolishness of my proclivities. No argument from me. Shirtless, my past battle-scars were evident and an invitation for her to editorialize. I didn't mind. Her ongoing monologue offered me a chance to think, consider my next steps. I kept coming up dry—Amsler was gone. Unequivocally. And it's a big world, and the trail was now cold, lost. Oh, man.

Smart money said she'd bailed yesterday. She wouldn't have left the security of the favela without travel plans. Still in Brazil? I doubted it. I now understood Amsler possessed a feral consciousness. She'd sensed someone on her trail. Headed for parts unknown with her package of horror. Left me with nothing—no inkling, no direction, no immediate action plan.

The blues smacked me upside the head as Novocain and stitches and sterile bandages were applied. From certainty as I stood at her doorstep to gone, gone. I'd missed her by one day. One damn day. Whupped, empty, adrift. The entire freakin' mess now depressed me.

Plugged, patched, with new attire. Another taxi delivered me a block from the hotel. I played it by rote—if there's a threat of getting whacked, don't give them the opportunity while you climb, vulnerable, from a vehicle. Approach on foot and, if necessary, go down swinging. Although I didn't have a lot of swing left in me.

We spotted each other at the same time. He sat at a table outside my hotel, mouth full, and waved a Popeye forearm to join him. Uri Hirsch, Mossad. Which brought me to a standstill. I wasn't in the mood, my tolerance level rock-bottom. But he might have something—fresh intel or spook-tainted insights. He managed to swallow and spoke as I approached.

"My friend, my friend! Join me. Sit."

"Hi, Hirsch."

"Allow me to move and make room. We will both have our backs against the wall and enjoy a drink together. Look at your attire. Have you decided to enter the medical profession?"

A Grey Goose on the rocks was a helluva temptation. I sat. He raised a hand and caught a waiter's attention. Ordered for us both. He remembered my preference and asked for a chilled bottle of white wine for himself. And two orders of feijoada—black beans and pork bits slow-cooked in a clay pot.

"Although on closer inspection it appears the medical profession entered *you*." A robust chuckle, a quail egg popped home, a small bread slice slathered with butter and consumed. "You were not hard to find, of course. But let it be said I wondered if you planned on staying here this evening. Eat something. Have an egg. You look as if you need it."

I was plenty hungry but craved the drink more. I kept an eye on my surroundings. Hirsh appeared sanguine about our wider-world exposure. I wasn't.

"Why would I wonder such a thing?" he asked. "It is simple. Far up the hillside, several miles away, an outburst of gunfire well above the normal amount. And it continued for some time... Ah, the drinks."

He poured wine, slurped, continued. "I thought to myself, these are the sounds of my friend Case Lee. A great deal of gunfire. An operational signature of yours, one must assume. No explosions, however. Did you forget the grenades?" He followed up with several snorts of laughter.

"She's gone."

No reason to beat around the bush. I sucked down half the vodka and cast an eye toward the night sky. Gone. What a freakin' mess and loss of life, and so, so close.

"As always, straight to the point." He took a long draft of water, a slug of wine. He belched. "Let us begin at the beginning. Or begin where you and I left off. Did you validate her discovery?"

I had nothing to lose, so I laid my cards on the table. He'd lie and maneuver and manipulate, but offer—maybe—a nugget or two.

"Yeah. Bad stuff. As bad as it gets. Airborne and maybe waterborne as well."

"Can you quantify it more?"

"Airborne, it kills a man in seconds. Not a pretty death."

"Ah."

Hirsch mulled it over, took another sip of wine. He wouldn't bother asking me if I knew the dead zone's location. Wasted breath. But he jotted a mental note—Kim Rochat had traveled with me. She knew. Mossad would approach her in Switzerland. She could count on it. Nothing I could do about that.

"Amsler captured a sample. Carries it around with her."

The feijoada arrived. Fine and good and much needed. I ordered another Grey Goose and waited for Mossad reciprocity. I wasn't holding my breath, but miracles do happen. He placed two tree-limb forearms on the table and got serious.

"We, you and I, must cooperate, my friend. We have entered a new phase. A most dangerous phase."

"Not your friend."

"I understand your feelings on the matter. But feelings must be put aside. There were developments while you lagged behind the rest of us."

"You may note I don't have a sophisticated spy organization providing intel. It's just me. Case Lee Inc. And you may also want to note I'm the one who found her lair in Rio."

"Which was empty, I shall assume."

"She split yesterday."

"We do not know that."

"I do."

He dived back into the feijoada, consuming massive spoonfuls between shots of wine or water. Apparently he required sustenance prior to delivering a bombshell.

"I observed an interesting conversation yesterday." I enjoyed a moment of respite while he shoveled the stew in his face, dabbed at his mouth with a napkin, and cleared his throat. "Kirmani and his killers met with the good Dr. Amsler."

It was too far-fetched for a lie. Too bizarre for a false flag. He had my full attention.

"You'll have to detail that out for me, Hirsch."

"When I realized you failed to find Amsler in the jungle, I tracked MOIS here in Rio." He shoved another spoonful home. "I had a strong inclination to terminate them. You may be certain. Especially after they turned the Swiss base camp into an abattoir. You must have felt terrible about that."

Wound, meet salt. Thanks, asshole. But I hadn't revealed the Swiss base camp situation to Ski. Hirsch must have accessed other backdoors for intel—the Swiss a strong possibility. Not surprising.

"I followed them instead," he continued, sprinkling malagueta pepper hot sauce on his feijoada. "You might not think I would excel at such endeavors given my physical profile, but I am quite good at it."

"You want a trophy? Or are you going to tell me what the hell happened?"

A smile, a shrug, more wine poured into his glass.

"They met yesterday on Copacabana. It was clearly arranged. A sidewalk café, similar to this one. During daylight hours."

Arranged through the Russians. Then they'd wash their hands, claim no knowledge of subsequent events. A layer of separation. High odds they took the Company's viewpoint—how dangerous could an organic compound from the wilds be?

"And?"

"And it is good you revealed Dr. Amsler carries a sample of this poison with her. I am relieved to report she did not exchange any containers of any type."

"And?"

"She and Kirmani held intense talks. Then they hugged. Hardly typical for a Persian male with a European female he'd just met. A true spirit of geniality. I did not like this. But a decision was forced upon me: who to follow."

"You followed Amsler. And lost her."

"A sad and sorry state of affairs, I am afraid. Yes, she leapt into a taxi. By the time I was able to do the same, there was no sign of her."

"Sounds like a serious failure on your part."

"An operational challenge. It happens, my friend, even to the best of us. So I returned and continued pursuit of Kirmani. It is most unfortunate, but he and his minions fled to the airport. Of course, I pursued."

Bad news piled on bad news. The Amsler and MOIS meeting was a witches' brew of future plans. Plans involving mass death. Hirsch paused, consumed several more spoonfuls, smacked his lips, and added more hot sauce.

"They beat me to the airport. Now, Mossad has several effective strategies for termination."

"Do tell."

"I do tell. However most of them apply to individual encounters. There were four MOIS agents, standing in line at Rio's airport. Hardly a place for the application of either stealth or hot gunfire."

"Where'd they go?"

"Venezuela. The current president-for-life in that country is quite close with the Islamic Republic of Iran. Strange bedfellows, indeed."

"Yeah, indeed. They still there?"

"No. Alas, we lost them. Perhaps a private charter to parts unknown."

Another drink arrived. I pushed the near-empty feijoada bowl away, hunger satisfied. But everything still felt lost, swirling. Gone, gone. She'd hauled it out of Brazil with grand plans.

"Before we dig deeper into your and Mossad's failures," I said, "assure me again that Amsler didn't reach into a large straw bag and hand a container to Kirmani before she fled the country."

He pushed back, refilled the wineglass, frowned. "Dr. Amsler remains in Brazil."

"No, she doesn't. Straw bag. Container."

We locked eyes. He attempted to wait me out. Get me to speak again. It wasn't happening. He broke eye contact, swirled the wine.

"No such exchange occurred between them. And no commercial or charter flights originated in Rio with her on board."

Ski would have assigned assets to cover Amsler's escape route. Fed Hirsch the information. But neither of them knew Amsler as I did. Clever, aware, cautious—a wily fox. She'd hire a car and driver, scoot via road to Belo Horizonte or another midsized Brazilian city. Charter a private flight from there. She'd know there weren't enough assets to cover all the options, the possibilities. Gone, gone.

"So Kirmani and his men flew out after a deal was made, actions assigned. Apocalyptic scenarios envisioned. A hug, great victories assured. And they aren't victories over Israel, Hirsch. Maybe later. But not now. It's my country she's after."

"We, together, can still stop her. Before she escapes again."

So you and Israel can nab the sample.

"Get this into your thick skull. She's gone. Count on it."

"We shall see."

"*You* shall see." I raised a hand, ordered another drink. "I'm outta here. It's over. Finito Benito. At least this part, this phase."

The drinks took the edge off the ache from the face and side wounds. But the big ache came from the sinking, the despair. So close. So, so close.

"I did not take you as a man who would throw up his hands and quit. No, I did not. But you do what you must do, my friend. I shall not quit. *We* do not quit."

"I'm not quitting. And I'm not your friend. I'll do a reset. Clarification on next steps."

"Ah. A rather unstable commitment. You do not have the assets, the organization to assist you. Which is why, more than ever, we must work together." He leaned forward and entered my personal space, face florid, eyes stone-hard. "This is serious business, Case Lee. Lives, many innocent lives, are at stake. Working together is our best chance."

I wasn't working with Mossad. And wasn't working with the Company unless I hit a stone-wall dead end. What I did have was a last-ditch ace in the hole. Jules of the Clubhouse.

Chapter 28

Booked an early a.m. stateside flight. End-point: Norfolk, Virginia. I wouldn't arrive until late, so I scheduled a morning Clubhouse visit. Sent Jules a message, dark web, the detailed content a first, and a breach of Clubhouse standards. Given her proclivities, operational details were handled face-to-face. Not this time. I kept the intel succinct but thorough. Background, events, contacts, and an informational dump on Amsler. The whole shebang. No choice. Jules represented my last shot, my last chance before handing what I knew over to law enforcement. A hand-off best avoided like the plague as such an act involved questions, with outside-the-law answers, delivered and logged and recorded. A last resort, but one I'd take if all else failed. This was too big, too dangerous: an embryonic terrorist attack with the potential for death on a scale beyond imaginable.

I sent my client, Global Resolutions, a mid-contract report. Another first. One which reeked of failure. I attached expenses to date and expected they'd pull the plug on the job. Surprised when they responded within an hour—continue my endeavors. Don't quit. Interim expenses paid. One possible translation—the Swiss pharma company working through Global Resolutions now had Kim Rochat's assessment. They understood the gravity and were freaked about corporate fingerprints on their wingnut's activities. Helluva jaundiced view, but welcome to the real world.

Nighttime found me plopped within an obscure bar alongside an obscure Chesapeake hotel, checking messages. Jules replied quickly, an affirmative toward the a.m. meeting. Then the vodka prompted musings on where I'd screwed up. I knew it would happen, fought it, failed. The blues washed over me with coulda-shouldas, and there wasn't a damn thing I could do about it. I could have hit Coari first, before initiating the search. Confirmed Amsler hadn't split the scene. Left a reward at the airport for intel. I could have been more emphatic with Bernie. Maybe saved his life. Could have asked Hirsch to look after him. I could have called for an evacuation of the Swiss base camp. Demanded they contact their Swiss company and announce a mandatory evac. All hands, get the hell out of there while Kim and I headed upriver. Could have hunted Kirmani in Manaus. Taken the SOB out after the opera house fandango. On and on and on.

A country singer on the jukebox wailed about being fooled again. Yeah, no kidding. The one avenue of solid relief—my friends. More than friends:

blood brothers. Brothers well situated and well experienced, delivering insights and advice and an exit strategy for the blues. The quiet corner booth provided privacy and a launchpad.

Bo first. Bo Dickerson, a man who dwelled among his own unique cosmic realities. And our former Delta team spearhead. The most fearless and strange warrior any of us had ever encountered. My best friend. He now lived on the island of St. Thomas, US Virgin Islands. He'd stayed behind after the chaos and horror of the Caribbean job. Drawn by his new love, JJ. Julie Johnson. An FBI agent stationed there. She represented the federal law I'd spill the beans to if necessary. JJ had more than an inkling about my background, and Bo's. If contacted, she'd focus on the issue at hand and leave the shovel behind. She and Bo had a tacit agreement—no grave digging.

"My Georgia peach! Wait one," he said, answering after two rings. A minute later he continued. "The sound and fury of surrounding tourists had an inhibiting vibe. I now stand before you, not quite naked but fully engaged. How be ye?"

"Holed up in anticipation of tomorrow's sit-down with your Clubhouse girlfriend."

Jules had met Bo prior to our Caribbean trip. A meeting for the ages.

"Provide her with my lasting admiration and affection. She occupies an enlightened place in the cosmos. Now tell me a tale. Where have your bedraggled buttocks ventured as of late?"

I gave him an overview, a few insights, and my current position as loser in the grand chase.

"It sounds like you punched the right cards, my brother," Bo said. "An admirable effort."

A high compliment considering the source; Bo was a tracker extraordinaire.

"Admirable doesn't always translate to success."

He gave a heavy sigh in response. "You lack perspective. An old story and one that wears on my tender soul. If I didn't love you, I'd get pissed at your usual lack of understanding. Think universal placement, goober."

"Yeah, well, right now the universe has placed my worn rear end in a corner booth. Near a neon beer sign whose first two letters pop and flicker at irregular intervals."

"Pay it no heed. A false metaphor. Your path will reveal itself. The mighty oracle awaits you in the morn. All is well."

"No. No it's not, Bo. This stuff is as bad as it gets. With ill intent stamped across the owner's actions. And I can't tote the burden much longer. So if I pull in the Feds, I'll start with JJ. At least I know her. And trust her."

"A valid consideration. But let's face it, kemosabe. That's a nuclear option."

I got it. Expired bad guys littered US turf. Bodies sprinkled across hell's half acre. Bodies me and Bo and Catch and Marcus had walked away from. Rooting around our home turf history wasn't a door any of us wished reopened.

"Yeah. I know. How's she doing?"

I held a warm spot in my heart for JJ. She'd joined me in battle on St. Thomas and more than held up her end. We shared a rock-solid bond.

"Fine as kind. Accepting. Loving. An old soul and one who, against all logic, finds herself attracted to me."

We chatted about life on St. Thomas. Bo worked as a snorkeling guide, quite popular by his accounts. I didn't doubt it. JJ was bored out of her mind. Not a lot of FBI activity within her Caribbean domain. We had a fine and pleasant chat, much needed and fulfilling. Bo signed off with words of germane wisdom based on his vast experience.

"Before you pull the Fed trigger, consider the hunting field."

"Okay."

"Your rabbit has gone to ground. This isn't unusual. But she'll stick her head up, my brother. Oh, yes, she will. So be still. Be patient. Hover high with the cosmic winds. Then strike with fury and finality."

Man, I missed hanging with him. Sort through the Bo universal perspective and discover hidden gems. He was right; she'd show. The nagging questions of when and where still weighed heavy on me. At some point, soon, I'd have no option but to contact federal authorities. Not the CIA and their mission-specific partner Mossad. For a variety of reasons, including agency turf wars, their feedback of findings to domestic US authorities wasn't guaranteed. So I'd pull the domestic Fed trigger at some point. Prudent, sure, but it reeked of handwashing.

Amsler would focus on the States. How MOIS played into it, unknown and disturbing. And here I sat in a hideaway drinking hole, having another. Bo's perspective, valid as ever, didn't alleviate the alone-on-an-ice-floe blues. Solo hunter, waiting. So I made another call.

Marcus Johnson represented a lot of things. Former team lead for our Delta unit. An excellent leader, one we all respected. A person who didn't mince words or actions or advice—a mild irritant at times, but one accepted as part of the blood brother package. He now lived as one of the few black ranchers amid the wilds of Montana, blanketed in isolation, nursing an attitude of leave-me-alone-and-I'll-return-the-favor.

"Impeccable timing as usual." He'd answered after three rings. "The hay is put away, the hard work accomplished. Your absence was noted."

I'd visited him a couple of months earlier. Left with the usual vague commitment of "See you soon."

"I know. And the guilt overflows. I left a man of your age stranded without the scooter I promised to get you between the house and the barn."

"Get your butt up here, and I'll show you stranded. I suppose you're calling to ask about the fishing and bird hunting. It's time. Although the hunts *do* require long walks. Are you still capable of those? Or should I plan on driving his highness across the prairie?"

We both laughed, tossed a few more jibes, and settled into the nature of the call. I filled him in with an overview, spared some details, outlined next steps.

"This proves, once again, you listen about as well as a rock," he said.

Marcus unloaded The Talk each Montana visit. Stop my current line of work, move to his neck of the woods, settle. Rinse, repeat. He'd delivered a bang-up rendition during my last visit.

"Could we not review my career choice deficiencies? And, I don't know, maybe focus on the issue at hand?"

"It sounds like you've already made your decision." His Zippo lighter flicked, a cigar lit. "You'll meet with the Chesapeake witch. And figure it out from there. Solid footing, son. Solid."

"Hold that thought while I get a mop and clean up the dripping sarcasm, Obi Wan."

Marcus held Jules in less than high regard. During our Delta days we'd worked with the CIA on a regular basis. Official spookdom wasn't his cup of tea either, but he internalized the need for clandestine efforts. Jules sat a far distance from official, and her loyalties, at least from Marcus's perch, were suspect at best.

"So give me more detail on this elixir." He avoided the use of "toxin" or "poison," knowing full well that even encrypted phones had potential, however minimal, for a security breach. "Are we talking be real careful or tighten your jockstrap?"

"Jockstrap."

"And this person is no fan of the homeland?"

"Card-carrying wingnut of the central committee."

"And she's got a few lights out on her string?"

"More than a few."

Silence while he mulled the situation. A slight groan—either brought on by my circumstances, or he'd stood up from a comfortable chair.

"When you fart around among those other places around the world, I get less than excited," he said. "But you're talking about home turf. Addressing threats here requires swift and sure action. I'm not hearing swift. You have no clue where she's gone. And guidance from the witch falls far short of sure."

"Bo says she's gone to ground but will stick her head up."

"You went and told the cosmic cowboy about this? What the hell is wrong with you?"

"Long list. But you and him have the same tactical solution. When it's time, hit hard."

"You are aware he sleeps with an FBI agent, right?"

"And she's the person I'll communicate with if the need arises."

A heavy sigh from Montana. Not evoked by the JJ option near as much as his head-wagging disgust over my participation in digging this current hole. The Zippo clacked again as he relit the cigar. I nodded affirmation toward the distant barkeep who'd shot me the universal raised eyebrows: "Want another?"

"What I'm saying next is not advice. It is reality," Marcus said. His voice adopted a lower timbre than usual. "The Feds contain legions of bureaucratic numbnuts. That's a fact. They won't move with speed. Or finality."

"Okay."

"Don't do that. I'm as serious as it gets."

Marcus couldn't stand my "Okay" rejoinders. For him, they meant I half-listened or half-accepted the information shared.

"I'm with you on the serious scale."

"So I understand you will want the law enforcement trigger pulled at some point. *When* is a personal decision. You have good instincts. You'll know."

"Not far from it now."

"Again, understood. But if you get wind of her, and she's heading this way or is already here, we will take care of business. And I do mean we. You and I."

My drink arrived. I took a sip while Marcus continued.

"If she pokes up her head, it becomes a matter of trust," he said.

"How so?"

"Do you trust any government with the elixir? Including our own?"

"No. No, I don't. Maybe the Swiss. Otherwise, this stuff requires a deep shoveling and a lifetime shut up."

"The Swiss have an issue."

"What's that?"

"They're human."

"Yeah." I rubbed my face, internalized his point. "Yeah. I get it."

"Right. So we're full circle. Back to you and me. Don't even think about flying solo on this one. The risk is too high, the stakes too high, and you'll require someone to cover your back. That would be me."

There wasn't a finer man on this good earth to fulfill the role.

"No argument here, Marcus." Took another sip. "Moment's notice, right?"

"Hell, yes. Locked and loaded. Tell me when and where. We'll clean house, end it, bury it."

I halfway committed. A blood brother, former Delta, and rock-solid character might join me if Amsler was headed our way. Events now hinged on the Clubhouse. And if Jules set her mind to something, mountains moved.

Chapter 29

The sawed-off double-barrel shotgun rested on the desktop. Door locked, eyepatch once again jet black, the large Cirque du Soleil flyer replaced with the previous occupant—a *Casablanca* movie poster. She twirled the sealed tip of her cigar against the embedded Ka-Bar knife and eyeballed me.

"You've brought back Bogart and Bergman," I said and adjusted my seating position. The stitched side wounds stung.

"You've brought back more physical artifacts. I would venture they extend well beyond the one exhibited on your cheekbone."

"Not a big deal."

"Hmm."

She fished in a shirt pocket, produced a kitchen match, and fired it along the arm of her chair. I took her Case Lee perusal as an opportunity to slide my index card across the worn wooden surface. Three names and phone numbers—Kirmani, Hirsch, and Ski. A credit for my account, balanced against the information she'd supply. A sealed fingertip pulled the card closer.

"Iranian, Israeli, Company?"

I nodded back. She puffed, leaned forward, elbows tucked on armrests. A bony hand lifted a corner of the old wooden abacus and let it drop with a resounding clap.

"This shall not be a transactional visit. Larger considerations loom. I say this due to your lengthy missive. It was most prodigious, Shakespeare."

"Sorry. Protocol broken, I know." She was referencing yesterday's detailed report I'd sent her way via the dark web. "But I'm borderline desperate, Jules. I've got nothing. No trail, no hint."

"I shall forgive you. This time."

"Thanks. About those larger considerations?"

"In due course. Now if you would, dear, edify me. I require context, so leave no stone unturned."

I reviewed the entire mess. The Manaus riverside bar and the mistake of arming myself in plain sight. The chat with Kirmani. Hirsch's introduction, the opera house shoot-out. The exploration with Kim, the dead zone and its effects on the two MOIS agents. Bernie's murder, slaughter at the Swiss base camp, events at Coari. Ski in Rio, the favela shoot-out, and Hirsch's reappearance. The Amsler and MOIS meeting. Everything.

Cigar puffed, eye squinted, several more *hmm*s delivered. As I wrapped up, she leaned back, the chair squeaking, and stared upward. Smoke collected across the ceiling.

"So that's where I sit," I said, wrapping up.

A single raised eyebrow as her head lowered, the bird-of-prey stare locked and loaded.

"I shall posit questions, as is my wont. Do *not* raise the usual hackles. We engage with serious business, Mr. Lee. Most serious business."

"Yeah. It is."

"Three people know the toxin's source. Do you trust Dr. Rochat?"

"Yeah. I have to."

"You most certainly do not."

"She understands the potential. Her knowledge will fade into obscurity."

"Hackles raised."

"Disagree. She's trustworthy. A simple reality."

A Case and Jules stare down ensued. Neither unusual nor prolonged. It usually happened when she presented a conversational path best avoided. I felt no desire to plumb her concerns over Kim Rochat's trustworthiness. In Jules's world, actions toward Kim could be intimated if not initiated. Then her face softened as she slumped and cocked her head.

"Your attempt at casting a protective cloak around Dr. Rochat is admirable. Let us move on. A brief detour, and one we have discussed several times before. I shall repeat it." She tapped two fingers against the desktop for emphasis. "I fear one of those bullets you dodge during your gymnastic field endeavors will find a terminal home. You are no longer a young man. And I would miss you, Case Lee."

That came from out of the blue. Jules—such a strange bird. The weird affectations, deep shadow life, inviolate Clubhouse rules. But she had a soft spot for me. And, truth be told, me for her.

"I'm not a knife-between-the-teeth-and-storm-the-barricades kind of guy anymore, Jules."

"Our perspectives on that would vary greatly."

"This started as a simple search-and-rescue gig. The escalation, bullets included, weren't part of the plan."

An empathetic nod and sigh, the cigar inspected.

"I have always admired your endeavors to straddle this muddy stream of mine. And you have made consistent and valiant efforts to avoid wetting your feet. But avoidance, dear boy, is seldom an option. Which brings us to those larger considerations."

"Okay."

"Do understand the grand finale of this current situation will involve shadow players."

"Not if I isolate her. Her and the toxin sample. MOIS might be involved. I can handle them."

A part of me wished they were involved—in particular Kirmani. Dead man walking.

"A possibility, yes. For she will make a mistake. I shall do what I can to capture the mistake. And back to the larger considerations."

"Okay."

"The major players. They are engaged now. Word has spread. I would suspect the Company leads the charge, although you shouldn't discount others."

"What I'm hearing is it's liable to get crowded."

"And be aware one of the crowd's predominant members may have altered course. Over the last twenty-four hours the tea leaves would indicate as much."

"Okay."

Drove me nuts. The Clubhouse, and spookville in general, dealt with the obtuse. Why? Because, as per the clandestine world, we lived and communicated within a spatial environment. Nonlinear, they would tell you. Just flat drove me nuts.

"I fear you shall greet the news with less than open acceptance."

"Jules, I'm begging. Just tell me."

"The Russians, dear."

I sighed. The Suriname and New Guinea jobs had placed me high on their shitlist. Avoidance was my prime tactic. Whatever altered course they'd taken, I had high hopes Case Lee wasn't perched on the road they now barreled down.

"Well, I have open acceptance they want me dead. So, yeah, there *is* that."

She tapped a bony fingertip against the desktop.

"Remove yourself from this. It is not about you."

"It's about stopping a world-class terror attack. I get it. Now what's up with the Russkies?"

aforementioned tea leaves suggest they have lost control. Their
) longer communicate."

ıne Iranians?"

"Yes." She scratched her head with the cigar hand. "In the past you have
often brought tasty offerings. Confections. Has this wretched creature
offended you somehow?"

Licorice. Jules had an extreme fondness for licorice, and I often
delivered her a small supply. I hadn't done so the last two visits. These
strange conversational detours she often employed had a more complex
purpose. At least for her. I didn't have a clue.

"Sorry. I've been remiss in the licorice department. So MOIS has gone
rogue?"

"So it would appear. If an attack on the US became a reality, Russian
fingerprints on the event would be evident. As a general rule, one would wish
to prevent a cool war from becoming hot."

"I didn't share the Russian connection with anyone."

"Again, it is not about you, dear. I would rather imagine our Israeli
friends have leveraged the Russian-Iranian relationship for their great
advantage. Upped the ante, as it were."

"Okay. Thanks and good to know. Lots of activity, the big boys
engaged. Got it. Except for the Russians. They'll back further away."

"Or not."

Yeah, or not. Russians tended toward full frontal—see a problem,
address it straight on.

"All of which raises the question," she continued. "How far are you
willing to go with this endeavor, Poirot?"

An item I'd given more than a passing thought to for the last twenty-
four hours. A mental line drawn in the sand, with a simple realization—small
Case Lee fish, big clandestine pond. I wouldn't chase her to London or Paris
or Singapore. A position hardened with Jules's revelation that the major
players had joined the hunt. But US turf was another story, and tied into
Marcus's admonition. When the time to strike fast and sure presented itself,
fast and sure actions were mandatory. Plus the major matter of the toxic
sample was a mental irritant. I didn't trust anyone with it. Period. Except,
perhaps, the Swiss. They'd bury it under a mountain. Maybe. Although since
this gig had morphed with dramatic fashion into a remove-the-problem

operation, I doubted the Swiss would mind if I handled the matter, sample and all. Hard to say. Man, what a freakin' mess.

I expressed thoughts and concerns to Jules. She accepted them without judgment, and walked a conversational path under the premise of Amsler's domestic activities. And under the premise I, and the Clubhouse, would remain engaged. Fair enough, and better than dwelling on things well outside my control.

"How far am I willing to go? Pretty damn far. On US soil, to the hilt."

"Such ferocity is both laudable and, I'm afraid, required. Now tell me what you know of Dr. Amsler's red-white-and-blue ire," she said, scratching under her chin.

I did. Included Kim's input along with Vampire's words and poster collection.

"Would you assess her intentions as viable?" Jules asked. "Mass death, civil disruption?"

"Yes. She's clever and committed. With a feral component. She smelled me, Jules. Knew I was homing in on her."

"An attribute often found among her ilk. Those of ill intent. This would fall under the category of bad news."

"No kidding. She's capable of carrying out whatever plan she's cooked up with the Iranians. Yeah, she's serious as a heart attack."

Jules placed the cigar on the edge of the old desk and slid open a wooden drawer. Dropped my index card in and produced another. Slid it across the desktop, kept her bony fingers pressed against it while she talked.

"Global possibilities abound. Let us focus on but one possibility. One which coincides with a few points of connectivity."

She released the index card. It contained a San Diego address and a phone number. I memorized both and returned the card. Clients weren't allowed to leave the Clubhouse with hard copy.

"Okay. Got it. Who is this?"

"Your all-too-risky report mentioned Dr. Amsler's beau. A Dr. William Archer."

"You think she's headed in his direction?"

Jules snorted, shook her head, slumped back. She eyeballed me and delivered another headshake.

"I do not *think* any such thing. This shall devolve into the tedious if you continue your nasty habit of assumptive conditions."

"Yeah, well, it's what I do."

"And a cross I must bear. We have no idea where Dr. Amsler currently resides, nor her destination. None. Assumptions under these conditions have no footing."

"Okay."

"We are discussing an amalgam of intersecting, and interesting, facts. Points of connectivity."

"Okay."

Satisfied with her chastisement, she sat back up and continued. Life in the freakin' Clubhouse.

"He is a biochemist. Birds of a feather in more ways than one."

"How's that?"

"He has expressed anarchist tendencies within internet chat rooms. Nothing that would alert the authorities, mind you. Personal opinions cloaked with banality."

"So he's another wingnut."

A tight-lipped smile returned. "Oh to live with such a black-and-white worldview."

"I'm a simple man."

"You are a good and fine man. Simple in some regards, yes. However I am stout of back and able to bear several crosses."

I smiled back. "Good knowing."

"It is Dr. Archer's workaday world we must consider. His employer is a large manufacturer of agricultural chemicals. *Do* mull that over for a minute, dear."

I did. The connection was nebulous at first, followed by horrific awareness. Ag chemicals. Applied most often in one of two ways, the most prevalent method through large sprayers and irrigation equipment. The circular fields across the States, viewed from any airline window, used center-pivot irrigation systems. Massive aluminum arms performed a slow roll and dispersed irrigation water… as well as chemical herbicides, pesticides, and fertilizers. If a center-pivot wasn't utilized, agricultural chemicals were applied in the same manner through spray arms behind a tractor. Dispersed effective application, the hallmark of agricultural chemicals.

Another application technique: aerial. Crop-duster airplanes. Either way, it didn't take a great deal of imagination to visualize a dozen ways large population centers could be exposed to the toxin. Tap into the water supply.

Small street bombs with toxin rather than shrapnel the killing element. Or a crop-duster flyover. With enough toxin synthesized, one pass over New York or Los Angeles or any large city and millions would be killed. Oh, man.

I rehashed what I could and should have done differently, reflections on how the gig had evolved and the luck of the draw. Circling whirlpool thoughts. Shovel. Hole. Kept digging. I faded away for a few seconds. Jules struck another match and relit the cigar, snapping me out of it.

"Tiptoeing through the woe-is-me tulips, dear?"

"A little bit. This is nothing but bad wrong. About as bad as it gets. What a mess."

"What we must bear in mind is that several steps must occur for such an endeavor to reach fruition."

"Yeah. Synthesis on a decent-sized scale. But not a massive scale. Depending on potency, a couple gallons of this stuff would fit the bill. She'd also require help. Help beyond her wingnut lover."

"You have always had a talent for segue. Allow me to do so."

"This whole mess stacks up. Lover boy, ag company."

"There is more. Another fact that may come into play. A buttressing of the possibility we discussed."

I sighed, shook my head, and acknowledged my white-hot anger toward Amsler. Followed by an acknowledgement she hadn't done anything harmful. Yet.

"Don't know if I can take any more good news."

"Understand we discuss one of multiple possible scenarios. There are no guarantees we track the appropriate avenue."

"Understood. But still."

"But still, indeed. Southern California is well known as the home of the largest Persian concentration of espionage activity."

"Iranians?"

"If you so choose—they've been Persians for two thousand years. Since the early eighties, a great number of Persians fled their country. Regime change, the Ayatollah, et al. Many settled within Southern California and with great success integrated into society. Scientists, engineers, and academics. By and large, productive citizens. Tehran did not view this in a positive light."

"Lot of defense contractors within the area as well."

"The Clubhouse is rubbing off on you, dear. Well done. The point is, Tehran focused on the Golden State's southern section for espionage incursion. They attempted to apply leverage against the US Persian expatriates. Intimidation, threats—the usual. They are still there. In force."

Motivation—check. Amsler and Iran's government despised the US. The Great Satan.

Technical resources—check. This asshat William Archer would lend his expertise toward synthesizing the toxin.

Peripheral support—check. MOIS in SoCal.

"It all adds up. So what's the catch? This is too clean. The dots connect too easily."

"Truly my ministrations over the years have produced fruit. Why, you are positively *imbued* with skepticism!"

She leaned back, chuckled, puffed the cigar, and hummed an off-key show tune. "Cabaret", maybe. Hard to say.

"Glad you're happy. I'm not. You think I should head to San Diego and shadow Archer?"

She sat up, remnants of what may have passed for a smile displayed.

"No. A premature act. If our Dr. Amsler possesses a fine nose, as you've stated, she may pick up *your* scent and alter her plans. Wait for the trail to appear, Daniel Boone. I would suggest you wait and prepare."

Another pause. I sat with hands across belly, legs extended, and shifted in the hard chair for a comfortable position. She smoked and eyeballed me.

"Allow us to take succor and nourishment from the ongoing effort," Jules continued. "Larger players now have the good doctor on their radar. I shall do the same. She will make a mistake. A credit card used, a bank transaction, an errant phone call. A trail will appear. The Clubhouse shall hear of it. A bit late, perhaps, but I shall hear."

"Alright. I'll be on standby, twiddling my thumbs."

"Twiddle away. But a final thought if signs point toward Southern California. Are *you* committed?"

"When haven't I been?"

"If the possibility we discussed becomes reality, it will be on homeland soil. Where governmental department power plays and politics hold court. Are you committed to ensure it doesn't arrive at their operational doorstep?"

She and Marcus had the same mindset. Both intimated terminal conclusion for Amsler. And now Archer as well. Toss in a handful of MOIS agents and a decent-sized body count could mount. With Jules's cryptic worldview, a mere drop in the bucket. Marcus understood the reality of violent death all too well, but maintained his usual sanguine black-and-white, good-and-bad perspective. Not me. Not yet. A back-pocket option—the original terms of my contract—remained. Haul Amsler back to Switzerland. Handcuff her, hogtie her, whatever. The Swiss would have a transatlantic private jet at my disposal pronto. The toxic sample was another issue. But first, find her crazy butt.

"You, me, Kim Rochat. The only three people who know of the boyfriend connection. Unless Kim spilled the beans with Swiss authorities. So I'll have an open playing field. At least for a while."

"Within which you will stop them. On US soil. You may note I did not say catch or capture them."

"Understood."

"One of innumerable dark events lost forever in the fog of history, dear boy. With resolution swift, sure, and final."

I returned a hard stare, a sufficient answer for the moment. Jules, well aware of my violent background, construed the look as agreement. She returned a half-smile, closed her eye, and delivered a formal head-nod. A Clubhouse done deal.

THE AMAZON JOB

Chapter 30

The *Ace of Spades*, moored in New Bern, pulled hard. Family pulled harder. I booked a flight to Charleston, South Carolina. Home of my mom, Mary Lola Wilson, and my sister CC. Sanctuary and a respite while waiting to hear from the Clubhouse.

Mom took back her maiden name after cancer caused Dad's passing. Along with the move from Savannah to Charleston, it added a layer of protection for her and CC against people who sought leverage against me. Bounty hunters.

My younger sister CC. No one ever used her given name of Celice as she wouldn't respond to it. Born with an intellectual disability, she was capable of simple health and safety skills and participated in activities. Unknown to CC, she was my anchor. Where I lived far too often amid chaos and shadows and death, CC ensured grounding among those things most important. The small miracles, the surrounding marvels. My lifeline to the real. Soul-filling experiences of the wondrous kind. I loved her, and Mom, with core-driven passion.

Marcus Johnson called as I waited for my flight. Not unexpected as he considered himself now engaged. I had a different opinion. One based upon necessity. At this point, his help wasn't needed.

"What's the word?" he asked, skipping niceties.

"On standby."

"While the witch stirs her cauldron?"

"Yeah. And if you have a better idea, oracle on high, lay it on the table."

"Here's the best idea for the moment. I'm packed. Give the word, and I'll be there. So what's the latest intel? You *did* visit her."

I spilled the beans, explained possibilities, with a heavy focus on Amsler's boyfriend and his work experience. Marcus didn't require elaboration about the potential hellish scenarios. The encrypted phones we both used were sufficient protection for such a conversation. And if not, if the NSA could crack the algorithm, so be it. Come join the freakin' party, boys.

"So here's the operational reality," he said. "You will pull your usual go-it-alone BS until things get too hot. Too hot in this situation means too late. Are you listening to me?"

"Hard to avoid."

His declarative statements, a Marcus Johnson hallmark, brought a grin to my face. And the perversely pleasurable urge to wind him up. I loved the guy, would follow him into hell and back, but years had passed since Delta days. While the rest of us—me, Bo, Catch—had changed and perhaps mellowed, Marcus donned the team lead hat without hesitation. Which included operational declarative directives.

"What you might want to *avoid*," he said, "is swallowing dumbass pills by the handful. Engage me as soon as you hear something."

"Man, I miss your dulcet tones. You ever consider a career in advertising voice-overs?"

"You're an idiot. I'm part of this solution, so accept it."

"I'm thinking those Just For Men commercials."

The last couple of years showed graying hair peeking below his Stetson.

"I'm thinking I'd like to crawl through this phone."

"We're talking erectile dysfunction ads, arthritis meds, lounger ads—you, a crackling fire, dog at your feet."

"You through?"

"Almost. The deal is I *will* call you. And Lord knows, I appreciate the help. But there's little point unleashing the Montana Kid until actionable items appear."

"Listen to me. As hard as that simple act is for you. Listen. If you travel domestic regarding this threat, actionable items will already be present. Period. You require a partner."

Point taken. I told him so and signed off. I altered my potential plans with a stop in Billings, Montana, a decision made less with a sense of relief than one of surety. Surety toward any subsequent activities. Marcus was as solid as they came, and tough as they came, and possessed a decisiveness that I, on occasion, lacked. And something told me rapid and final decisions were part and parcel of whatever would come down. *If,* the big *if.* If she showed in the US. Better odds than fifty-fifty. But still.

When I informed Mom I was heading her way, she offered several declarative statements of her own.

"Wonderful! It is always a pleasure and joy to see the prodigal son. And you will be relieved to know that I've maintained my no-matchmaking status, even though it pains me to no end."

For some time, Mom would arrange dates for me with a Mary Lola Wilson-vetted candidate. Nice ladies, every single one, but nothing had ever clicked. To Mom's dismay and borderline disgust. So she'd finally abandoned her efforts.

"A wise decision, Mary Lola."

"It has nothing to do with wisdom, son of mine, and everything to do with exasperation. I have not ceased prayers in that regard, but personal efforts will remain on hold. When are you getting in?"

I told her, and explained I'd take a cab from the Charleston airport.

"You will do no such thing. Peter will pick you up. This is quite the treat, you arriving by means other than your rancid leaky boat."

"I'll ask the *Ace* to forgive you for the descriptive."

"Ask all you want, and tell your old tub it's time for the boat boneyard. We'll eat supper outside. It's cooled off. CC will be thrilled. We'll have fried chicken as way of celebration. And pecan pie with vanilla ice cream. You and Peter stop on the way home and pick up the ice cream."

Peter Brooks, Mom's beau, was retired from the insurance business and impressed me as a solid individual. A good man.

"Will do. So, how are you and Peter doing?"

"Fine, and we just ended that train of conversation. You, my loving son, are about the last person on earth to provide insight into relationships. Is chicken alright, or would you prefer something else?"

Mom's fare—the personal well-being penicillin for pretty much anyone and any ailment. I'd be the last person to argue against it.

"Chicken sounds great. How's CC?"

"Since the weather cooled off, she's taking Tinker on longer walks. I swear, she and that dog communicate. I don't know whether thanks or worry is called for. She'll be so happy to see you."

Tinker Juarez, a mutt of indeterminate lineage, was CC's constant companion.

"Same here. And same for you. Anything you want me to tell Peter? Some subject you're too shy to broach?"

"Hush. Hush and hurry up and get here."

We signed off. The best mom on the planet, bar none. The flight, uneventful. The reunion, joyous. CC slammed into me with a hug that wouldn't quit. I sucked it up and pretended the stitches along my side didn't holler. Mom applied a gentle hug and kissed me about seventeen times while a tear or three fell. Tinker leapt and barked. Makes a person feel more than welcome and fine.

"And why is there an oversized Band-Aid on your cheek?" Mom asked.

"Hit myself with a wrench. I was tugging at a rusty bolt on the *Ace*, and it snapped. Not to worry, I found a good horse doctor who applied a few stitches."

"Reason number seventy-seven to ditch your boat. Now stay out of my kitchen while Peter and I cook."

I did. CC insisted we lay in the backyard grass. I was more than fine with the suggestion and grabbed a cold beer. We stretched out on our backs, the grass cool. CC placed her head on my belly, perpendicular to me. Both of us stared at the predusk sky and giant oak limbs and hanging Spanish moss. Tinker plopped down with CC and nestled his head on her stomach. Puzzle pieces fitting with perfection, glued with love.

"I heard geese last night," CC said. She turned her head and ensured I understood the import. We cast loving eyes in both directions. "At night! How do they see?"

"Most animals can see pretty well at night. Like Tinker."

"Tinker Juarez."

"Like Tinker Juarez. Humans don't have the same night-vision ability."

She accepted the answer and moved on. Tinker raised his head at the mention of his name, ensured all was well and that no food was involved. Then he laid his head back down.

"This is the best," she said.

"Yes, it is, my love. Yes, it is."

She meant the moment, this exact snippet of time. Snippets most of us allow to slide past without acknowledgement or wonder. We chatted about her special school and the new friends she'd made and the new friends Tinker had made on their long walks around Charleston. Mom's call for supper drew us out of our reverie but didn't break the spell. We maintained it throughout the meal.

CC and I both relished fried chicken legs. And prior to either of us digging in, we'd wait for the other to lift their chicken leg. As two wineglasses clinked in a salute, we'd tap drumsticks and share a secret smile. Our private toast. My special CC.

An evening spent with loved ones on a screened-in Charleston back porch. Gentle conversations, the light clink of cutlery on plates, night sounds as insect choruses kicked off. Peter told a funny tale or two, his voice low and slow and loaded with gentle humor. Mom spoke of the small things that constituted life's binding agents—marriages, divorces, new babies brought into the world, who'd packed up and moved, who died. CC and I tapped drumsticks, she'd sneak Tinker bits of food, and the quiet conversational pauses were filled with contentment, connectivity, love. Sanctuary realized, soul replenished. Necessary, craved, and welcomed with open arms.

Ensconced in the spare bedroom late at night, I checked messages. Only one, but one with violent hooks pulling me back into another world. One with massive implications. From Jules.

Not fresh. Mexico City.

Amsler had poked her head above ground in Mexico. Jules implied it was a less than current data point. A couple of days old. It set off the head claxons, a call to action. The Clubhouse had heard it late, which meant the major players were all over Mexico City, hunting Amsler.

But the major players didn't know what Kim and Jules and I knew. The boyfriend. Dr. Archer. Amsler was headed north. Private charter flight to Tijuana. She'd cross a porous border into SoCal and hook up with her comrade-in-arms and fellow wingnut. Odds were high that the major players wouldn't have this bit of information. But I did. A trail, a scent. Swift and sure, Amsler. Swift and sure and somehow final.

THE AMAZON JOB

Chapter 31

Predawn and logistics loomed. Commercial flights were not an option. Charter jet services weren't open for business yet. My weapon selection remained on board the *Ace of Spades* in New Bern. It didn't matter. A trail sniffed and the hunt active. Coffee preparation stirred thoughts of Team Marcus. It was a solid move engaging him and one no longer edged with a desire to go it alone. Coffee prep stirred Mom as well.

"I take it you are leaving." She entered the kitchen and nudged me aside. Took full command and control of the coffee preparation.

"I'm sorry to scoot on such short notice, but it's something of an emergency."

Her sole response—a silent pad to the fridge and the retrieval of breakfast food.

"I'm not real hungry," I said and checked the hour for the umpteenth time. A charter jet was my first priority, and I'd already tried calling several outfits. None answered. "Last night's meal did me in."

"Sausage, eggs, biscuits, and gravy," she said, pulling mixing bowls and utensils out of cupboards. "You will not leave here without sustenance."

It was too early to call Marcus. He was two hours back in the Mountain Time Zone. I didn't sweat weaponry as he'd equip me. Marcus would foist an HK45 pistol on me in lieu of my preferred Glock but beggars, choosers. Mom rattled a few more pans, fired the stovetop and oven, then poured coffee for us both.

"These emergencies," she said, blowing across the top of her cup. "They show up more often than you might realize, son of mine."

"I know. Most fall under the category of nature-of-the-beast. Job related. This one belongs in a class by itself."

"You know I worry. I try and hide it, but the worry exists. Prayer helps. It helps me a lot. But I'm your mother. So I worry. Do you want your eggs over medium?"

"I know you do and I'm sorry and yes please."

More than sorry. Unfair and a strain and ever-present. The engagements, yeah, plus the bounty.

For the engagements, I hid their nature as best I could. The wounds and scars I incurred were treated with healing lag time prior to a Mom visit. And she understood the jobs often held a challenging element.

The bounty was another issue. I'd asked her twice to head for the hills when I suspected that danger approached her and CC. Bounty hunters. A special code was well established for emergency communications. You have to take a break, Mom. Today. Right now.

She'd pack up, grab CC and Tinker Juarez, and leave town for her still-spry mom's place nestled among Spartanburg County's rolling forested hills, three hours away. Temporary sanctuary with Grandma Wilson who kept a pack of loud, alert dogs nearby and knew her way around a firearm. Mom understood, accepted, and did nothing but warn me about taking care of myself. A world-class mom.

None of the tuck-Mom-and-CC-away exercise negated the requirement to end the bounty issue. A high dollar figure had been stamped on our heads—me, Marcus, Catch, Bo—during Delta days. A million bucks each. Offered by a Yemeni sheik, perhaps. Somalian warlord, Malaccan pirate, Taliban mullah—all possibilities. A burden we'd carried too damn long. We'd come close to discovering the source, the paymaster, during the New Guinea job. Until our informant got himself whacked, right freakin' in front of us.

Finding the source was a consistent priority one. Jules tried, to no avail. The Company—Marilyn Townsend in particular—knew about the bounty but claimed no knowledge of the paymaster. A possible lie, but there was damn little I could do to wrest the information from her. But bottom line— the bounty placed an added burden on my family. I held tight to one sliver of silver lining. Marcus, Bo, and Catch were each prepared for action at a moment's notice once the paymaster's identity became known. Movement and plans and activities directed with a single purpose—end it. Remove the source, eliminate the issue. None of which helped at the kitchen table as biscuits cooked and Mom prepared the gravy.

"It's not about apologizing. I know it bothers you when I worry." She stopped the stir-and-scrape gravy ministrations, turned, and addressed me. Slurped coffee and loaded a salvo. "Which leaves a simple solution on the table. A fix we've talked about until I'm blue in the face."

"I try, Mom. You'll remember the last job was a sedate investigation on Long Island."

Mom didn't know the sedate gig included whacking a guy in the Hamptons, a terrorist attack, and the bullet-flying pursuit of a turncoat spy.

"Yes. And I was thrilled to hear about it." She turned back toward the stovetop and waved a wooden spatula as she talked. "But once again you're carrying an injury on your face and Lord knows where else. What in Sam Hill happened to *sedate*?" She scraped cooked sausage bits from the iron skillet, then whipped around. "The way I see it, you didn't give sedate much of a stretch. Were you bored with normal?"

I couldn't help but smile. She was wound up, and only a fool would do anything but ride these moments out.

"I'm all about normal."

"Prove it, my son." She checked the oven and stirred the gravy again. "And another thing. You aren't a spring chicken any longer. Do you ever think about that?"

"Boy howdy. Which is why I took this current job. A simple search and rescue. Right up my alley."

"I take it things didn't pan out as you'd planned. Which is why we sit here before the rooster crows while you prepare to hightail it off somewhere."

"True enough. But this one is different. We're talking about preventing harm to lots of other folks. Innocent folks."

Satisfied with the gravy's progress, she turned off the stovetop and checked the oven again. Poured us both more coffee and sat across from me.

"Well, I know you'll do the right thing. You always have, and I *do* take comfort in that. Just be careful. I worry."

"I know, Mom. And I'm sorry as can be. And I'm trying for a career redirection. Honest."

I was. I continued to push for lower-key gigs with Global Resolutions. The Caribbean job had started sedate. And this job had had no indicators it would turn gnarly. It happens. But I'd continue the course change with solid and sincere intent. Although sedate and normal and low-key were out the window when me and my blood brothers discovered the bounty source. We'd land on that son of a bitch like a ton of bricks.

"You and I both know a good woman would help with the proper path. A steady, normal path." She slurped coffee. "But I know how it riles you when I talk about it, so I won't. Although it's several years since Rae passed, and you're not getting any younger, and I'd like some grandchildren before I've got one foot in the grave."

"Glad you won't talk about it," I said, a mile-wide smile plastered across my face.

"I can still reach across this table, young man. And don't you forget it."

She rose and started egg prep. Man, I loved her. Greatest mom in the world.

I found an amenable and available jet charter out of Raleigh-Durham. Two factors favored the charter flight: Global Resolutions would pay (they always did for any job-related expenses, no questions asked); and a private jet avoided the hassle of checking weaponry as luggage. Not an issue for most states, but California had the potential of unwanted state official eyeballs. I wasn't sure, and I wasn't risking it. The jet would land in Charleston midmorning, and we'd head for Billings, then San Diego. Long flights, arriving at our destination midafternoon with the time changes.

Teaming with Marcus had allowed me ample simmer time the last twenty-four hours, but the reality sunk in with the charter booked. I didn't mind one iota teaming with Marcus—hell, I looked forward to it—but the act contained a whiff of failure. My failure. Hard to shake the sensation, but there it was. I called Marcus with the jet's ETA for Billings.

"So the witch delivered a definitive operational area?"

"No. Not really."

"What does that mean?"

"Our wandering wingnut showed up in Mexico. A day or three ago. It's not fresh intel."

The Zippo lighter clacked open, his cigar fired.

"What's your gut say?" he asked, puffing.

"She's boyfriend-bound. Or already there."

The Zippo clicked shut.

"Of any of us, you've always had the best gut feel."

"You may have more confidence than me. But it's all I've got. And I can't afford not acting on it."

"Understood. Let's saddle up. Head toward SoCal."

"I'm a long way from the *Ace*. I'll arrive in Billings naked."

A complete reliance on Marcus for weaponry. I'd miss one or two personal favorites, but he owned a substantial mini-armory. As we all did. Habit, I suppose.

"I'll handle it. As long as you don't whine about selection."

"Speaking of which, we'll be operating within an urban environment. Remember those?"

"I have a vague recollection. You're telling me there's more people than cattle?"

"Exactamundo. So noise suppression would be appreciated."

"Yeah, got it."

"And a wide selection as well. We don't know how this will go down."

"Are you really telling me how to prep for an operation? What the hell is wrong with you?"

"How much time you got? And one last thing. I appreciate this, Marcus. It feels right and tight."

"You're not carrying any need-help-because-I-screwed-up BS, are you?"

The man could always read me—and the rest of the team—like a book, one of the aspects that singled him out as an excellent leader.

"A little."

"I expect any and all such attitude long gone when you get here. You copy?"

"Yeah. I copy."

"And one last thing before we get the ball rolling. If this situation is half as bad as you've let on, we end it. No moral musings on your part. Which you tend to do. Sabe?"

"Yeah. Yeah, I get it."

I did. Marcus referenced my tendency to struggle with violent terminations when other options—such as delivering Amsler to the Swiss client—existed.

"I'm serious as a heart attack, son. I'm not walking into this without confirmation your mindset is adjusted."

He was right, as usual. The potential for hundreds of thousands killed. Innocents wiped out. This toxin had the capability of widespread annihilation, and heaven knows how much of the stuff Amsler and Archer would synthesize and distill given the opportunity. Marcus, and Jules too, were right. End it. An event shoved into history's dark shadows. A place I was all too familiar with.

Chapter 32

No caped crusader ruminations, no avenging angel fantasies on my part. Instead, filled with tight-lipped intent, I began my mission. Small remnant doubts nagged me after takeoff, soon swept aside by the onset of an active hunt. I'd never seen or met Amsler, but I knew her, had learned her trails and traits and tendencies. She would meet up with Dr. William Archer. Cook and synthesize the toxin. Seek perverted revenge over perceived slights. Deal death without regard for the victims. I had no idea where the lab work would take place, but my gut said Archer's house made for a good start.

Charleston, South Carolina, to Billings, Montana. Eighteen hundred air miles. A thousand miles from Billings to San Diego. We lived in a big country. Marcus stood outside the glass door of the small private air terminal lounge. His attire consisted of a Stetson, western-cut jacket, jeans, and western boots. A rucksack lay near his feet along with two large aluminum-sided weapon cases. Marcus Johnson was good to go. While the jet refueled, we reviewed the operational plan.

"When we get airborne, I'll show you the layout," I said after handshakes and pats on shoulders and sides. My other blood brothers, Bo and Catch, tended toward bear hugs. Given Marcus's previous position as team lead, the three of us hadn't crossed the hug-Marcus line. And Marcus was more than okay with the arrangement.

"Give me an overview," he said and waved an airport employee away from our rucksacks and gun cases. We'd carry them onboard. He head-signaled toward a small grass plot outside the terminal area. A quieter place, where he fired a cigar.

"We arrive late afternoon, rent a car, drive to Archer's place. He lives alone. A house in the suburbs on a cul-de-sac. Nice neighborhood. Cedar fences hem the backyard. Single-level house. Looks like a three- or four-bedroom with attached two-car garage. This guy makes a better than good living with the agricultural chemical company."

"How much of this effort is attributable to him?" Marcus asked.

"Don't know. Although high odds he's a wingnut."

"Roger that. Weather?"

"Clear, mild. High sixties. Mild breeze north to south."

"Neighbors?"

"Unknown if they will be home."

199

"Alarm system?"

"Unknown."

"Pets?"

"Unknown. No indications from the aerial view. Single front door. Concrete deck at back door. Back door composition unknown, but street view indicates lots of ambient light inside, so I'd bet on a large sliding-glass door."

Which provided lots of visibility to the backyard for anyone inside. Not good.

"Garage entrance?"

"Aerial view shows concrete paving stones leading from the back of the garage. Indicates a small door."

"Good. Neighborhood kids will return from school within this window?"

"Borderline. The timing is close."

"A consideration. Go on." He puffed and waited.

"Roof is composition shingles. No chimney. Stucco construction. Small front yard tree, two larger ones in the back. The lot abuts one of those power line easements they've turned into a greenbelt. Walking and bike paths. That's our approach."

"Good. Bushes outside the fence for cover?"

"Yes. The fences along the greenbelt have hedges. Extra privacy."

"Do we anticipate him home? Or is he at work today?"

"Unknown. I've called his office number. Straight to voice mail. But I do expect she's at work today. His garage, maybe. Prepping their special presentation."

He shook his head, stared into the big lost and contemplated a laboratory effort with one of the world's deadliest toxins within a quiet US suburb. Jaw muscles working, he spit, then said, "I have a sense they wouldn't cook in the neighborhood. This Archer fellow may have rented a small warehouse. An isolated location."

"Agreed. But they'll sleep at Archer's place. We'll be there to meet them."

"Alright. Let's get this show on the road."

We did. I requested cabin privacy from the two pilots after takeoff. I unclasped the shipping cases and reviewed Marcus's weapons' cache. Two Colt 901 rifles, .308 caliber. Each with an Elcan Specter scope wired for night vision. Two HK45 pistols, semiautomatic. Suppressors for the pistols. When attached, the pistol/suppressor combination made for an awkward length. Marcus also brought two shoulder holsters to accommodate the added size.

"Do not even think about giving me grief about the HKs," Marcus said. He knew my preference for Glocks.

I didn't. Heckler & Koch manufactured a fine firearm. The pistols were chambered in .45 ACP, a no-nonsense round and more than satisfactory. Marcus also included two Remington Model 870 12 gauge pump shotguns. Just in case.

"You forgot the blowguns," I said, admiring the collection.

"Funny. We should handle most any situation with this assortment. Unless you plan on an underwater assault."

We both snoozed the flight's final hour. Wheels down woke us both. The Pacific glittered under the cloudless sky, the weather perfect. At the car rental counter I used a false driver's license and a legit credit card tied to a Cayman Island bank and found an obscure side street. Parked and kept the car idling. Pulled a GPS detector from my rucksack.

"What are you doing?" Marcus asked.

"Locating the GPS device."

"Why?"

"Hard lesson learned."

On a previous gig the Company had tracked me through a rental car's GPS. Wouldn't happen again. The detector signaled a location tucked behind the left front bumper. I stretched out on the asphalt and found a small card-deck-sized gray box. Removed the device's battery.

"I'd forgotten you lived such a spook-filled life," Marcus said, watching.

"When in Rome."

"Just to confirm. We anticipate the operational area's a spook-free zone, right?"

"I think we're ahead of the pack."

We headed for Archer's house. Traffic was bad, bumper-to-bumper in stretches. Marcus rolled down his window, produced a cigar, and clacked the Zippo open.

"You may note," I said. "This is a nonsmoking rental car."

"You may note the state of California wouldn't be happy about any of the hardware we carry." He paused and fired the smoke. "Why, between the cigar and exotic weaponry we're a regular Bonnie and Clyde."

It struck me that this was the first time Marcus had teamed for a domestic operation. We'd performed missions throughout the world together. Both rural and urban environments. Along with our Delta Force brothers. Post-Delta, the lone incident where he'd engaged happened on his ranch near Fishtail, Montana. Far from an urban setting. An ugly and intense and bloodletting event, but on such isolated geography as to make civilian involvement moot. This was a different ballgame. A mission more attuned to my recent endeavors, recent contracts. Marcus had no truck with such a world.

Offsetting that was the simple fact that there wasn't another person on this good earth I'd rather have with me, covering my back. A man who defined tactical and ensured the operational *t*'s were crossed and *i*'s dotted. Blunt, direct, perform the mission. A man who'd lay down his life for me. And I him. A stone-cold fact overriding any other factor.

Traffic cleared as we approached Archer's subdivision. A slow drive-by of the cul-de-sac's entrance revealed a sedan parked in Archer's driveway. Excellent. Someone was home. The Amsler radar tingled, the period at the end of this long and bloody series of events within reach. I expressed as much to Marcus. He, of course, focused on the immediate.

"Ingress and egress via the backyard," he said. "Take our time, pick the proper moment. We're two locals on the hike path. Nice day for a walk."

"Roger that. Tuck into the bushes along the fence, visually assess the backyard and house."

"Then over the top. Quick dash toward the garage back door. Assess, act, execute."

Execute was a performance indicator within our jargon, and a terminal implication as well. Ugly stuff, but I focused on Amsler, now at last within reach. A headshaking hard-to-believe. But she was here, or close by.

A small parking lot afforded a semblance of solitude alongside the power line greenbelt. Two other vehicles, empty. The owners jogged or walked or pedaled along the two paved paths. We both kept our light jackets on—cover for the shoulder holsters.

"Are you still contemplating the Swiss option?" he asked.

"Yeah."

"I'm not," he said and chambered a round.

We locked eyes.

"Give me a chance to talk with her. All I'm asking."

He shifted his gaze out the front windshield. A nostril sigh, a light headshake.

"You'd best hope she talks fast." He opened his car door.

"You losing the lid?" I asked. Marcus still wore his Stetson.

"Why?"

"It might be worth a mention the key for a civilian incursion is ensuring no witnesses can recall anything. Like a black guy in western wear and Stetson."

Without comment he removed the wide-brimmed hat and tossed it into the backseat. We left the vehicle and strolled the quarter-mile toward the back of Archer's house. I kept my hands in the front pockets of my jeans, a casual stroll.

"If she's here, what about the stuff she's been brewing?" he asked. He'd pulled a cigar, thought better of it, and returned the smoke to an inside jacket pocket.

"Play it by ear. See what's there. Containerize whatever we find. Head to the hills and bury it. Your point about the Swiss being human was well taken."

"Miracles never cease."

"But I'm still leaving the haul-*her*-back-to-Switzerland option open."

Marcus ignored my statement, but he clearly grasped the toxin's mysterious nature and didn't press for more detail. Uncharted turf—on both our parts. A fact, a gray area, not affecting the core mission, which was: stop this madness. End it.

"She's got a sixth sense," I said as we approached the tall cedar fence around the half-circle of Archer's cul-de-sac. "She'll run if there's a whiff of pursuit."

"All the more reason for rapid action."

We halted at the intersecting fence line of Archer and his neighbor. We stood back to back and scoped the area, the pathways, sought movement of any sort.

"Clear," I said.

"Clear," he repeated.

We ducked into the thick, shoulder-high bushes and peeked over the fence. A sliding-glass back door, sure enough. With the curtain drawn shut. All good. The garage back door where expected. No dog, at least not outside. And no noise. Dead still. I dug into a pocket and pulled out two sets of blue latex gloves. Handed Marcus a pair. His initial reaction was to stare at the offer as if it were some foreign object, unrelated to anything he might require. I got it. Fingerprints weren't an issue in Yemen or Afghanistan or Angola. But this was domestic turf, and there were fair odds we would leave bodies behind.

He internalized the need, delivered a brief and quiet snort of disgust. We stretched the tight latex and covered too-large hands. Then over the top, fast and silent. We pulled our weapons and dashed toward the back door of the garage. Halted, listened. Littering the ground at our feet were a half-dozen Davidoff cigarette butts. Each with but a few puffs taken. I indicated the butts for Marcus, gave a thumbs-up. We had her. Maybe. I should have felt a greater sense of exultation, or at least satisfaction. But the moment was tinged with something else. A sense of wrong trail, wrong place and time. A gut thing, but one persistent and polluting. I shook it off. Amsler could be positioned on the other side of the door, stirring her cauldron. No time for doubts.

Chapter 33

Silence. My ear near the back door, my expectations set for the clink of lab glassware, movement. Nothing. Two unseen joggers chatted as they loped past along the greenbelt path. A commercial jet far overhead exited San Diego airspace. Birds chirped on a gorgeous day. I heard a voice, too muted for recognition, too distant to have originated inside the garage. A male voice. Inside the house.

I hand-signaled Marcus, enquired if he heard anything. He returned a slight headshake. No. But it sounded somewhere inside, no doubt. The voice stopped. I placed a hand on the doorknob, the other with weapon ready. I glanced at Marcus. He nodded. I'd go first, low, and eliminate threats. Marcus, on my heels, would handle any remaining issues. Which included a possible Amsler kill shot. He'd also cover my back, with an eye toward the inside garage door leading into the house.

A single rapid and smooth motion. The door opened—with minimal noise from hinges—and a pistol-first slide-through, targets sought. I stepped into emptiness. A plain-vanilla car garage. Shelves with yard implements and stored household items. A lawnmower, workbench with tools, old cardboard boxes filled with whatever. No lab, no Amsler, no indications of cooking. Then the voice again. A phone conversation—one-sided from our perspective. A straightforward chat, businesslike. But not English. Or Farsi, or Swiss.

It was a Russian. He spoke without a care in the world, paused, spoke again. All indications pointed toward complete unawareness of our presence in the garage. What the hell?

Marcus picked up on the voice and remained in pure operational mode. A silent stride across the concrete floor and alongside the door leading to the house's interior. An adamant head indication to get my ass in gear and prepare for another entry. The Russian voice had thrown me, and I stood stock-still. The weird factor cranked up.

Marcus glared, gave another head jerk. Both actions filled with, "Hey, dumbass. Follow standard operational protocol."

I can't say I fully snapped out of it. But his directives prompted the appropriate reaction, although distraction and confusion reigned. It made no sense, none. A Russian jabbered away inside the house. I had a quick flashback of Jules's skeptical response to my certainty that the Russians would now back away. But she'd intimated their potential involvement would not be to further Amsler's effort. So why this Russian?

Get real, Lee. Get operational. I stood on the killing floor, safety off, soon to deliver quick and sure violence on the other side of the door. Two wooden steps led to the entrance, Marcus and I positioned at either side. I stepped onto the second step, focusing my weight placement above the underneath wooden support structure to minimize creaks. The Russian—clearly having a phone conversation—continued talking. His voice's volume raised and lowered dependent upon what direction he faced. The guy strolled around as he conversed. I tested the doorknob. Unlocked. I nodded toward Marcus; a return nod indicated all green. Waited for the moment. Waited until his voice pointed away from us, his back in my direction.

No stealth. Burst in and gain the target. I did. The weird meter cranked up several more notches. Between us on the kitchen counter was his weapon. Another suppressed semiautomatic pistol of Russian make. He stood five paces past his weapon in the middle of the open living area. The Russian turned with a casual air, acknowledged our presence and the two pistols aimed his way with an agreeable nod. And the crazy bastard kept talking on the phone! His other hand gesticulated as he emphasized verbal points. Nearby, a couch. A couch with a dead man, eyes open, a perfect centered red hole in his forehead. The dead man had the visual appearance of a MOIS agent. What the hell?

Marcus brushed past me, gun trained, while the Russian continued his conversation. I eased closer as well. The guy wore a light-blue windbreaker, khakis, buzz haircut. Nondescript as could be.

"Don't know," I said. "Don't know what the deal is or what's going on. I just know this is beyond strange."

The Russian captured my comment and spoke into the phone again, cool as a cucumber.

"You think, James Bond?" Marcus shook his head and shot me a quick glance. "I thought you said we were ahead of the spooks."

"Apparently not."

"You think?"

Marcus would take action within the next several seconds. Either allow me management of the current reality or put a bullet in the Russian's head.

"Let me handle this," I said.

A preemptive move on my part, ensuring the Russian remained vertical until we gained answers, more insight. In midsentence the guy pronounced "Case Lee" into the phone. Oh, man. The last freakin' thing I wanted to hear.

"Sure," Marcus said. "You handle this. The two of you being on a first name basis and all. You handle this until I get uncomfortable, which isn't too far away. Then I handle it."

The Russian ended his call, kept both hands visible, and tossed the phone onto the couch alongside the dead Iranian.

"This is a cleanup operation," he said. "As you know."

I didn't know jack except we faced an FSB hitter. The Russian spoke English with a heavy accent. The FSB, Russia's version of the CIA, ensured their field agents were polished and professional and operated within areas where their language skills could pass for a local. Not this guy. Nope, here stood a wet-work specialist. A professional killer. Ice water ran through his veins, attitude assured and nonchalant.

"Iranian?" I asked, nodding toward the couch's expired occupant.

"Of course."

The MOIS agent constituted the Case Lee greeting committee. They'd covered their bases in the event I'd tracked Amsler this far. That part I understood. Other pieces fell into place as new questions arose. MOIS had gone rogue. They'd teamed with Amsler and disregarded their patrons, the Russians. That wouldn't do. At all. A valid puzzle piece. But this hitter's appearance said others knew of Archer. Only the Russians? Amsler had told them of the plan while in Rio?

"Amsler and Archer?" I asked.

He shrugged. "Not here. And not here for a day or two. Maybe three. A pity."

Yeah, a pity. This guy could have whacked them both and taken the sample back to mother Russia. A pity.

"So what now?" I asked.

Important question on many levels. Amsler and Archer had split. I doubted this guy had any clues about their whereabouts. Plus the Russians wanted me dead because of past activities in Suriname and New Guinea. I wasn't exactly top of their shitlist, but I was on it. This guy had ID'd me, knew my name. Exhibited peculiar behaviors in my direction. Behaviors that indicated a teammate, a fellow comrade. At least for this mission. And if such were the case, this presented an opportunity to leverage the situation and shove me further down their kill list. Not off it, perhaps, but a notch or two lower. Become a catch-as-catch-can hit. Self-serving given the current situation, but when life gives you lemons…

"Now? We are happy you are here. Best of luck."

The accent so thick as to forestall any nuance. Still, more pieces fell into place. They were handing this off to me—lock, stock, and barrel. It told me that when it came to next steps, they had no clue.

The wake-up light flicked on, and more puzzle pieces fell into place. Russian fingerprints on the Amsler-Iranian hookup. MOIS gone rogue. Amsler disappears. I didn't know the murky espionage world to any great depth, but I did understand one cardinal rule, one Jules had emphasized: don't take action that could escalate events onto a global stage. Everyone in spookville got it, with few exceptions. The Iranians were one of the outfits who'd failed to grasp the concept. They didn't care.

"Well?" Marcus asked.

"Wait one. Working on it."

The FSB was throwing the Company a we-tried bone. We tried to rein in the Iranians, they'd say. Put a stop to it. Even killed one of their agents. But your guy arrived. That Case Lee fellow. So we're all on the same page. Let's stop this madness.

I fell far outside the realm of a CIA "guy." The FSB knew it. But they also understood I had some form of connection to the Company, however tenuous. From their perspective, a positive connection. I failed to hold the same view.

"You got anything resembling a trail?" I asked the Russian. "Any leads?"

Straws grasped. He shrugged.

"May I light a cigarette?"

His accent weighed thick; his stance remained matter-of-fact.

"No. So this is it? You're walking away?"

"Wait a damn minute," Marcus said.

"I follow instructions," the wet-work specialist said. "As do you. They are not here. This Iranian *was* here. I completed my work."

Sent to clean house, he'd done his part. Sleuthing, investigation—not among his skill sets. The one thing he did offer was a halfway good word passed up the Russian food chain. Ran into Case Lee. Reasonable fellow. Yes, I'll put a bullet in his head if you'd like, the next time we meet. As for Amsler? Who knows?

"Okay. Out the front door."

I signaled with the pistol's barrel. Marcus shot me another are-you-nuts look until the trust element took over. He gathered himself, snorted loudly, and led operations.

"You will exit through the front door," he said, addressing the Russian. "You will not walk past your vehicle. Cut across the lawn. Any sudden movement, and I will kill you. Understood?"

"I would like my weapon. And my phone."

"Come back for them in one hour. If you come back earlier, I will kill you. Drop your car keys on the floor."

The Russian glanced my way, sought support. I shrugged in return. Out of my hands, bud. Marcus Johnson called these shots. He slid his hand with a slow and gentle motion into a front pocket, retrieved the keys, and dropped them on the floor.

"You will walk to the end of the street. You will turn right. You will continue walking for an hour. Understood?"

The Russian nodded back, unafraid but accepting. Part of the job, a pain in the ass, but not unreasonable requests.

"Do anything wrong, anything, and I will hunt you down and kill you."

He would. Neighborhood or not, he'd hustle along the street and plug this guy. Without a doubt. Even if the Russian pulled an ankle-holster firearm and prepared a defensive position. Didn't matter. Marcus Johnson would keep coming. Do what he said.

"What is your name?" the hitter asked.

"The pale rider," Marcus said. "Now get your ass out the door."

The Russian did as he was told. Marcus stood at the open entrance and watched, the pistol alongside his leg. He lit a cigar and spoke while his eyes remained glued on the Russian's retreating figure.

"Can I make a suggestion, son?"

"Please don't."

As expected, he ignored me.

"I would suggest you seek other forms of employment. One where you can get up in the morning and not wade through dead bodies and Russian spooks."

No argument from me.

Chapter 34

"They left a trail," I said. "Somewhere in this house, they left a trail. Help me find it."

Marcus closed and locked the front door.

"Why not ask the Iranian if he knows anything?"

"Could use help searching for clues. And I could use an attitude adjustment, Marcus."

"If I find a bottle, sniff it, and keel over dead, does that count as a clue?"

"Attitude, please."

I started with Archer's office. Hit pay dirt right away. More than pay dirt. Scattered across the messy surface lay receipts and packing slips. Lab equipment. A great deal of lab equipment—expensive, sophisticated stuff. A recent delivery.

Tracks, evidence—and the fire within stoked. I knew something wasn't right about this incursion. Something empty. But the lab receipts, for the first time, confirmed absolute intent. Amsler was cooking. Somewhere, she'd attempted synthesis of her discovery. She'd teamed with the Iranians—the dead guy in the other room was proof aplenty—and was hell-bent on delivering. Delivering mass death. Well, screw that noise.

The receipts were also death warrants, plain and simple. I no longer considered the capture-and-deliver-Amsler option. I would terminate her, and her sidekick, with extreme prejudice.

Marcus wandered into the office. I handed him a few receipts. Didn't take long for him to digest it. The receipts, and the Russian hitter, removed his last vestige of buried skepticism. Skepticism I understood and expected. He hadn't viewed the dead zone. He hadn't watched a passing dragonfly crash and burn from airborne toxicity. Hadn't seen a stretch of Amazon jungle sick with mummified bird and monkey corpses. Or the real-time lesson of two MOIS thugs exposed to the toxin.

"To be crystal clear, Marcus, I no longer require a chat with Ana Amsler."

"And to be crystal clear on my part, attitude adjusted. Let's find her. Terminate this."

We nodded simultaneously. It was game on, and Marcus Johnson wasn't standing on any sidelines. Neither was Case Lee.

"Let's focus." He continued puffing the cigar. "They *did* leave one lead. Too bad the dumbass Russkie shot him."

"The Iranian was my welcoming committee. He may not have known Amsler and Archer's whereabouts."

"It's a moot point now. Let's gather the basics. They drove somewhere. You don't have a bunch of lab equipment delivered then get on an airplane."

"Gotta assume he's already set it up. These were delivered a week ago," I said and waved a handful of receipts.

Amsler had communicated with Archer while in Brazil. Dark web, most likely. No tracks, no traces. Communiqués buried within a murky world that frustrated sniffers and electronic bloodhounds. We both stood still, absorbed the implications.

"I'll take the living room and kitchen," Marcus said.

"Roger that. I've got the office and bedrooms. We've got to hustle. The Russian will be back."

How had the Russians tracked to Archer's house? Kim Rochat? Mossad? Somewhere in the deep background, information trickled. White noise now, shoved aside. Time to circle, sniff, and ferret out the trail.

"Don't worry about the Russian," Marcus said.

"It's not me I'm worried about."

"Then I hope it's him you're worried about. As for me, I may shoot his ass on general principles."

We both went to work. I pulled drawers, rifled through papers and supplies. Searched cabinets and closets. Sought indicators, hints, potential destinations. Amsler and Archer were cooking. A sophisticated lab established, synthesis underway. I should have known they wouldn't attempt such an endeavor within a neighborhood. Prying eyes, noses, ears. No, they'd packed up and headed for a spot where they could pull it off. MOIS had helped, and we could count on Kirmani's involvement as well. The son of a bitch was here in the States, no doubt.

No evidence, no clues. A carpet outline in Archer's closet where a suitcase once sat. The dresser drawers with empty areas. Toothbrush and shaving kit gone. We found no weapons, although we did find a half-filled box of .357 pistol ammunition tucked away on a closet's upper shelf. And no sign of Amsler other than the cigarette butts outside the garage door. She hadn't stayed long.

"What are we missing?" Marcus asked as he pulled the dead man's wallet and checked his pockets. "There's a record here somewhere of intent. Direction."

"The kitchen. People hide stuff in food containers and cans."

We ripped it apart. Panic's insidious edge entered. We had no game plan, no active fallback if we failed to find evidence of their lab's location. Marcus was experiencing the anxiety as well, and he hypothesized as we tore open cereal boxes and frozen items.

"They may have rented a place near a rural airport," he said. "Where crop dusters are available."

"Or close to San Diego's water supply. Or LA's. We can check those out."

Needle. Haystack. But I felt the same desperation. We both understood the immediate alternative. Contact the Feds. Contact Marilyn Townsend, the Company's head spook. Unleash the hounds. And they'd start with this house and the dead MOIS agent and our involvement. It would get worse from there. Deep research into Case Lee's domestic activities. Lots of expired hitters and bounty hunters sprinkled across *that* landscape. With no assurances, none, they would handle this current situation with the appropriate level of gravity. While Amsler and Archer cooked, planned, arranged. With the help of SoCal MOIS agents. Together, they crafted horror beyond a 9/11 scale. Oh, man.

"Hitting the garage," I said.

Marcus continued his desperate kitchen disassembly and responded. "Roger that. I'll search the attic crawl space next."

I flicked on the garage lights with no concern for neighbors noticing activity. I was beyond such considerations. Dusk settled. Muted light filtered through the lone garage window. Two overhead bulbs helped. Workbench— nothing. Shelves of fertilizer, insecticide, garden tools. Old rope, a rusty chain, several opened paint cans. Old wallpaper rolls, a small roll of linoleum flooring tied with chord. I was creating far too much noise, flinging items when they stood in the way of something behind them. I didn't care. Time ticked; people would die. A great number of people.

Several old cardboard boxes had been shoved on the highest shelves. They came tumbling down. One held Christmas ornaments. Another filled with seldom-used kitchen gadgets—food processor, pasta maker, George Foreman grill. One box contained old documents. I moved it over to the workbench and flicked on the available gooseneck lamp. Legal documents from Archer's parents. He'd been the executor of their estates. Archer's tax records—nothing jumped out after a cursory reading. An old article from a scientific journal. Search, fling, search. An old multifolded blueprint.

Bingo, maybe. A construction blueprint. A house or a cabin. My heart pounded; the years-old paper was stiff and resistant to unfolding. The construction company was listed on the blueprint's left side. The lower right of the two-feet-by-three-feet document stated the content:

Country Cabin. Designed and Built for Theodite, Inc. A Nevada Corporation.

Below the verbiage, a set of coordinates. This cabin didn't have an address; it was so far in the boonies they'd used geographic coordinates.

"Marcus!"

He strode through the kitchen as foodstuff and packaging crunched underfoot.

"Finished the crawl space. Not a damn thing." He stepped into the garage. "What do you have?"

"Call these coordinates to me in a minute."

I pointed toward the spot on the blueprint. He grasped the discovery as his face formed a tight half-smile. I stepped outside the back garage door and picked up a satellite phone signal. Left the door open. The garage lights created a rectangle of light across the grass.

"Who is Theodite?" Marcus asked. "A Nevada Corporation?"

"Archer."

"How so?"

The satellite signal locked in. I said a quick prayer. Make these coordinates nearby. Remote but nearby.

"Nevada has an unreal privacy level for corporations," I said, waiting for the overhead big bird's signal to settle down. "You don't have to file owner names with the state. No public record, no secret record. Not there at all. Folks hire an attorney to serve as the person of record. Anonymity, big time."

"You *would* know that."

"Feed me coordinates, oh sour one," I said as my hopes rose and my excitement built. The blueprint was old, but the trail was now hot, the scent fresh. This had to be it.

Marcus spoke the coordinates. I used Google Earth. A challenge on a handheld device, but I zoomed in. A clearing. And a structure smack-dab in the middle. Slow zooms out and I discerned a long winding forest road, connecting with another. Zoomed farther out. San Bernardino National Forest. Archer owned a tucked-away private plot in the middle of a national forest. I oriented myself with nearby towns and stepped back inside.

"Temecula."

"A town?"

"An hour north. We can get a room and reconnoiter. His cabin is in the national forest maybe an hour or so away from there."

He exited the garage, folded the blueprint, and shoved it into his back waistband.

"What does your gut say?"

"They're there. This is it."

His half-smile increased.

"Then let's roll."

We did.

Chapter 35

Several hours later, laptop open, drinks ordered. A Temecula hotel's quiet lounge. A couple in another corner chatted, two business people sat solo at the bar, checking their phones. Low music—an old Three Dog Night tune—provided conversational cover.

Marcus insisted we stop and gather supplies during the drive from San Diego. We collected a grab bag of situational tools: rope, chain, shovels, duct tape, plastic sheeting, zip ties, crowbar, bolt cutters. Not a stop I would have made, but Marcus called the shots when it came to preparedness—team lead tendencies pulled from his background. No argument from me.

The laptop's larger screen allowed for an excellent view of the cabin and surrounding area. It was more house than cabin. The rustic look was built-in with purpose. Single level, log construction. Attached two-car garage. Large propane tank behind the structure, an elevated gas tank nearby for vehicles. The structure was centered within a hundred-yard vaguely circular clearing. A deliberate firebreak. The surrounding forest was interspersed with rock outcrops and large boulders. Big mountains eastward. The turf to the west similar to the Temecula area—large hills, stony outcrops, arid.

"What's with the private property in a national forest?" I asked. Marcus lived in an area surrounded by national forests. He'd know.

"You see it often. Old established homesteads remain in private hands. The Forest Service provides a permanent easement for a private access road. This guy tore down an old cabin to build his Shangri-La. Check the weather."

His team lead tendencies at work again. Gather the variables, plan, execute.

"Early morning light rain, drizzle, mist."

"Good. Wet undergrowth, muffled noise. Low light, no sun glints off equipment. Let's talk targets."

I sipped my vodka-rocks, half hiding a smile. He knew the targets. And their fate. Operational protocol, as per Marcus Johnson.

"Amsler. Archer. MOIS agents, maybe."

"Other players perceived as friendly?" he asked.

"You mean Russians? Company assets?"

"Yes."

"Marcus, when I say we're ahead of the gang, this time take it to the bank. We both know some spook outfits are a helluva lot better than others at tracking. But this cabin intel, the blueprint, is ours alone. Gotta be."

"Nothing is got to be with spooks."

"Fair enough. But let's bet on targets confined to Amsler, Archer, and MOIS agents. And as for MOIS, they're thugs. Killers. I wouldn't expect great battle experience."

"Hmm." Marcus took nothing for granted.

The barkeep wandered over. Marcus ordered another beer; I remained good with the dregs of mine.

"What if they haven't synthesized any?" Marcus asked. "What if they're still working on it? Makes our job a lot easier."

"Unknown. But those receipts for lab equipment are a week old. He prepped for her arrival. She hit the ground running."

"Which still doesn't tell us anything about their cooking progress."

"Yeah, but I know one thing. A collection of purple plants wiped out life across an area the size of a football field. And if they can synthesize it, they can concentrate it. Don't know the best way to describe it. But a gallon or two of concentrate offers the possibility of terror on a scale you and I can't imagine. This stuff is potent beyond belief."

"I'm uncomfortable sitting here. Come on. Outside."

We wandered onto a small empty patio attached to the bar. Told the barkeep we were fine on drinks. Traffic minimal, the night cool, and somewhere east of us in the San Bernardino Mountains two wingnuts worked away. Marcus fired a cigar, cogitated, and stared into the sky.

We developed an operational plan with the full understanding it constituted a framework only. Prone to go to hell in a handbasket—combat always altered plans—but this was an assault on a lone building's occupants. The framework's key attribute: get as many of them as possible out of the cabin.

We counted on MOIS's presence, and having them holed up in their Alamo made for a high-risk situation. We didn't possess the appropriate firepower for an assault on a house full of armed enemies. No grenades, no shoulder-mounted rockets. Our best option avoided having them hunkered down inside. Get their sorry asses out in the open. Terminate them. Doubtful if Amsler and Archer would join the fight. We'd handle them after removing the high-velocity bullet threats.

A short and mild disagreement ensued regarding our positioning at the cabin, expected and settled.

"You circle north," Marcus had said. "Take the back and north side."

"Nope. You take it. I've got the cabin's front and south."

Odds were high much of the action we encountered would show at the front, including the garage entrance.

"My mess. My cleanup," I added and patted Marcus on the arm. He'd attempted to remove the battle's hot spot from my tactical responsibility. No further positioning discussion ensued. He understood and respected my perspective.

"Nothing indicates power lines to the cabin. They'll have a generator or two somewhere. We could start with them," Marcus said.

"Won't draw much of a crowd. Whoever is on watch—if anyone is standing watch—will wander over and check it. I doubt if much of a crowd will join the generator inspection."

"Fair enough," he said. "There's always the old standby."

Fire. A large fire brought an atavistic reaction. People rushed about, clamored to escape or move closer for a view. Fire got people's attention, pronto.

"I like it."

"The elevated gas tank," he said. "The hose is gravity fed, no noise. Douse the ground around the tank. Light it."

As with innumerable remote ranches and cabins, Archer owned an elevated fuel tank for his vehicles. It appeared as a hundred fifty to two hundred gallon tank mounted on a steel stand, maybe six feet in the air.

"It might run downhill and soak the back of the cabin as well."

"Good," Marcus said. "Smoke them out."

I related the vignette on the river when Kim and I had stripped and burned our clothes. Yeah, fire appeared to take care of business with tiny doses of the toxin. But a full-blown conflagration with distilled toxin could send deadly stuff into the atmosphere. The propane tank popping off ensured uncontrolled fire. How far such a smoke cloud would drift, unknown. The potential to wipe out a small city like Temecula loomed. A distinct possibility.

"If the cabin starts burning with whatever amount of toxin is inside, run like hell, Marcus. I'll be with you stride for stride."

"This stuff is seriously that bad?"

"No question. And I can't have a potential death cloud killing everything downwind on my head."

We both internalized the thin ice we would tread the next morning. Delta-style assaults, sure. Fast, violent, deadly. No worries. But handling and disposing of a substance this dangerous was well outside our shared experience.

"As for post-engagement," I added. "*If* we've captured the toxin, sure. We burn the cabin to the ground, bodies included. We don't need tracks of our involvement when the law arrives, if it does."

Bodies included. Such cut-and-dried callousness. Time's passage, life lived, now altered my perspective toward discussions of a mission's aftermath. It was part of our past shared experiences, but I now viewed these activities through a different lens.

"I still like the old standby to draw them out. Ideas?" he asked.

"Yeah. The garage is the lab. Gotta be. So vehicles will park in front. If it's a solo vehicle, MOIS isn't around. We ease inside and take care of business."

"I'm with you. And if there are multiple vehicles?"

"I'll cut one of the fuel lines. Fire it up. They'll come scrambling out the front door once the vehicle-on-fire alarm is raised. A turkey shoot ensues."

"Most vehicles have metal fuel lines. Not rubber. You'd know that if you'd spent an honest day working with me on the ranch."

"Well, here's the deal, aged one. Someone I know insisted we buy bolt cutters along with a bundle of other crap not two hours ago. Those cutters will do."

He drained his beer, puffed the cigar.

"You got a penlight?"

"In my rucksack."

"Lighter?"

"Same rucksack."

"It feels too Hollywood. Car fire, the enemy scrambles through the front door, we clean house. Is there a pretty girl involved who swoons into your arms at some point?"

"I'll stand here for a while so you can conjure up a better approach."

He stubbed the cigar into a large dirt-filled planter. Turned my way, stood closer.

"Alright. It's a plan. We'll execute it. Now I want to go over a central issue. The one involving you and your trigger finger."

"Went over this at Archer's place," I said.

Classic Marcus Johnson tactical redundancy. Address the perceived operational weakness, confirm solidity.

"How many missions did we pull off in Delta?" he asked.

"Plenty."

"And in how many of those did we state, 'Hands up, you're under arrest'?"

"Zero."

"We went in hot. Every time."

"Yeah, and I get it. Message received."

My protestations had no effect. I didn't mind, knowing Marcus would beat on the subject awhile.

"I wouldn't bring this up with Catch," he said.

"I know."

Catch engaged with a ferocity and surety few could match. No prisoners, no one left alive.

"Or Bo."

At the mention of Bo Dickerson, I developed a smile. Marcus didn't.

"You might not bring it up with Bo," I said. "But Bo would bring *lots* of things up with *you*."

"I'm not talking about cosmic ruminations, and you damn well know it."

"Fair enough. My head's right, Marcus. Good to go."

An insufficient declaration. He edged closer.

"The people at this cabin intend to kill thousands of citizens. Maybe hundreds of thousands. We're talking about slaughter on a huge scale. Our fellow countrymen."

"Understood. Big time."

"They have full intent and malice. We stand between them and execution of their plan. You and me."

"I know."

"So we are clear on this mission's resolution? None of this back-to-Switzerland crap?"

"We're clear."

Locked eyes, tight nods.

"We saddle up at zero dark thirty," he said. "Bring the hammer down on these bastards."

My gut knotted, nostrils flared. This was it. A long, strange trip, Amsler. At dawn tomorrow, it ends. You and Archer and whatever MOIS agents are with you. You might sense me again, but too late. Case Lee and Marcus Johnson have you on high ground. You're trying to sow the wind, Amsler. Prepare to reap the whirlwind.

Chapter 36

A half-mile from Archer's road I doused the headlights and found a semiclear patch of ground off the road. I eased into a conifer grove and parked. We'd walk the rest of the way. The wet gravel road indicated our pullout location, but we'd have to live with it. We prepped in silence; car doors closed without a sound. No jackets against the misty drizzle—it would introduce an extra element of fabric noise. Webbed battle vests, pockets filled with loaded rifle and pistol magazines. Marcus insisted we both carry the pistol suppressors within the vests as well. Contingency planning. I shoved the bolt cutters into my back waistband, confirmed the lighter and penlight inside cargo pockets. Rounds chambered in pistols and rifles, a final radio check. Tight nods, good to go.

We stayed off the forest road, worked parallel. We both used the Elcan rifle sight, night-vision function flicked on, as a movement tool. Pitch black among the trees and rocks and boulders. A dozen steps, stop, scope, ascertain the terrain's next short stretch. Night-vision goggles were perhaps preferable, but you make do. We made good time regardless. Quick, sure steps, movement through sense and feel, the pace eating ground. We halted at a rock outcrop near Archer's private road turnoff. Used the rifles and scoped the area. Always a chance MOIS had placed an asset at the road's entrance.

The vague outline of a large hinged gate, closed, nested between two eighteen-inch posts—one to hang the gate, the other for wrapping a secure chain. No movement, no noise other than a few birds sounding predawn chirps. The smell of rich earth and wet conifer needles and wild country rain filled our world.

"Wait ten." Marcus, positioned thirty feet away, spoke low into the earbud radio.

His voice arrived both assured and reassuring. Yeah, I had no issue performing this assault solo and would have committed without hesitation or concern. But there's an operational comfort blanket present with a blood brother at your figurative side. Someone to share the foxhole with. Someone I'd worked with in more tight spots than we'd care to think about.

"Roger that."

I knelt near a large boulder, leaned against it, and waited. Such moments afforded the opportunity to become part of the environment, a living component, nonintrusive. Primal synapses reengaged, senses tuned. Whole-being integration with earth, vegetation, other hunters, and prey. A place few visited with regularity. I sensed Marcus's presence, and the absence of other two-legged critters.

"Let's move."

Marcus. His statement marked the end of our progress together. He'd cross the road and advance along the north side, parallel to Archer's half-mile private road. I'd do the same along the south side. The vaguest outline of a dark figure disappeared into the woods. Odds were high that I wouldn't see him again until it was over, although radio communication with whispered voices would remain active.

Fifteen minutes later I positioned above the cabin, hidden among rock outcrops and conifer trees. Collected drips from overhead limbs landed on my head and neck as I positioned seventy-five yards away, wet pine needles as a cushion. A nearby owl sounded low night hoots and confirmed my quiet approach.

We'd caught a break. The long covered front porch light remained on. It provided more than sufficient light for a detailed riflescope situational scan. One glaring fact didn't require the scope. A MOIS agent sat, smoked, and drank coffee on a front porch bench. An AK-47 automatic rifle rested alongside him.

Three SUVs and a sedan were parked across the open area in front of the porch. If Amsler and Archer accounted for one vehicle, that translated into six to ten MOIS agents resident. The SUV farthest from the porch and closest to me constituted the initial target. More of a challenge with an enemy on outside watch, but the proper angle and low quick movement would afford undetected access. As long as the porch guy stayed put. So ingress was covered. Egress was another story. Once I lit gasoline, porch guy would snap upright and come running. And maybe start yelling.

I scoped the wider surroundings. The garage roof displayed a large vent. It hadn't appeared in the Google Earth image. A new addition. An exhaust vent for the homemade lab. A dim light inside—high odds it was low kitchen illumination as the night shift made coffee. No interior movement. No exterior movement other than the enemy on the porch. Steam from his coffee and cigarette smoke rose in the cool predawn air. The nearby owl continued its soft hoots.

Timing had become critical. A semblance of daylight was thirty minutes away. Given the vehicle fire objective, darkness was my friend. And with night-vision scopes we held a distinct advantage once the shooting started. I checked with Marcus.

"I'm set," I said, a kick-off plan formulated. I could handle the porch enemy with minimal fuss.

"Give me five."

"Roger that. Three vehicles. Night-duty target on the porch, AK visible."

"Can you pull it off?"

He referenced the car fire.

"Roger."

Enough said, no elaboration required. I waited five minutes as he gained a northern position with a rear view of the cabin. I gave a silent thanks for Marcus's fixation with preparedness. The pistol suppressor I'd seen little point carrying was now attached to the HK45. The front porch target yawned.

"I'm go," Marcus said.

His declaration acted as a starter's pistol. The watchman yawned again, stood, and walked to his right. He faced Marcus's direction and peed off the porch.

"How's the view?" I asked into the ear mic. Couldn't help it.

"Shut up and execute."

I did. Fast and low with rifle, pistol, bolt cutters in hand. Dashed across the open area and hunkered down at the nearest SUV's front grill. With the wet earth, the crunch of road gravel was minimal. The night guard wandered back to his coffee and smoke. The porch's wooden planks sounded light creaks in protest.

I stretched out alongside the vehicle and scooted halfway underneath near its rear. Small rainwater rivulets dripped off the SUV's side as the vehicle's body collected the ongoing drizzle. I sighted along the ground. Another SUV and part of the sedan blocked any view from the porch. Important because the penlight, while casting a minimal light, would be evident within the enemy's line-of-sight.

Beneath the vehicle's fuel tank, I flicked on the light and found the fuel line. Transferred the penlight, held it with my mouth, and slid the bolt cutters toward me. The bolt cutter's open position gap was small and wouldn't reach around the entire metal fuel line. No worries. A pinched cut would be more than adequate. I ensured my body position remained well clear of the soon-to-be gasoline flow and nipped the line. A small, steady fuel stream developed, soon enough sufficient to light as it pooled beneath the vehicle. I sliced a cloth strip from my pants leg and soaked it with fuel. Scooted back from under the SUV, penlight off, and waited. The minimal sounds of my ground movement were well covered by both distance from the porch and the light rain.

Wait time. The porch remained quiet; the enemy sipped coffee and smoked. The owl called with soft hoots, a gentle rain fell, and in moments I would kill a man. My lone concern was his potential hue and cry as he ran toward the fire. Others dashing out the front door as I handled close-quarters business would create an OK Corral scenario. Not good, and not much I could do about it other than ensure my initial shots delivered an immediate kill. Fuel continued flowing. The smell reached me perched near one of the front tires. It was time.

Delta execution—perform with ultraviolent impact. Strike with full fury and terminal intent. With a flick of the lighter the gas-soaked cloth strip torched. I tossed it under the SUV. The universal *swoosh* of a gas fire igniting was followed with two rapid footfalls on the wooden porch. No yells, no cries. Then wet, pounding steps approached as I waited with a two-handed pistol grip. The footfalls sounded a hundred feet distant, seventy, fifty. At thirty feet I popped up from the burning vehicle's front grill. Took calm aim and delivered a double tap to the running figure. Two rapid chest shots. He staggered, AK-47 still in hand, crumpled. I put another one in his head. To be sure. Not a soundless five-second event, but damn quiet.

Pistol shoved into my waistband, I dashed for the body. Dragged it, and the AK, around to the front of the torched vehicle. The next targets dashing from the front door wouldn't key on anything but a car fire. I hauled ass, full speed, away from the cabin's clearing and up among the rocks and trees. Unscrewed my weapon's suppressor, stowed it, and holstered the pistol. No more silent shots—big bang would now rule. Still no movement from within the cabin. That would soon change.

Vehicles on fire don't explode. Except in Hollywood. But they do burn like a high-octane torch. Plastic, rubber, upholstery, wiring—crackles and pops and the ongoing escalating roar of an out-of-control fire. The cabin's inhabitants would awake in short order if they hadn't already. A quick glance out any front window would send them running outdoors. Didn't take long.

The first flung the front door open and scrambled outside, followed by two more. Each held AKs. The first called out a name—the porch watchman no doubt. The three circled in different directions toward the flaring vehicle, yelling for their comrade and at each other.

"Two exited the back door. Armed. Working their way toward the tree line," Marcus said, his electronic voice calm, factual. "They won't reach it."

Translation—he'd begin shooting in seconds, take out the back two targets before they gained the cover of trees and rocks. It also highlighted at least two of them had military experience. Gain the high ground, fire and maneuver.

"Roger that. One down, three active in front."

Six enemies accounted for. I held one in my riflescope's crosshairs and hoped more from the cabin would join the party. Split seconds before either Marcus or I fired. My trigger point would be the discovery of their comrade's body tucked under the blazing vehicle's front bumper. So far, their awareness was limited to a strange and alarming car fire. The discovery of their dead comrade would kick their actions into a different realm. They'd take cover. I'd squeeze the trigger prior to that happening.

Marcus's first shot kicked things off. His second came as I squeezed the trigger. My target went down hard. Acquisition of the second target a split second later prompted my second shot. He crumpled, dead. A safe assumption the two at the rear had met the same fate. The third target ducked behind one of the SUVs and sprayed automatic fire in my general direction. Hot flashes of light in the predawn black. Bullets slapped trees and foliage ten yards away from my position.

Three down in front, one alive. Two down in back. Six targets. Couldn't be many more. I scooted through darkness on my left, low and sure. Skirted boulders, kept among the trees. Headed for a clear fire position.

Marcus would assume I'd hunt the last outdoor shooter. The SUV blazed as the undercarriage—still fed gasoline—powered roasting flames across the gravel and up the vehicle's sides. The cabin's entire front face was now illuminated with wavering, flickering light. My target remained hidden behind his chosen SUV. Voices called from inside; the front door slammed shut. Shattering glass sounded as windows were broken outward to allow firing. At least one if not several more MOIS agents remained inside.

My outside target screamed at the cabin's occupants. Voices, in Farsi, called back. Two AKs from two different windows spit fiery lead across the hillside I traversed. Cover fire. I dropped to a knee, focused on the space between my target's hiding spot and the cabin's front door. Ten yards to the porch, two more flying steps would make the door. He broke cover under the gunfire delivered from his comrades and headed for the cabin. He didn't make the porch, landing face-first in wet gravel, dead. In response, the AKs inside pointed toward my muzzle flash and sprayed lead. Bullets thwacked ground and rocks, ricocheted off boulders. I hugged dirt until they quit. Shifted position back toward my original location with a view of both the cabin's front and the south side of the garage. The flames from the car licked higher, roaring, as four dead men occupied the fire's illumination ring. A post-apocalyptic scene and deliverance of what we'd been trained to do.

As I repositioned under the cover of darkness and terrain, movement came from the structure's south, a garage side door. A figure with an AK-47 dashed full speed toward the adjacent rise with its trees and rocks and boulders. I slammed on the brakes, assumed a standing aim. Gained then lost the target as it disappeared into the covering hillside. But I'd seen enough, had captured a sufficient glimpse through the night-vision scope. Kirmani, exhibiting the exact behavior he'd shown at the opera house in Manaus. Cut and run, save his skin. Too late, asshole. You're next on the hit list.

No sign of Amsler or Archer. But their fear, their certainty that death knocked, was emphasized with each shot Marcus and I took. With each MOIS agent killed. Amsler and Archer's fate was sealed, their precious time on this good earth reduced to minutes. I felt no sympathy, no empathetic reaction toward them. And no remorse.

Chapter 37

"Status?"

Marcus required a tactical update and confirmation I remained vertical.

"Two enemies with AKs inside. Along with prime targets one and two. Another target on the hillside, south side. I'm headed his way."

"Roger that. I'll shift west."

He'd move his firing position and cover the cabin's front where the lion's share of the action emanated from. Cover the lone viable escape route. I tapped a forefinger against the earpiece mic. Two taps—an electronic "Roger that." No more spoken words while I hunted. Wet pine needles muffled my footsteps, my pace rapid as I covered the hunting grounds. I knelt under a large tree and scoped, the occasional needle-collected rain droplet hitting my head and neck.

Kirmani wouldn't travel far. There was a chance his group would overcome our attack. Kill us. So he'd hunker down nearby, wait for daylight and outcomes. The bastard was smart enough to comprehend that his best bet for immediate survival was stillness. Zero movement. Situate himself against a large boulder and wait. From the battle noises he'd grasp the nature of my weapon: semiautomatic, one shot each trigger pull. Reliance on accuracy. He held a different tool. The AK-47 would spit a large number of bullets with a single trigger pull. No great accuracy, with reliance on the sheer volume of killing lead filling a general location. A tool best applied up close and personal. So he'd hide, motionless, until a nearby target appeared.

I scoped for movement along the hillside. Nothing. He'd gone to ground and waited. The sky's eastern rim displayed signs of the new day. The overcast rainclouds toward the east were lighter, defined, as the sun rose. The advantage of darkness slipped away.

I angled uphill and kept among the thicker vegetation. Five or six cautious steps, dropped to a knee, scoped. Repeated until I covered another forty yards. Ahead and downhill was a large cluster of boulders. If I'd been Kirmani, I would have headed for those. So I eased toward them and stopped at their edge, a ten-minute trip. Crouched against a truck-sized boulder, its surface rough and wet. He'd blast away at any movement or sight of me, but I required his exact position. Take him out with a well-aimed single shot. No time for cat and mouse, and no sense of his current rabbit hole location. As daylight increased I pressed against stone and opted for a long-odds tactic.

Rifle laid down, the .45 pistol pulled. I slid the phone from a battle vest pocket, turned it on. No cell phone service for miles, but overhead a communication bird hovered in geosynchronous orbit. The phone gained a signal. The satellite would act as a cell tower and forward my call. I found what I wanted in the device's contact list, pressed dial.

The *William Tell* Overture sounded. Opposite me, on the other side of the large boulder. The dumbass had kept his phone active. He shut the ring tone off and now sat freaked and trigger-happy. With my quarry located, I reverted to primitive deception, tried and true. Grabbed a nearby stone and chucked it downhill toward a small copse of trees and brush. The stone landed, rolled, and drew his fire. He emptied a half-magazine of ammo toward a ghost. I flung myself around the boulder's uphill side, the .45 leading the way.

He stopped firing and heard the rough scrape of fabric against rock at his rear. Within the split-second moment, he understood it was over, finished. Death knocked on his life's door. Sitting up, back toward me and AK aimed downhill, his head turned, sufficient to display the raised-lip sneer.

"We should talk, my friend."

Whether he suspected it was me or had merely tossed out his habitual opening statement would remain unknown. But I ensured his executioner was revealed.

"I don't think so, you son of a bitch."

I put a bullet into the back of his head. The .45's unique retort echoed across the area. A signifying boom as opposed to the loud crack of the Colt or AK rifles. Marcus knew it well.

"Report."

"Target terminated."

My shot also sounded as an escape signal for the two MOIS agents remaining inside.

"We got runners," Marcus said.

I scrambled back around the boulder, holstered the pistol, and retrieved the Colt rifle. Flipped the scope to daylight operation and leaned back against the boulder, steadying my aim. Below, the SUV blazed as black smoke funneled upward. Bodies were strewn across the front drive gravel. And two MOIS agents ran toward an available SUV, which was parked facing the entrance road. The passenger side target never made it as Marcus's shot cut him down. The other attained the driver's side door, blocked from Marcus's aim by the bulk of the vehicle. He wasn't blocked from mine. A trigger squeeze, the Colt barked, and he died extending a leg into the driver's side. His body collapsed alongside the black SUV, a foot resting on the vehicle doorsill. Amsler and Archer remained the sole survivors.

"Repositioning west," I said.

Amsler and Archer wouldn't attempt a back door escape. A dash into the hills behind the cabin didn't fit their profile. No, they'd hole up. Marcus and I would flush them out.

"Roger that. Maintaining position."

Marcus assessed the situation and concurred with my belief that cabin front was action central. I side-hilled at a fast pace, remaining covered among trees and brush and rocks with the exception of short sprints across open ground. No telling if Archer kept a scoped deer rifle inside. I took a position behind a jumble of rocks, forty yards from the cabin's front.

"Got you visual," Marcus said.

He could see me. I searched the hillside across the entrance road, spotted him as well. He sat on knees, pressed against a large tree trunk, rifle aimed toward the cabin.

"You too."

I lifted a chin in his direction; he returned the favor.

"I'd bet on hands raised, don't shoot," he said.

A scenario where the two exited, hands high, a surrender. Followed with a BS story of their kidnapping by foreign agents and, from their perspective, more than a fair chance of getting off scot-free. A viable path if you were in their boots, but I couldn't see it. It didn't fit Amsler's style and didn't matter. They were both walking dead.

"Nope. Bet on batshit crazy. Something dramatic."

On cue, the loud grind of an electric garage door lifting sounded across the area and mixed with the torched vehicle's heat-generated pops and cracks.

"Here we go," Marcus said.

One set of feet were revealed, wearing house slippers. Long thin legs in PJ bottoms. Behind, another set of boot-clad feet and jeans. Archer, standing behind Amsler. The curtain rose on this final vignette.

The cool drizzle continued as the scene entered the big strange. A burning vehicle, dead bodies sprinkled across the gravel turnaround, blood washed with rainwater soaking into the ground. Amsler wore a jacket, her hair disheveled, eyes wild. Clutched against her chest was a three-gallon container more than half-filled with pinkish liquid. Viscous, it sloshed in slow motion as she walked forward. The lid appeared as some type of vacuum seal with a plastic hinge and clasp. Their prize, their hopes and aspirations delivered from the bowels of hell.

Archer, midfifties, remained at her heels, his brought-from-home .357 pistol held at his side. His appearance lacked Amsler's fevered zealotry. Fear, panicked fear, washed across his face and body movement.

"Is it glass?" Marcus asked.

Helluva good question. If plastic, we wouldn't sweat her dropping it as she died standing.

"Don't know. Let's keep her moving forward. Get her off the concrete."

Concrete extended seven paces from the garage entrance. If it was a glass container, a kill shot sent it onto a rock-hard surface. Bad news.

"I know you can see me!" Amsler's voice, loud and emphatic with a Swiss-German accent. "Can you hear me?"

"You might as well," Marcus said over the earpiece, an indication I should talk with her. His voice bordered on desultory, bored. I knew why. Every fiber of Marcus Johnson was focused on keeping his rifle's crosshairs on Amsler's head, finger resting against the trigger.

"Yeah. I can hear you."

She twisted her head toward my voice, a snap move, birdlike. She stopped her forward progress, now on gravel, and stood still. Archer remained behind her and stared wide-eyed toward my general direction. Again it struck me how otherworldly this scene was. Mist, drizzle, the dull light of overcast daybreak. Bodies sprawled, and a vehicle burned and crackled while a Swiss scientist in slippers, PJs, and jacket held distilled evil.

"Do you know what this vessel is? This container?"

"No."

My voice was sufficient to carry the thirty-odd yards separating us. At last—Dr. Ana Amsler. The endgame. I had a perverse urge to stretch this out. Engage while she still lived. Gain insight or knowledge or a semblance of rationale. Or perhaps relish the moment—I had her. Finally had her. She lifted the large jar higher, the lid underneath her chin.

"'Now I am become Death, the destroyer of worlds!'"

Spittle formed at the corners of her lips. She clearly hadn't slept for days. I had a close-up view, the Colt's crosshairs steady on a spot between her eyes. Amsler waded the deep end of crazy. Her efforts—conjured, planned, coordinated—now brought to fruition and held tight against her chest. Madness, absolute madness.

"Okay."

What the hell else do you say to an insane wingnut? Her head tilted at my reply.

"Did you really just say okay?" Marcus asked, his voice a monotone.

"Gimme a break, Marcus."

"If I spill this, if I drop this container, we all die!" Amsler screamed. "You cannot escape its effects. It will mix with the atmosphere, the air. And it will drift. It will move! A vast area of death!"

"Do you think she's BS'ing?" Marcus asked. "She may not have had enough cooking time. It could be pink gelatin for all we know."

"No. Between her and Archer they cooked. That jar contains the real deal."

There was a strange comfort to holding a near-silent conversation with Marcus. An electronic sounding board for the weirdness before us.

"Do you think it will break on the gravel?" he asked.

"I know where it *won't* break. I've got this."

Marcus trusted me, trusted whatever action I'd concocted. A trust indicated through his silence in my earpiece.

The hellish scene presented an opportunity. A just-crafted plan driven by circumstance, sure, but also one affording a close-up with Amsler. My quarry. A wild ride through a twisted body-strewn trail. I ached for face-to-face closure.

"Hey, lady! I'm coming out. Unarmed. You and your magic potion hang tight. And tell your friend not to shoot at me."

Confusion crossed both their faces. I laid the rifle down, removed the .45 from its holster, and slid it into my back waistband. Stood with palms extended. Not a hands-up, but rather an indicator I intended no harm. The idiot Archer raised his pistol and aimed in my general direction.

"My friend and I were paid to eliminate a group of Iranian spies," I said. "Our contract doesn't include killing civilians. Are you German?"

I continued a steady stroll in their direction, toward flame and death and insanity. Amsler frowned, perplexed. Unkempt hair now matted with rain, Archer assumed a wide-legged stance, pistol still aimed.

"We want to ensure we got them all. So we're going to inspect the house. You got a problem with that?"

"Who do you work for?" Amsler asked. Her eyes glistened with madness and confusion.

"Not going to tell you that. But my buddy on the hillside has *you* in his riflescope." I pointed a finger toward Archer. "So stop aiming the pistol at me."

Amsler and Archer exchanged looks. Archer lowered his pistol. I sidled closer, hands on hips. Lifted a chin toward the spread-out scene as if inspecting our handiwork. The urge to disclose, to reveal both my identity and intent, burned strong. Tell Amsler of Kim Rochat and the base camp slaughterhouse. Bernie the pilot and Vampire and the dead favela soldiers. I was hard-pressed to keep the moment a large lie.

"We're private contractors," I continued. "I'd suggest you two haul ass. Now. We never saw each other."

With a deeply furrowed forehead and crazed eyes wide, she shot quick glances toward the hillside where an unknown person aimed a weapon their way. She shot a quick glance my way, then shared another look with Archer. Her head movements were rapid, jerky. The jar of distilled toxin wasn't the object of everyone's attention. Her great discovery, her fantastic accomplishment, was no longer center stage.

"This vessel." She lifted the bottle a few inches. "This container holds the deadliest substance on earth. Do you understand?"

"Sure, lady. Whatever."

We exchanged unblinking stares. I'd failed to deliver the appropriate respect, the requisite awe toward the leashed terror within the container. A high-risk option presented itself: edge closer, pull the pistol, kill them, and catch the jar before it hit the ground. I weighed the risks and stuck with my original plan. Mist and raindrops collected and flowed downward on the outside of the oversized glass jar—and it was without question glass. Amsler twitched as the burning vehicle's engine compartment sounded several loud pops.

"Look," I said. "I don't give a rat's ass about some crazy German lady and her special elixir. What I *do* care about is you two getting out of our hair. So vamoose. Scoot. Get the hell out of here before we change our minds about killing you."

Face contorted with confusion and anger and insanity, she shot a rapid glance over her shoulder toward the cabin, back to me, and scanned the hillside for Marcus.

"We must get a few things," she said, brow furrowed.

"You're not listening, lady. Leave. Now." I quit my inspection of the burning vehicle, the dead bodies, and the cabin's front windows. Turned their way. "You're making me *upset*. When I get upset, my friend with the rifle pointed at you gets *very* upset."

The urge to shoot her, end it then, was powerful. But I hadn't sidled close enough to ensure I'd catch the jar. And I wasn't thrilled about handling the container without protection.

The two exchanged glances again. Archer was more motivated and eased past me. He headed for the SUV with the dead body draped near the open driver's door. He stood for a moment alongside the MOIS agent, then used his foot to lift the dead man's leg from the doorsill, letting it drop on the ground. Archer shot Amsler a let's-get-the-hell-out-of-Dodge look and climbed into the SUV. A key ring sat on the dashboard, and Archer shoved home the ignition key as the open-door alarm pinged. Driver's door shut, he waited for his partner.

Amsler and I still hadn't faced each other. She stood toward the SUV, while I continued viewing our handiwork. Side to side, I turned and addressed her.

"Remember, lady, you never saw us. I'll return the favor."

Hesitancy, a frown, and wild eyes—bright green eyes—locked with mine. She started toward the SUV. I followed. The low rumble of distant thunder sounded, her footsteps flat as if walking through a dream. I stayed close behind as she opened the door, one hand clutching the glass container.

She slid into the passenger seat. I placed myself in the line-of-sight between her and Marcus. Marcus had the clear shot, but I wouldn't let him take it. My mess. My cleanup. Archer waited, his pistol on the console between them. The door remained open as she buckled the seat belt, strapping it across her body and the container, locking the precious cargo tight against her belly. The rain's intensity increased. Large droplets smacked vehicle rooftops while the car fire still raged nearby.

As she extended a hand to pull the door shut, I stepped into the gap and prevented its closing. Pulled the .45 from my back waistband. Her hand still gripped the interior door handle. We locked eyes, and she knew. A feral realization, a moment balanced on the razor's edge. She knew who and what I was. The guy who'd chased her through jungles and slums and needless death. Her executioner.

"Ana Amsler, my name is Case Lee."

Then I put a bullet in her head.

Archer, with her blood and brain matter splattered across his face and body, stared wide-eyed. A second shot blasted and it was over. The entire damn thing, over. I felt a hollow, borderline indifference toward this inevitable outcome. Stunned with anger at the entire job, at Amsler and the entire bloody chain of events. Raindrops splatted against my head and shoulders, the burning vehicle hissed in protest, death and blood were strewn across the landscape. Helluva way to live.

Chapter 38

Gravel crunched as Marcus strode toward me. I didn't turn and acknowledge him, which prompted a gentle shoulder squeeze.

"I'll go check the cabin," he said. "What about the jar?"

"We'll wrap it in plastic layers. Tape it like a mummy. Head into the mountains."

He didn't reply and headed for the front door, rifle ready. I snapped out of it and followed, covered his back. The inside was a mess but no more targets, no enemies. The garage contained a formal lab setup. Glassware, burners, a small centrifuge, and electronic equipment beyond my understanding. Several beakers held liquid, which we left alone.

"Have to risk burning this entire mess down. Don't know what else to do," I said, my voice flat inside the garage. The large overhead door stood open and framed a view of the last hour's actions.

"Agreed. I don't see another option."

Time to haul it. First, go Roman on the area—burn it to the ground, scatter the stones, salt the earth. Then haul it.

"We have to clear this area, Marcus. Rain and clouds and isolation will help, but fair odds the cabin fire will draw attention at some point. Let's sweep the area and hit the road."

"I'll go get our vehicle."

"I'll start at the perimeter and work inward. Start with spent brass."

Our semiauto weapons ejected empty brass cartridges when fired.

"Why?"

"Fingerprints. Yours mostly."

He shot me a hard stare, a quick headshake, and took off toward our hidden SUV. I worked the Kirmani area first, found the spent brass, and dragged him downhill and into the open garage. Such a strange and over-practiced process—grab ankles and pull dead weight across pine needles, rocks, and gravel. I didn't blink an eye doing it, but the passage of time and place emphasized how bizarre it was performing such duties. And a painful acknowledgement that once again I was walking within such a dark world when my best efforts had been to back away from it.

The rain lessened, my mood worsened, and my anger toward Amsler and what she'd wrought boiled. I returned to my initial firing spot and collected more ejected brass casings. Headed downhill and crossed the killing floor. It struck me again that Marcus shouldn't be obligated to help sweep away my mess. I'd brought him into it. So while he retrieved our vehicle, I took over body collection. I opted to leave Amsler and Archer where they were. I'd collect the toxin, torch the vehicle. The MOIS agents, including Marcus's two kills behind the cabin, joined Kirmani inside the garage. Quite the collection. There were several cords of wood stacked along the back side of the garage. I'd construct a one-time-only crematorium. Build a funeral pyre for the lab equipment and MOIS agents. With added gasoline, it would burn white hot.

I headed uphill to Marcus's original position and found his spent casings. Side-hilled toward my Amsler contact spot to retrieve the Colt rifle and start prepping the bonfire. Wrap and seal the toxin container using rubber gloves. Then bury it within the remote wilderness. The final act. I bent over to retrieve my rifle and froze at the sound of a known voice.

"Leave it, my friend."

Hirsch. Uri Hirsch, Mossad.

"And turn only to the right. Please do not force me to shoot you."

I straightened up, made a slow right turn, keeping my holstered pistol within his eyesight. The friar's fringe of hair was plastered against his large skull, the pistol pointed toward my chest aimed with a steady paw. He stepped from behind a large tree trunk, seven paces away. He wore street clothes, soaked, his shoes covered with a mud-and-pine-needle mixture.

"I did once tell you of my abilities with regard to tracking, did I not?"

He smiled.

"Yeah, Hirsch. Yeah, you did."

"We must move with speed, you and I. Your friend will return soon."

I'd let my mind wander, dropped focus on the moment. Hirsch's incursion within the scene was a stark reminder of what happens when you let your guard down. It irritated the hell out of me.

"You're not taking the toxin."

He ignored me. I ignored his immediate threat, filled to the brim with enough and no more and shove-it-where-the-sun-don't-shine. He'd get off a shot or two before I drew and fired. Yeah, I'd get hit, maybe die. There was no maybe about his death.

"I will lock you in the back—the trunk, you people call it—of the smaller vehicle. Your friend can retrieve you when he arrives. I will have departed by then. It is a good plan."

"No, it's not. I'm not getting into any car trunks."

"Then I will be forced to shoot you. I do not wish this, Case Lee. But my people, my country, require Dr. Amsler's toxin. It is for our survival."

The side of his head exploded. The crack of Marcus's rifle followed a split second later. I remained stock-still, absorbed in the presence of another senseless death. No aspersions cast toward Marcus—a blood brother doing what was expected. Covering my back. But another death sucked into Amsler's conspiracy. A man gone and soon enough forgotten. Except by me. My anger toward Amsler ratcheted up another notch.

I retrieved my firearm and waited for Marcus. He trudged from the thick vegetation on the opposite hillside, crossed the gravel access road, and climbed my way.

"Thanks," I said. "Our conversation wasn't going well. Guess who he was?"

"I know who he was. A man pointing a weapon at you in a hot-fire zone."

End of story, as far as Marcus was concerned. Fair enough, and no further discussion ensued regarding the Mossad agent except for body disposal.

"Let's leave this one," I said, indicating Hirsch. "It'll give the authorities a goose chase. They might pin him as the instigator."

Marcus spit and pulled a cigar. "I am *not* enthused about how your mind works these days, son." His lighter clacked open. "It's cleaner to stack and burn them."

"Don't want clean. He's a spook. Hell, they're all spooks except Amsler and Archer. Leaving him here keeps it muddy. Helps cover our trail."

A brief eye lock followed, but he didn't press the issue. Marcus left my world to me.

"Why'd you backtrack?" I asked, wondering what prompted him to abandon our vehicle's retrieval.

"A set of car tracks. They stopped at our pullout. Footprints indicated someone had walked to our vehicle and returned. Then they drove on. I didn't like it."

"Well, thanks again. This guy must have followed the Iranians here a day or so ago. He had a talent for tracking MOIS agents. Too bad it rained. Tire tracks did him in."

"Yeah. Too bad," Marcus said, turning. "I'll get the vehicle. Try and avoid more vertical spooks."

He strode away, headed back toward our parked SUV. I made for the garage, opened the back door, and loaded a wheelbarrow with cordwood. Piled it across bodies. Several trips created a decent stack of conflagration kindling. I was still at it when Marcus drove up.

"I'll pop the propane tank valve out back," he said, searching for a wrench. "Let it empty. We don't want an explosion ruining our campfire."

I continued hauling wood. When he finished his chore we swapped duties.

"You go wrap the prize to your satisfaction," he said. "I'll finish here."

I snagged a pair of thick rubber lab gloves from a makeshift counter and retrieved plastic sheeting and two rolls of duct tape. Removed the glass container from Amsler's lap with great care while giving little consideration toward the previous owner. She'd tried and failed and paid the price. Instigated pain and death across a wide swath of her trail. I damn near felt like shooting her again.

Once finished, the container wrapped in plastic and duct tape appeared as a large dull silver egg. It would do. I nestled it in our SUV's backseat. We finished the firewood duty. Placed two entire cords over the bodies and across the floor, with another pile underneath the lab equipment. We grabbed two five-gallon gas cans, full, and set them near Amsler and Archer's vehicle. Marcus wired open the gas nozzle from the elevated gas tank. Fuel flowed, and small streams made their way against the back of the cabin and garage.

He and I shared a nod before he set off the cabin with a gas-fueled roar. I doused the inside and outside of Amsler's vehicle with gasoline. Lit it and climbed into our SUV. Marcus slid in, and we both viewed our handiwork. The cabin and garage would burn to the ground, no doubt. Amsler's vehicle would become a mess of melted plastic and upholstery and bodies. Smoke billowed against the low overcast sky. The drizzle—now light—prompted the use of windshield wipers as we observed the brutal aftermath. We didn't linger long.

"Let's get the hell out of here," Marcus said.

"Roger on that."

I turned toward the gravel exit road and goosed it. Left the entire mess in the rearview mirror. We didn't speak another word for ten minutes. I drove east toward towering mountain peaks. The gravel forest road allowed decent speed, and we ate miles. Marcus rolled his window down and lit a cigar.

"You are aware," he said, breaking the silence. "We did the right thing."

Cool damp air rushed within the vehicle, and the windshield wipers slapped a slow and steady beat.

"Yeah. Yeah, and I'm glad it's over, and I appreciate your help more than you'll know. It's the anger I can't drop. One person, one wingnut kicked this off and brought about the final outcome. I'm mightily pissed at her, and maybe pissed at the human condition that creates these things. These plots, these insane conspiracies."

"If your head is grappling with the human condition, chase your tail while you're at it. Now pull over at the next trailhead. Let's check the map."

We did. The small parking area was empty. Not a good day for hikes, given the weather. The oversized plastic-covered topo map displayed trails throughout the thirteen hundred square miles of national forest. Marcus pinpointed another trailhead farther up the road.

"A single loop trail," he said. "It doesn't intersect with any others. We'll hike in a couple of miles and turn north. Bushwhack for several miles. About as isolated a spot as we'll find."

An hour later we parked and took off, the silver egg strapped to the back of my battle vest. Marcus carried the shovel and small hatchet we'd purchased. I toted the heavy crowbar. The trail angled uphill, toward the no-longer-distant mountains. It felt good to stretch out, sweat, scramble. Cleared the head, reset attitude. The burning anger dissipated, and acceptance rolled in. A sense of victory, accomplishment, and doing-the-right-thing took root.

Angling off-trail provided a true sense of isolation. Hikers wouldn't venture in our direction. A deer hunter, maybe. But this was a vast area, and the odds of another human stumbling across our burial spot was beyond remote. Besides, we were adept at covering our tracks and our digging spot. Two hours later we came to the edge of a high mountain scree field.

"At the scree's edge," Marcus said. "We can use rocks as a final cover."

"Too open. Let's dig here, under cover of these pines."

"What do you mean too open?"

"Big birds overhead. The sky might clear. Can't chance it."

Marcus, sweat and rain running down his face, shook his head.

"Just out of curiosity," he asked. "Do you drop the cloak and dagger crap when not on a job?"

I unloaded the prize and stripped off my vest and shirt.

"It requires a constant state of alertness," I said. "So I wouldn't expect your understanding. Those days are long gone for you."

"Shut up and dig. It will do my heart good to observe you putting in honest labor."

"Happy to. Please don't help. Otherwise I'll have to perform CPR and haul your butt back down the mountain."

"A frail attempt at covering the true nature of our situation. My skills are best applied in a supervisory capacity. Dig away, grunt."

I did. I kicked the pine needles and forest duff aside for reuse. Started with a four-foot diameter hole. I used the crowbar when I encountered large rocks, the hatchet for roots. The strenuous exercise provided head-clearing relief and closure. I hit a clay layer and shoveled it aside for earth-sealing the container.

Six feet deep. Clay dropped and stomped into the bottom. The wrapped container next, and it too surrounded with clay. Then dirt, dirt and rocks, and a final foot pounding. The pine needles and duff reapplied. Marcus helped with the surface cleanup. Done and done.

"Glass doesn't decompose," I said as my normal breathing pattern returned. "Good for a million years. At least."

"This is high country," Marcus said, sniffing the air. "It will be snow-covered in a few weeks. Come spring, after snowmelt, there won't be a blade of grass out of place."

"True enough."

"Which leaves you and me as the sole proprietors of this burial location. And leaving you and the other Swiss scientist as the keepers of the source material location. It's worth noting that the common denominator is you."

"An international man of mystique."

"You mean mystery."

"Not if you ask Bo."

"I do not *even* want to know. Suffice it to say you're a man who relishes the placement of his butt in a sling. I swear, Case. I swear."

The cool mist and light rain settled on my bare torso as a distant crow cawed across wilderness. My breath was visible, and the sweat running down my torso turned cold. Over and done and move on. I quit leaning on the shovel and patted his side.

"Me too, Marcus. Me too."

Epilogue

Tinker Juarez stood at the prow of the *Ace of Spades*, nose to the wind, our own private figurehead. We cruised off Port Royal, second day of the trip, taking our time. Salt marsh islands, small towns, a light fall weather chop across the larger bay crossings where I'd let CC steer. Fine and good and fulfilling time spent, staying in the moment.

"If we are about to crash, will you help?" CC asked for the third time that hour.

"Of course, my love. I'm standing right here."

"What if we hit a whale?"

"We say, 'Excuse *me*.' Whales expect you to be polite."

She threw back her head and laughed. Wind through the open wheelhouse windows ruffled her hair.

"Excuse me, whale!" she yelled.

"Excuuuuuse me, whale!" I yelled back.

We both roared, CC slung an arm around my side, and we shared pilot duties—each with a hand on the wheel. Tinker glanced back, gave a tail wag or three, and reassumed his personal water route inspection.

A text message from Kim Rochat arrived after I'd returned to the *Ace* in New Bern and headed south toward Charleston.

How are you?

I am well. And you?

I am also well.

We left it at that, hanging, incomplete, filled with faltering poignancy. There was no great love or passion between us, but I missed her. Plain and simple, missed her. She made a great partner, and once personal layers had been peeled away she'd displayed a depth I hadn't explored. Lost opportunity, mild yearning, pleasant evening ruminations of "What if?" I disliked leaving it in such a manner—a suspended state I was all too familiar with.

The *Ace* slid into small burgs along the Ditch or hamlets perched on the banks of small rivers within South Carolina's Lowcountry region. We'd take walks, let Tinker do his business, eat burgers and fries. Light jackets the order of the day as fall announced its southern presence. Near a small village near Hilton Head, I asked if CC would enjoy a milkshake.

"Yes! Strawberry, please!"

"Maybe a dirt-flavored milkshake for me."

CC frowned. Jokes were an iffy proposition with her, and this one created consternation.

"I don't think I'd like that, Case. Not dirt."

"No dirt. My mistake. May I have a strawberry milkshake like you?"

"Of course!" A few seconds later she added, "Tinker Juarez likes vanilla."

"Then a strawberry milkshake for CC, a strawberry milkshake for Case, and a vanilla milkshake for Tinker."

"Tinker Juarez."

"A vanilla milkshake for Tinker Juarez."

I filed a final message with my client, Global Resolutions. With other engagements they always received a detailed report that outlined the who, what, where, and when's. Not this time. Too much at stake, too many eyes and ears involved. So I shot off a short and sweet missive with an attached expense report.

Contract complete. Terminal resolution.

Enough said, and they concurred, my invoice paid and expenses reimbursed within four hours. My concern lay with their perception. I'd pushed for more sedate gigs, and this one had "Case Lee, Hitter for Hire" painted across it. I'd follow up in a few weeks with another communiqué and enquire about gumshoe gigs. Messy divorces, embezzlement, white-collar crime. Well below the espionage radar.

I'd cook onboard the *Ace* in the evenings—fish, hot dogs, tacos. CC's favorites. After cleanup, CC and Tinker would head belowdecks and crawl into her bunk. I'd pour a Grey Goose and lounge on the throne—an old recliner patched with a roll or two of duct tape and situated under the foredeck tarp. I cogitated, without too much concern, spookville's alignment and reaction and plans moving forward. The Company's Marilyn Townsend understood my involvement with the Amsler pursuit at some undetermined level. The Russians more so. Mossad and the Brits and Chinese—who knew? There was one bright and shining element of relief. Given the state of the world, a disappeared Swiss bio-prospector with her alleged killer jungle juice wouldn't make it far up the clandestine priority list. Fine by me. On the other hand, MOIS would kill me on sight if we bumped in the night. So would Mossad, maybe. Hard to say, and I wouldn't lose any sleep over it. Screw 'em.

"I've made a decision," CC said.

She sat sideways in a large South American hammock—courtesy of Bo—strung across the foredeck. Tinker jumped in with her and slept with his head on her lap. Her feet dangled, the breeze blew, and the hammock developed its own rhythm, working with the wind and roll of the *Ace*.

"What's your decision?" I asked.

"Either five or six or seven days."

I'd left our trip itinerary open and ensured Mom we'd be back before she missed too much school. Mom called each evening and checked on CC. Not to ensure she was well and cared for, but to ascertain if she felt any pangs of homesickness. Greatest mom in the world.

"I think that's a good decision. We'll play it by ear."

"No, Case. Not ears. Here on your boat. Here on the *Ace of Spades*."

"Of course, my love. Sorry. Yes, it's a good decision. Five or six or seven days."

I'd scheduled a bird hunt and fly-fishing trip in Montana. Marcus and I shook on it at the private air terminal in Billings. We'd departed from LA via private charter.

"Why LA?" he'd asked. "What's wrong with San Diego?"

"Tracks, trails, footprints."

"If you lived with me and had a normal job, you could drop all the I Spy junk."

"Allergic to cows."

"Allergic to normal."

We both drank too much on the victory flight and reminisced about Delta days. Laughter, painful memories, and a shared acute yearning for a world with well-framed missions and black-and-white outcomes. The tiny world of Delta Force, the inhabitants relating on a plane unavailable—and unattainable—for most everyone else on the planet.

Languid days, traveling at a sedate twelve knots. We fished, watched birds and marine life pass, and took walks on salt grass islands. Salt marsh cut-throughs the preferred waterways as the *Ace* drew but three feet of water. Few other vessels, isolation, precious time spent with CC.

I rented a golf cart on Daufuskie Island—standard transport for the two-by-five-mile time capsule. No bridges joined the island to the mainland, which ensured the clock moved at an older pace. CC, Tinker, and I cruised sandy dirt roads while CC waved at each passerby. Without exception, they waved back. Isolated beaches, ancient moss-draped oak trees, bright smiles.

We ate lunch outside at a popular eatery. Lowcountry fare—fried shrimp and grits, deviled crab, collard greens. CC's eyes were bright and absorbing, pointing out people and other dogs and fall flowers. Evident miracles, too often unnoticed.

"This is so good. So very good."

"The shrimp?"

Incredulous eyes and arms widened.

"Everything, Case. Everything!"

I sat in the moment, swaddled with love. Throughout our trip, I captured those jewels of time and place, precious, and locked them away.

Bo called one morning as the *Ace's* belowdeck diesel engine rumbled assurance with its blue-collar rhythm.

"I sense a calm within the universal fabric. A tranquility sought and fulfilled. A goober tranquility as opposed to the higher-order repose of yours truly."

"Well, we lower-order creatures have to take what we can."

Always a joy, a Christmas-light flare-up within my soul once we made contact. When it was revealed CC traveled with me, he insisted I pass her the phone. The subsequent conversation included CC asking Tinker questions for the benefit of Bo and CC giggling nonstop at Bo's comments and questions. It went on for fifteen minutes until CC, eyes filled with tears of laughter, handed me back the phone.

"I understand Tinker Juarez is navigating."

"Yes, indeed. And doing a sterling job of it. We haven't held a straight course in days."

"As it should be, my brother. As it should be. Tell me a tale. I require sustenance—preferably legume-based—filling me on my favorite goober's wellness."

We chatted, laughed, made nebulous promises of soon-enough visits. And covered the recent job with sidestepping obscure details.

"Tell me of our fearless leader, a man prone toward rigidity but filled with an old soul," he said after I'd broad-brushed the operational framework.

"Solid as a rock, as always. Invaluable. Somewhat disgusted with the whole affair."

"Disgusted with the whole affair. Not a bad name for a rock band. Our leader is a fine and good and solid man. Glad he was helpful, although I expected to fill the role of aiding and abetting."

"He was more than insistent."

"Another admirable trait, one you and I have experienced with him multiple times. Damn the torpedoes, saber drawn. No physical totems acquired for either of you?"

He asked about wounds, injuries.

"I picked up a few in Rio. Nothing serious."

"They are *all* serious. In the metaphysical sense. Tales told, markers laid. How's your headspace?"

"I was angry as hell at the main perp. She brought on a barrelful of pain and premature demise."

"Negative energy, my brother. Foul and corrupting. Let it go."

"I have. Sort of."

"You'll keep remnants, as always. It feeds the Georgia peach waterwheel of angst."

I asked about JJ, their relationship, and future plans. We signed off with poignancy and a desire for closer proximity.

During the watery trip toward Charleston to pick up CC, I'd anchored for the night within a Ditch slough and settled into the throne, Grey Goose in hand. I fired off a short Clubhouse message, dark web. I owed her a wrap-up.

Mission accomplished. Job complete and buried.

Jules wouldn't require further elaboration. Her response, late at night, arrived quicker than usual.

Excellent. Now rest, dear boy. Soon enough the hounds shall bay again.

ABOUT THE AUTHOR

I've lived and worked all over the world, traipsing through places like the Amazon, Congo, and Papua New Guinea. And I make a point of capturing unique sights, sounds, and personalities that are incorporated into each of my novels.

The Suriname Job

I worked a contract in that tiny South American country when revolution broke out. Armored vehicles in the streets, gunfire—the whole nine yards. There's a standard protocol in many countries when woken by automatic gunfire. Slide out of bed, take a pillow, and nestle on the floor while contemplating whether a coup has taken place or the national soccer team just won a game. In Suriname, it was a coup.

There was work to do, and that meant traveling across Suriname while the fighting took place. Ugly stuff. But the people were great—a strange and unique mixture of Dutch, Asian Indians, Javanese, and Africans. The result of back in the day when the Dutch were a global colonial power.

Revolutions and coups attract strange players. Spies, mercenaries, "advisors." I did require the services of a helicopter, and one merc who'd arrived with his chopper was willing to perform side gigs when not flying incumbent military folks around. And yes, just as in *The Suriname Job*, I had to seek him out in Paramaribo's best bordello. Not my finest moment.

The New Guinea Job

What a strange place. A massive jungle-covered island with 14,000 foot mountains. As tribal a culture as you'll find. Over 800 living languages (languages, not dialects) making it the most linguistically diverse place on earth. Headhunting an active and proud tradition until very recently (I strongly suspect it still goes on).

I lived and worked deep in the bush—up a tributary of the Fly River. Amazing flora and fauna. Shadowed rain forest jungle, snakes and insects aplenty, peculiar ostrich-like creatures with fluorescent blue heads, massive crocs. Jurassic Park stuff. And leeches. Man, I hated those bloody leeches. Millions of them.

And remarkable characters. In *The New Guinea Job*, the tribesman Luke Mugumwup was a real person, and a pleasure to be around. The tribal tattoos and ritual scarification across his body lent a badass appearance, for sure. But a rock-solid individual to work with. Unless he became upset. Then all bets were off.

I toned *down* the boat driver, Babe Cox. Hard to believe. But the actual guy was a unique and nasty and unforgettable piece of work. His speech pattern consisted of continual f-bombs with the occasional adjective, noun, and verb tossed in. And you could smell the dude from thirty feet.

The Caribbean Job

Flashbacks of the time I spent working in that glorious part of the world came easy. The Bahamas, American Virgin Islands, Jamaica, San Andres, Providencia—a trip down memory lane capturing the feel of those islands for this novel. And the people! What marvelous folks. I figured the tale's intrigue and action against such an idyllic background would make for a unique reading experience.

And pirates. The real deal. I was forced into dealing with them while attempting work contracts. Much of the Caribbean has an active smuggler and pirate trade—well-hidden and never posted in tourist blurbs. Talk about interesting characters! There is a weird code of conduct among them, but I was never clear on the rules of the road. It made for an interesting work environment.

One of the more prevalent memories of those times involved cash. Wads of Benjamins—$100 bills. The pirate and smuggler clans, as you can well imagine, don't take credit cards or issue receipts. Cash on the barrelhead. Benjamins the preferred currency. It made for inventive bookkeeping entries.

The Amazon Job

I was fortunate to have had a long contract in Brazil, splitting my time between an office in Rio de Janeiro and base camps deep within the Amazon wilderness. The people—remarkable. The environments even more so. Rio is an amazing albeit dangerous place, with favelas or slums crammed across the hills overlooking the city. You have to remain on your toes while enjoying the amazing sights and sounds and culture of Copacabana, Ipanema, and Leblon.

The Amazon rainforest is jaw-dropping in its scope and scale. 20% of the earth's fresh water flows down the Amazon River with thousands of smaller rivers and tributaries feeding it. The Amazon rainforest is three million square miles, and during flood season is covered with ten to twenty feet of water.

The wildlife is, of course, amazing. After a long field day, I'd often take one of the small base camp skiffs and fish for tucunaré (peacock bass). I'd figured out their preferred watery environments. And learned where the piranhas were less plentiful (although it's worth noting those fierce little chompers are both easy to catch and quite tasty—karmic justice, perhaps). So I was fishing a remote lagoon a mile or so from the base camp. Lily pads, tannic water, dusk and isolation. Howler monkeys broke into a verbal ruckus among the treetops circling the lagoon. When those raucous critters took a break—dead quiet.

Then soft blowhole exhales no more than five feet away. Scared the bejeesus out of me. It was two botos. Rare Amazon river dolphins. Pinkish-white, curious and content to check out the new addition to their lagoon. We shared the space a full four or five minutes until they eased away. A magic moment, etched forever.

About Me

I live in the Intermountain West, where wide-open spaces give a person perspective and room to think. I relish great books, fine trout streams, family, old friends, and good dogs.

You can visit me at https://vincemilam.com/ to learn about new releases and writer's angst. I can also be visited on Facebook at Vince Milam Author.

Made in the USA
Monee, IL
17 December 2024

74131705R00152